ONE FOOT IN THE GRAVE

A LOU THORNE THRILLER

KORY M. SHRUM

Copyright © 2023 by Kory M. Shrum
Cover design by Christian Bentulan
Editing by Toby Selwyn

ISBN: 978-1-949577-64-8

AN EXCLUSIVE OFFER FOR YOU

Connecting with my readers is the best part of my job as a writer. One way that I like to connect is by sending 2–3 newsletters a month with a subscribers-only giveaway, free stories from your favorite series, and personal updates (read: pictures of my dog).

When you first sign up for the mailing list, I send you at least three free stories right away. If free stories and exclusive give-aways sound like something you're interested in, please look for the special offer in the back of this book.

Happy reading,

Kory M. Shrum

1

When the little girl pointed the gun at Louie Thorne and pulled the trigger, Lou sidestepped through the dark, reappearing in the shadow of a snow-covered cedar. But not before the bullet cut a line of pain across her ribs.

Blood bloomed from Lou's newest wound, soaking the left side of her body.

She couldn't blame the kid for mistaking her for the enemy. Lou had been the one to step into the middle of this mayhem.

Lou took a second step and came out the other side of the darkness, reemerging into the night with more distance placed between her and the girl.

The snow was bright with moonlight. The single car sitting in the driveway outside the still house was quiet.

Lou didn't see any lights—from houses or streetlights or cars. This darkness went on for miles. Lou didn't even have a good sense of where the hell they were, except somewhere wild, where nature prevailed with the exception of this solitary house.

From this new angle, Lou could see the girl, but the girl couldn't see her.

She was small, no more than eight or nine years old. She still pointed the gun at the place where Lou had stood a moment before.

Her chest heaved. Her eyes were wide with fear, shimmering, as she searched the night for Lou, the gun swinging left and right.

Lou recoiled, standing closer to the base of the pine tree. The scent of pine tar, as pleasant as it was, wasn't enough to distract her from the burning ache in her side, or the sticky feel of the blood cooling on her skin.

"Come on!" the boy called. He pulled on the girl's free arm. He was older, Lou guessed. He stood over the girl by four or five inches.

"Where did she go?" the girl screamed. "Where did she go!"

But the boy was behind the wheel now, cranking the car to life. Red light from the brakes fell across the snow, giving the impression that the girl was standing in a blood bath.

The impression was strengthened by the two dead bodies at her feet.

"Kaia, let's *go*!" the boy called from inside the car. "We can't wait! Someone's coming!"

Was Lou really going to let two children—one of them armed and certainly neither of them old enough to legally drive—speed off into the night alone?

The only reason she'd come to this shootout at all was because her compass had demanded it. One minute Lou had been enjoying an Italian sunrise, a cup of black coffee in her hands. Then between one sip and the next, she'd been consumed by an intense pull ricocheting through her, a call as desperate as a prayer and as clear as an alarm bell.

And Lou had answered that prayer, as she'd done countless times over the years, having learned to trust such impulses when they arose. Knowing that when fear and panic welled up within her like that, it was best to act first, ask questions later.

So she'd come. She'd pulled on her leather jacket, her mirrored sunglasses, and had grabbed a gun.

Only to step from the darkness in time to find a little assassin shooting at anything that moved.

Lou turned her attention to the men.

They'd been the ones who'd looked dangerous. They'd been the ones trying to subdue the kids and force them into the vehicle. Without much thought, Lou had fired a shot through the man unfortunate enough to be closest to her. His eyes had widened only a moment before his brains sprayed across the snow, looking black even in the moonlight.

She had also shot the second man—a quick double tap under his chin—before turning to find that the girl had a gun of her own.

And she'd aimed it at Lou.

Lou hadn't even seen her pull it. She didn't know if the girl had been packing her own heat—which seemed unlikely, given her age—or if she'd pulled it off one of the men while Lou wasn't looking.

Now, as her body throbbed and blood continued to pour from the gash beneath her ribs, Lou thought it hardly mattered.

The girl climbed into the back seat of the car.

Am I really going to let them go? she wondered again.

No sooner did the car door shut behind the girl than a gunshot blew out the passenger-side window.

That's what I get for leaving a gun in a child's hands.

A second shot followed and then a third. The children were screaming, and Lou realized the shots weren't being fired from inside the vehicle.

A burly man with more neck than head stumbled into view. He was already at the car, wrenching the front passenger door open before Lou spotted the .357 Magnum in his swollen fist.

Five steps were all it took to close the distance. Five steps and Lou threw her body against his, slamming him hard against the metal frame. Still screaming, the boy shifted the car into drive.

It lurched forward and Lou, trying to shove the man's weight away, found her wounded left side would not cooperate. She ended up on her back in the front passenger seat, the man collapsed on top of her.

The car swerved across the road, the headlights still extinguished. The man on top of Lou growled as his legs were dragged across the road. The friction ate away his pants, then the flesh beneath. The ravenous road also ate away the heels of Lou's boots.

Yet the boy behind the wheel didn't stop. Instead, the car went faster. Lou's gun and hand were pinned between their chests, and she couldn't rotate her wrist enough to fire a decent shot at her assailant.

With her other hand, Lou managed to free a second Beretta from its hip holster and press its barrel against the man's neck. She pulled the trigger and his head rocked violently to one side.

As he brought up his hand to cover the burbling wound, his body dropped away. Free of his weight, Lou hauled herself up fully into the passenger seat and closed the door.

She had only a moment to register this before movement caught her eye.

She snatched the gun from the girl's hand before she managed to fire it.

"*Stop* trying to shoot me," Lou said, holding the gun aloft. "I'm helping you."

Kaia tried to grab the gun from Lou but was impeded by the seatbelt strapped across her chest.

Lou almost laughed. Given what she'd just witnessed, seatbelts seemed like a trivial consideration at a time like this. But at least the girl meant to stay alive. Lou could give her that.

"Now," Lou said, turning to the boy. "Who's trying to hurt you? What—shit."

Lou saw the outline of the truck only a second before it slammed into the driver's-side door. It had kept its lights off.

The children screamed. The car lurched, shoved to one side of the road, pushed off course by the force of the oncoming vehicle.

Lou had turned the girl's confiscated pistol in the direction of the attacking vehicle with the intention of firing shots at the driver's-side window.

But the boy had evidently not been wearing a seatbelt as the girl had. He flew across the front seat of the car and collided with Lou before she could fire a clean shot.

Lou had a moment to choose between firing blindly at the driver or opening her arms and catching the boy's body before he began pinballing the interior of the car.

She chose the boy. And she'd only just pulled him to her, wrapping her arms protectively around him, when the car began to roll.

Lou's head hit the roof and her ears rang. She shifted through the dark without thinking, still holding on to the boy.

They materialized outside of the car, the snow cold against her skin. The car tumbled past them. Seeing it, the boy screamed, "Kaia!"

"I'll get her. Stay here. Don't let them see you." Lou pushed him beneath the cover of the nearest conifer laden with snow and slipped. When she reemerged, she was back in the car only to find the girl fighting with her seatbelt.

She had a fresh cut on her forehead, no doubt from flying glass, but she looked otherwise unhurt. As soon as she saw Lou, she reached for the gun.

Lou moved them both before she could take hold of it, reuniting her with the boy.

Just in time for Lou to take a bullet for him. It ripped through her shoulder.

She swore and aimed her gun. She blew out the shooter's face without ever getting a good look at it. Now her right shoulder burned along with her ribs.

But better my shoulder than his skull, she thought, and pulled both the children through the dark and across the world.

Somewhere safe, she told her compass. *Somewhere remote, somewhere they can hide until I figure out what the hell is going on.*

When the world reformed from its nothingness, a cabin stood before them.

Lou recognized it, though she hadn't been here in ages, not since healing from a near-death experience while still hunting for Fernando Martinelli all those years ago.

As soon as she released the children onto the porch, she knew she couldn't stay. Her vision was tunneling. Darkness was pressing in on her from all directions.

Never a good sign.

She lifted the carved bear which stood beside the door and found the key. She handed it over.

"Go inside," she instructed. "There's heat. There's water. I'll bring food soon. No one should come here, but if they do, hide."

"Where are you going?" the boy asked.

"Give me a gun," the girl demanded.

Lou was not going to give her a gun. "Stay inside and stay warm until I come back."

Lou hoped she would come back. Leaving two kids in the Canadian wilderness, a good fifty miles from the nearest town, would prove just as deadly if she didn't. Using her GPS watch, she marked their location.

"Wait, lady, can you—"

Whatever the boy meant to say was swallowed up by Lou's encroaching unconsciousness. She fell backward, all strength leaving her body. She had a passing thought that her back would hit the cold snow at the bottom of the cabin's steps. Instead, it hit a tiled floor half warmed by Italian sunshine.

Before her eyes fluttered closed, a familiar face peered down at her.

Lou recognized her.

Isadora, Konstantine's personal physician, an Italian woman with dark brows and a stern expression, cried out.

"*Porca miseria!*" The doctor set her half-finished espresso down on its saucer. "Why did I think this would be a quiet morning?"

LOU SLEPT.

When she woke, it was briefly, mere moments at a time.

She slipped in and out of consciousness, and when awake, she caught only glimpses of the doctor's face, half covered by a surgical mask. Magnifying glasses enlarged her eyes to insectile proportions. In a commanding tone, the doctor gave orders to her subordinates, nurses that Lou might have been able to recognize under better circumstances, but for now, they were little more than gray shapes moving urgently around the surgical table where Lou had been placed.

And there was the incessant glare of the overhead light, horribly bright and unbearable.

At one point, Lou thought she saw Konstantine's face, felt

his cool hand on her feverish brow. Heard his calm reassurances in her ear.

But when she finally woke, rising to true wakefulness, she
was alone on a hospital cot.

Her body was sore. Her head was spinning.

She wore clean clothes. Gauze had been taped over her
wounds. Her mouth had the telltale taste of metallics,
confirming she'd been drugged, no doubt for her own
comfort while Isadora dug the offending bullet out of her
shoulder and replenished the lost blood.

Lou heard Isadora's footsteps before she saw her enter the
room. She tried to sit up and was forced to cradle her head
with shaky hands.

"Easy, *Strega*," the doctor said. "Don't move too quickly."

She examined her again, without comment, as Lou struggled to gain her bearings.

"Not bad," the doctor informed her. "Should I tell you to
take it easy? Or is that a waste of my breath?"

"A waste, probably," Lou said. She pinched her eyes shut
against the spinning room. Something cold was pressed into
her hand a moment later, and Lou opened her eyes.

Isadora offered her a cup of water and two large white
pills.

The doctor gave her a moment to take the pills and drink
before speaking.

"You will make a full recovery, but your back may scar.
Especially if you do not take care of your stitches," she said.

When Lou stretched, she felt the thread pull and the
gauze shift.

The doctor went on, "The bullet in your shoulder was
removed and you have a bump on the top of your head. I
removed the glass in your cheek and arm as well. But you'll
recover."

"Was Konstantine here?" Lou asked. She was certain she'd seen his face. Or maybe she had been dreaming.

"*Sì*," Isadora said. "I am to tell him *every* time you collapse bleeding at my feet. At least this time it was my kitchen floor. Which I can mop. *Grazie*."

Lou wasn't surprised her compass had brought her to Isadora. It was habit now. Isadora was employed solely in the service of the Ravengers, Konstantine's gang. If Konstantine or any of his men were shot, maimed, or otherwise injured, they went to Isadora. They relied on her for her medical expertise, but also her discretion.

Konstantine had once told Lou that he'd hired the doctor because he trusted Isadora with his life.

That was why Lou had begun to trust her too. That and the fact that Lou hated hospitals. The harsh fluorescents ran counter to her gifts. They exposed her. Nullified her ability.

And while Isadora's clinic did look and smell like a hospital, it was infinitely more palatable, in Lou's opinion.

"Thanks for the help." Lou slid off the cot. "Sorry about your kitchen floor."

"Wait," Isadora said.

"What is it?" Lou held on to the cot with a steadying hand.

The doctor took a deep breath.

Lou stilled herself. Whatever Isadora had to say next, she didn't want to say it. That was enough to make Lou's insides harden. "*What?*"

"You're pregnant," Isadora said.

Lou's heart skipped a beat. "How would you know that?"

"I do a pregnancy test whenever I operate on a woman. I confirmed the pregnancy by ultrasound post-surgery, *after* I sent everyone home, mind you. You are eight or nine weeks. There is a heartbeat."

Lou sat back down on the cot. She hoped the shakiness in

her knees was from dehydration and not the all-encompassing fear radiating through her.

"None of the medications I gave you should have a negative effect. I always err on the side of caution with a woman of childbearing age," she said.

Childbearing age.

Lou's birthday had been just six days ago. As she'd extinguished twenty-eight blazing candles with a single breath, she'd been blissfully unaware that another life had begun inside her.

"Did you tell him?" Lou asked.

Isadora's brow pinched. "Who?"

"Konstantine. Did you tell him I'm pregnant?"

Isadora barked a harsh, short laugh. "Do I look like I want to die?"

Lou frowned, confused. "Why would he kill you?"

"*Strega*, what if the child is not his?" Isadora's hands became very Italian suddenly. "You come and go all hours of the night. I do not know *where* you go or *who* you spend your time with. I am *not* going to tell the most dangerous man alive that his *amore* may be pregnant with someone else's child. *Col cavolo!*"

How to explain to the doctor that while it was true that Lou spent her nights with plenty of men, it usually ended in their murder. Regarding paternity, there was no question. Konstantine had been the only one in her bed for years.

Unless there was something freakier about La Loon's waters than its healing properties, Lou didn't think she'd conceived a child by any other means except the most obvious one.

"Is this the part where you tell me to lay off the red wine?" Lou asked. She was trying to find some ground under her feet despite the panic rising up within her.

Isadora laughed again, this one less strained.

"First of all, Italian women enjoy wine while pregnant. A glass or two a week? *Niente di grave.*" The doctor shrugged. "Wine is not your problem. It is a miracle that you did not miscarry after last night. And any other night where you insist on taking a bullet as if you are made of stone and not flesh and bones. Keep doing that and your chances of miscarriage will increase. Also, I cannot tell you what effect that place will have on your child."

That place. She meant La Loon, of course.

"We know that the microbes in its waters heal you, and we find them in your blood. Will they cross the placenta?" Isadora shrugged again.

"You want me to stop hunting?"

"No, *Strega.* I'm telling you that if you want to keep that child inside you, you will have to be more careful." She escorted Lou to the door of the clinic, opening it for her. "For at least four or five months. And unless you want to leave an orphan behind in this world, then another eighteen years beyond that."

Isadora closed the door on her, leaving Lou on the clinic steps in the predawn light.

Church bells rang in the distance.

For a moment all Lou could do was stand there listening to the sounds of Florence waking up all around her.

Mopeds honked. Tires bumped over the uneven roads. Pigeons cooed. Someone further down the street hummed a tune.

Lou started walking in the direction of the Arno River, toward the villa she shared with Konstantine.

What she would tell him when she saw him, she wasn't sure.

Maybe I won't tell him anything.

A flock of pigeons startled, escaping her path by scattering in the early-morning mist hanging above the damp cobblestone streets.

Lou hardly noticed.

Her mind was several places at once.

It was in the cabin with the children that she needed to check on. It was in the villa, looking into Konstantine's eyes.

It was everywhere but here with her.

The rising winter sun brightened the horizon, and with each step, Lou struggled to breathe.

Nine weeks pregnant.

I'm pregnant.

Fuck.

2

R obert King stepped away from the protection of Café du Monde's green awning, and a cold wind rolled off the Mississippi River, striking him square in the face. The skin on the back of his neck iced. He ducked his head and pulled his coat tighter, looking both ways before crossing the street.

As the cold tried to slither beneath his collar, King had to remind himself that he preferred winter in New Orleans to its summer. If this were August, a forty-eight-degree morning would feel blissful by comparison. A chilly, overcast day would be the type of day he'd prayed for as sweat poured from his body and the oppressive heat overtook his mind.

Besides, the wind was less brutal once he crossed Jackson Square and turned onto Royal Street, finding protection between the low-slung buildings facing one another. He passed storefronts showcasing styled mannequins, candle displays, and the colorful work of local artists. Souvenir shops offered a menagerie of promises, everything from half-price cocktails to fortune-telling.

King walked on as 777 Royal Street came into view. Its

large glass windows read *Crescent City Detective Agency* in the early-morning light.

He twisted his key in the lock and pushed the door open with a bump of his hip.

The office was quiet.

Piper wasn't in her apartment upstairs. She'd told King last week that she had an exam for one of her courses and would be two hours late.

What had the class been? Victimology? Abnormal Psychology? He couldn't remember.

That was just as well. He would use the quiet time before she arrived to complete some overdue paperwork. They could debrief each other on the status of their pending cases this afternoon.

And he had at least four hours before his lunch date with Beth Miller, the DA. Beth was his current—what? Girlfriend? Was that what he should call her? He had to admit he wasn't entirely sure where their relationship stood, and at his age, with the love of his life already in the grave, he was fine with that. Still, he was looking forward to her company and the turkey bacon club that he'd been craving since she'd suggested Ralph's Subs two days ago.

King had only just settled behind his desk, having arranged the paperwork in a pleasing formation for the sake of efficiency, his cup of coffee resting on a coaster he stole from the bar around the corner, when the bell above the door rang.

He looked up, half expecting to see Piper enter the agency.

But it was a woman he didn't know.

She hesitated in the doorway, holding her threadbare coat close to her body. Her legs were covered by nothing more than tights stretched thin. Even for New Orleans, her clothes weren't warm enough. She reeked of cigarette smoke and her hair was mostly blond. It had been dyed a long time ago, the roots never retouched. The dark part of her hair had grown out to almost her ears.

He thought he saw a hint of makeup on her face, though if it had been swiftly applied that morning or left over from the night before, he couldn't say.

One thing was for certain, she was in distress.

"Can I help you?" King asked.

"I'm looking for Robbie King," she said in a small, squeaky voice.

Robbie. Someone from the station referred her then. Only the officers around here called him Robbie.

"I'm King," he said, rising from his seat. He extended his hand toward her. "It's nice to meet you, Ms..."

She looked back at the door as if she intended to run. Something must have made her change her mind. "Carrie. My name is Carrie Bright."

She inched close enough to give his hand a weak shake.

"Can I offer you a seat and a cup of coffee, Ms. Bright?" He gestured at the unused coffee station on the opposite wall beside Piper's clean desk. "I have tea too, if that's your preference."

"No, no. Thank you. I can't stay."

King took his seat and she still stood. "How can I help you, Ms. Bright?"

He hoped his voice might ease her. But still she looked to the door as if she wasn't sure she wanted to be here. It had been a long time since he'd seen someone so skittish standing in the agency. The last time, it had been an addict looking for his dealer. He hadn't wanted to tell King about their relationship or why he'd been so desperate to find the man, though King had ascertained both rather quickly.

Unfortunately, King's search ended tragically when he discovered the dealer's body in a graffitied warehouse just outside Metairie. He'd been shot four times in the back of the head, his killer never apprehended.

"Whatever you want to tell me will remain in the confidence of this office, Ms. Bright," King said, gesturing to the chair opposite him again.

With her arms wrapped around her, the woman took the offered seat, barely perching on its edge.

"Most people only come to a detective agency for two reasons," King began. He felt like he was the one who should be talking, given her reluctance to do so. It left him with no other choice, really. "They come to me either because they're looking for someone, or perhaps some*thing* if it was a theft, or they want to find out something. Like if someone is having an affair or—"

"Nothing like that," Ms. Bright said.

"Then may I ask who you're looking for?"

"My daughter," she said.

Not uncommon.

"How old is she?"

"Nineteen."

King was slightly surprised by the age. Ms. Bright herself didn't appear that old, but he knew that people had kids young.

King reached across the desk and grabbed an ink pen and his legal pad. "Her name?"

"Jenny. Jenny Bright."

King wrote down the girl's name and age.

"When did you last see her?"

The woman hesitated. King waited, knowing that silence usually forced people to talk. They were less comfortable with the pressure that built in those empty moments than he was. Of course, he had decades of experience as an interrogator for the DEA.

"Maybe this is a mistake," she said.

King took a shot in the dark. "Ms. Bright. I don't know your situation, but let me assure you that I don't turn anyone away, no matter their circumstances. Last week, I had four sex workers in here asking for my help in finding another working girl who hadn't checked in for a couple of days."

"Did you find her?" the woman asked hopefully.

"I did. Unfortunately, she was strung out on meth with an ex-boyfriend, but we found her, and she was alive. It wasn't the best ending, but all parties were satisfied."

Her brow furrowed. "But I thought you worked with the police."

"I do, sometimes," he admitted, stretching back in his seat. "But I'm an independent contractor. I'll help the police or local law enforcement with a case if they ask. I've got enough experience collecting evidence and interviewing witnesses to be of use to them, but I'm not a cop. I don't owe them anything. And I don't have the same rules."

God was this true. Especially in more recent years.

King had always been a rule follower.

But since Louie Thorne had walked into his life, he had done plenty of unlawful things. Hell, two weeks ago, he'd given her the names of two child rapists who'd escaped prison knowing full well she'd blow their brains out before his head hit the pillow that night.

What did that make him?

A handler? An executioner?

And he couldn't even say he regretted it.

The world view he held today was a lot messier than the one he'd formed while working as a DEA agent with Louie's father all those years ago.

"If your daughter is in trouble, I'm not going to hand her over to the police if I find her, do you understand?" he said at last.

At last Ms. Bright's shoulders softened, sagging. Then the tears came. She covered her face with her hands.

"I'm sorry. I'm just so tired of it all."

She lifted her head, revealing her tearstained face.

"Tell me what's going on and I'll see what I can do." King offered her the box of tissues on his desk meant exactly for such moments as these.

She took two. "And what if I can't pay you? I've got nothing."

"I have a pro bono fund for situations like this," King lied. "From time to time I take on cases without expectation of payment. Yours might qualify."

The truth was King had made plenty of money while he was working on the force. He made even more when he sold his house in St. Louis and moved to New Orleans.

Now he was in his sixties and wanted for nothing. He'd come to New Orleans to drink himself to death and ended up opening the agency instead. He could have lived off his retirement and pension alone for the rest of his life. But he'd touched very little of that since opening the agency. The work he did for the DA's office and the local police precincts was enough to cover his modest expenses.

That meant he could trot out this lie about a pro bono fund whenever an unprofitable case pulled at his heart strings.

"But I can't help you if you don't tell me what's going on," King said gently.

"What's going on? I think she's gone and got herself wrapped up in some sort of satanic cult, is what I think," the woman said. She dabbed her wet eyes with the tissue. "I think they've brainwashed her with that devil shit and now they're gonna kill her."

King kept his face neutral. "When's the last time you saw her?"

"It's been two months," she said. She rubbed her nose until it was red. "And last night—"

Her words broke off and the crying began in earnest.

King waited.

She finally recovered enough air to squeak out, "Last night I dreamed about her again. She told me she was dead. She told me he'd killed her. I'm so scared I'm too late."

King would have inwardly dismissed such a claim a year ago. But Melandra, his landlady and best friend, had saved a girl's life because of the dreams she'd had. More than that, King was pretty sure he'd seen his first ghost just a few months ago while working a murder case at a bayou plantation. Before he'd left, it had waved to him—as if to say thank you for capturing her murderer.

As a result, King wasn't sure what to believe these days.

"Tell me about the dream," he said.

The woman took a shaky breath and pulled her coat closer. "I've had it for three nights in a row now. I feel crazy. Hell, I probably seem crazy to you."

"I won't judge," King said. He was glad Piper wasn't here. She would have laughed to hear him say that. "It's more important right now that I have as much information as possible before we speculate."

She wet her lips and began. "It always starts the same. I'm outside, looking at the sky. It's like I'm waitin' for something. It's dark with storm clouds a'rollin' in. And the lightning is just vicious. When I realize it's starting to rain and there's a tornado forming, I run into my RV. Except it ain't an RV on the inside. It's—well, I don't know what it is. A room? A dungeon? I couldn't tell you."

"Describe it the best you can," King said, continuing to take his notes.

"What I see when I look inside is like rooms, but the walls are black. Or maybe there ain't no walls. I can't see so much as my hand in front of my face. But I hear my baby, I hear Jenny calling for me and I'm following her voice. I keep thinking I'm gonna run into something because it's so dark, but I don't. And it's got a strange smell. I can't even begin to describe it. It ain't like nothing I've smelled before in my life. A little bit like animals maybe, but that ain't quite right either. Anyway, I'm running and running trying to find her and then I see a light. I run toward it and there she is. She's laying on this rock, like it's a bed. She's covered in blood and she's crying. I go to her, and I take her in my arms, and I hold her like I did when she was a baby. She's crying and I'm crying. And then she says, 'He's killed me, Momma. He's killed me.' Then I wake up, holding myself."

"Do you know who 'he' might be?" King asked, looking up from his notes.

"She can only mean her cousin on her daddy's side, Tommy. He's been in that devil shit for a long time."

"Does Tommy have a full name?"

"Thomas Scott Wexler," she said. "He's got a place somewhere off Tchoupitoulas Street and he works for one of them ghost tour places here in the Quarter. But I don't know much else about him."

King continued to write while she spoke. "Does Jenny have an address? A job? A list of friends I can talk to? Anyone who might have seen her lately?"

Shame flashed on the woman's face. "I don't know any of that, I'm sorry to say. I've got one address, but I don't think it's her last. She was cleaning rooms at a hotel over on Fourth Street for a while, but I think she quit. I don't know what she did after that. We ain't been on good speaking terms for a while now. Part of that was her daddy's fault. We divorced when she was little. He went on to become a hot-shot attorney with the fancy car and a new life. We had a lot of fights about the way I lived. By the time she was a teenager, she didn't like coming to my place. I guess it was hard for her to be in the RV with Roofus and me when she could be in some four-bedroom mansion out in Mandeville. But it's my fault too, I suppose, for never doin' no better than I have."

"Is Roofus your husband? Boyfriend?"

Ms. Bright snorted. "He's a twelve-year-old peekapoo. He's all I got now."

King considered offering platitudes about how poverty is rarely due to a person's fault alone. Luck plays a part, not to mention the fact that some people are simply offered more opportunity than others. Instead of saying any of this and risk offending her, King pressed on.

"Do you live here in the Quarter?" he asked.

The woman snorted. "Naw. My RV is out in St. Bernard," she added with a touch of defensive pride. "I take the bus into the Quarter for my job. I work just a few blocks from here, off Canal."

"And who referred you to me?" King looked up from his legal pad.

"I went down to the station here"—she pointed up Royal Street in the direction of the nearest precinct—"but the cop blew me off. It was the nice lady at the desk who told me about you. She has the braids and them colored contacts. They're cool. Don't know how she works with them long nails though. I can barely type with just my fingers."

She must have meant Kendra, the precinct's receptionist on most days. King had talked to her on a few occasions, little more than short, polite exchanges.

He hadn't realized he'd made an impression.

"She told me that you might be able to help me and that you were just up the road. So here I am." The tears returned, filling her eyes. "I want you to tell me it's just a bad dream, Mr. King. Please find my baby so that I know she's all right. I don't even care if I'm crazy, as long as she's all right."

A fist closed around King's heart. "I'll do my very best, Ms. Bright."

KING ENDED up leaving the office before Piper returned from her exam. Ms. Bright's visit had put him in a bad mood. It wasn't her fault. The woman had done nothing wrong. But the exchange had put his mind into overdrive, and the more he reviewed the limited details he'd received, the sicker he felt to his stomach.

It wasn't that he thought he couldn't find Jenny.

True, there wasn't a clear place to start the investigation yet, but King had other ways of finding someone. There was always Lou, who could use that compass of hers to locate a person without a second thought. And even if Lou was tied up with her own hunt, King knew how to get ahold of Konstantine and his vast surveillance network. Then there were his friends in the DEA office back in St. Louis who could run the girl's name.

So, no. It wasn't finding her.

It was the dream that troubled him. The way that Ms. Bright so obviously believed in it. She knew she shouldn't, but she did. That much was clear to him.

Perhaps that was why King turned the sign on the agency's door from *Open* to *Closed* and locked up after only an hour in the office. Hands in his pockets, he headed straight to Melandra's Fortunes and Fixes around the corner where Royal and St. Peter intersected.

As was his habit, he placed one hand on the horse head post outside of Mel's shop and checked his shoes. He didn't want to track any dirt inside. And given the fact that the French Quarter streets were often filthy with far worse than a bit of mud—horse shit, spilled alcohol, vomit, gum, or once he'd even found the soles of his shoes covered in glitter—it was always best to check before he crossed her mat.

When he pushed open the door to Fortunes and Fixes, the smell of incense greeted him. The earthy tones of patchouli and something sweeter, jasmine perhaps, assailed his nose. A ghoul, a six-foot statue he'd helped Mel assemble a couple of years ago, shrieked. And the chandelier overhead moaned, its candles flickering as he passed beneath it.

Mel had worked hard to create the right atmosphere for her occult shop. He was proud of her and what she had built. He hoped she was too.

When he didn't find her behind the register and saw that the curtain to her fortune-telling nook was open with no one inside, he called her name. He heard the click of dog nails before he saw the Belgian Malinois, Lady, saunter into view.

"Hey, girl, where's Mel?" King said, and gave Lady a good scratch behind her soft ears. Louder, he asked, "Mel, you here?"

The storage room opened, and a dark head emerged. "Why are you hollering? What if I had customers?"

"I looked first."

Mel arched a brow. "What's happened? Why does your face look like that?"

He snorted. "Like what?"

She scrunched up her face in a pantomime of concern. "Like *that*. What's happened?"

King told her about Carrie Bright, about the missing daughter, about the dream.

Mel's eyes lit with recognition. "You thought I'd be able to understand the dream. You know I believe dreams tell us something. So, let's hear it then."

King recounted all he could remember of the dream before he had to pull out his legal pad and review his notes to make sure he hadn't forgotten anything important. Lady was unhappy when the petting stopped, but quickly found a spot to curl up at Mel's feet.

"I'm not sure what she meant by 'devil shit,'" King finished at last. He gestured at the shop. "For all I know, this shop would be considered devil shit. Or maybe a rock t-shirt and black nail polish is her definition of satanic."

Mel pursed her lips. "It would be hard to say. You didn't think to ask?"

King shook his head. He didn't want to admit that he'd been struggling to remain objective with this case. That fact alone probably told him he was the wrong person for the job, but it was too late to back out now. He'd already promised Ms. Bright his best effort, told her he'd cover the expenses with his so-called pro bono fund.

All he could do now was pray the investigation didn't end with him finding the girl's body.

Please let her be okay, he thought. *Don't let her be dead.*

"You've got all kinds here in the Quarter," Mel went on, unaware of the silent war waging within him. "You've got the emo goth kids who are fascinated by all things macabre. You've got satanists, sure. Mostly that's a counterculture movement more than any *actual* worship of evil. Then there are people who confuse hoodoo, voodoo, or other afro-centric religions with satanism. So, there's really no telling what this cousin might be into. As for the dream, which is what I think you're *really* asking me about, I'd believe her. Even if her daughter isn't dead, Mr. King, there's got to be a reason a mother is dreaming about her baby night after night like that. A mother–child connection is a sacred one. I'd bet all my savings that the girl is in some kind of trouble, be it satanists or something else. What do you think?"

"I think I trust your judgment," he said.

"Though it's true I believe in dreams more after what happened with Zoey Peterson."

Zoey Peterson. Melandra had never met the girl before she started dreaming about her, night after night, seeing the girl's death on repeat. With King's help, they'd been able to save her from that fate.

"So, what will you do?" Mel asked, adjusting her bangles. King liked the musical sound they made as they slid along her wrists.

"I'll start with the cousin. If I find him, maybe I can figure out if he's been in contact with Jenny. Then I'll go from there. Can you check your sources and see if there really are any satanic cults operating in the area?"

"Sure," she said. "But we both know it don't take a group of satanists to kill a girl. There are plenty of crazies out there who would do the job with no credit to Satan at all."

3

___

Konstantine sat behind his desk, rolling a pen absentmindedly between his fingers. His face was turned toward the fireplace burning on his right, the heat a welcome balm against the cold February day. He should have been concerned with the business before him. He needed to make decisions on several pending shipments. Which cargo companies to use. How best to cloak his actions without arousing suspicion from either the authorities or competing organizations. Not to mention he had nearly a ton of uncut cocaine sitting in a Colombian harbor and no destination for it.

But his mind was far away from these concerns. No matter how much he tried to focus on his duty to the empire Padre Leo had left him, his thoughts still returned to Louie.

Something was wrong with her. Or perhaps something was wrong with *them*.

Perhaps it was simply her latest hunt, her obsession with the mysterious children she'd rescued.

She was diligent, certainly. She checked on them several times a day, and when she was not ensuring their well-being and safety, she was hunting the people who were trying to find them.

She had not asked him for help.

It wasn't her independent nature or her unwillingness to rely on him that worried him, both of which he'd grown accustomed to with time.

It was the other signs of her restlessness.

One night, he'd mentioned a mere inconvenience. A shipment of guns was being held up in a Hong Kong port because a bureaucrat was pressing him for more money than they'd agreed upon. The bureaucrat wanted a larger bribe, but that was a simple matter. One that Konstantine could have dealt with swiftly.

Konstantine thought he was offering up this information in passing, an attempt to share the workings of his day with her. He did not, however, realize he'd signed the bureaucrat's death warrant.

An hour later Lou was in Hong Kong. She killed the greedy bureaucrat and half his dock workers. The next morning, just as Konstantine was noting Lou's bloody footprints drying on their bedroom floor, he received a very apologetic phone call from Hong Kong.

It seemed the new boss was more than willing to accept Konstantine's original terms and had approved the shipment before the details were even finalized. The shipment was now on its way to Naples, as agreed, and if Konstantine felt obliged, he could pay at his earliest convenience.

Or not at all.

Konstantine had ended the call feeling equal parts amusement and concern.

He'd seen this ferocity before, when something troubled her.

Yet he had not found the courage to ask her what was wrong.

He sensed it had something to do with him. He had no logical explanation for this belief, and yet he didn't doubt it.

Their lovemaking had not changed. That was true.

But she didn't linger in his arms anymore. It seemed that now she went from their bed straight out into the night on some mission rather than indulge in his company.

Was she tired of him? Dissatisfied?

In the years before they'd become lovers, Konstantine had tracked her movements with an obsessive passion. He'd noted that Louie had never spent more than one night with a man.

He'd been secretly pleased with himself that he alone had earned her repeated affections. She had also not lived with anyone else, and yet here they were sharing a villa overlooking the Arno River. He'd thought they were making progress.

But perhaps she was not happy. Perhaps after their months of domestic bliss, she was growing bored of their arrangement. Maybe three years of devotion was her limit.

Or maybe she's met someone else.

A knock on his office door pulled Konstantine from his thoughts. "*Sì?*"

Stefano entered. He was dressed head to toe in black Armani, his hair clean and pushed back from his face. The scent of his cologne filled the small office. "*Sei occupato?*"

"No, I'm not busy." Konstantine composed himself, doing his best to wipe the concern from his face. It was immediately clear that he had not done a very good job of it.

"You've been sulking in here all day. Those children keep asking me if you're going to eat lunch with them or not." Stefano nodded in the direction of the kitchen.

"*Sì, sì.* I haven't forgotten." He had promised Matteo and the others that he would dine with them today. He checked the time and saw that it was less than an hour until lunch.

Stefano lingered, pulling a cigarette from his pocket and putting it between his lips. He struck a match, cupping the flame until the cigarette began to burn on its own. But even after he took several drags and blew the smoke toward the ceiling, he didn't leave.

"What is it?" Konstantine asked.

"You tell me," his friend said. He gestured at Konstantine with his cigarette. "I know it's something. Tell me."

Konstantine fell back against his seat.

If Stefano had noticed his dark mood, there was a good chance that Lou had noticed too. Was it possible that his sulkiness was making matters worse between them?

"I should just talk to her," Konstantine muttered to himself.

"You're having problems with *La Strega?*"

Konstantine held up his hands, which was answer enough.

"Fix it," Stefano said. "*Ora.*"

Konstantine met his eyes. "Why?"

"I like this life. Things are very easy for me now. It's no longer *Stefano* go to Tokyo tonight. *Stefano* go to Rio tomorrow. *Stefano*, break your back getting rid of this body."

Konstantine laughed.

It was true that with Louie and her dark gift on his side, it was easier for Konstantine to quell problems around the world himself with her as escort. Teams no longer needed to be mobilized or coordinated. Furthermore, it terrified his adversaries to see her. The infamous witch, mistress of death, and themselves reflected in her mirrored sunglasses.

Was *that* the problem? Was Konstantine relying too much on her gifts? Was he *bothering* her?

"Champagne, flowers, a long weekend on a white beach," Stefano was saying. "Take care of it."

"She doesn't care for those things."

"Buy her more guns," Stefano said. "A rocket launcher. Whatever will make her happy."

"And what if it's someone else that will make her happy?"

Konstantine asked, his voice barely above a whisper. "What if *that's* what she wants?"

Stefano considered this. Then he shrugged. "We will kill him. Make it look like an accident. Then you can win her back with the leather and the guns. I will help you."

A swell of affection ran through Konstantine. He remembered Stefano as a boy, the way he'd been annoyed at first to have him following on Konstantine's heels. Now he couldn't imagine his life without him.

"*Tu sei un grande amico*," Konstantine said.

"No, not a great friend." Stefano laughed. "Only a lazy one."

Konstantine couldn't hold his friend's good cheer. His dark thoughts crept back in, his chest growing heavy with doubt.

Stefano finished his cigarette then ground it out on the stone floor before putting the butt in the trash can.

"Listen," he began. "I will not pretend to understand a woman like *La Strega*. But I know that you are drawn to each other. And I believe she loves you. How many times has she saved your life? How many times has she fought for you?"

"She's restless," Konstantine interjected.

Stefano held up his hands. "Perhaps no man can own a woman like that. Not entirely. Maybe you have to ask yourself if you would be open to sharing her. Only a little."

Konstantine considered this.

What Stefano said rang true. Lou *did* love him. She hadn't said it and might never say it. But she'd proven it a hundred times over in all the ways that mattered to him.

"Maybe you can forgive her for this," Stefano said.

"I'd forgive her for anything," he said, and he meant it.

"*Di preciso*. So if she sleeps with someone, okay. It happened," Stefano said, shrugging again. "So what?"

"I'm jealous just thinking about it." Konstantine would never have admitted this to anyone else.

"Then we kill him." Stefano pulled another cigarette from his pocket and lit it. "She has her fun then you have yours. It's only fair."

LOU WOKE TO A QUIET VILLA. She had a vague memory of Konstantine kissing her cheek before hearing the door close. She rose, stretched. No sooner did her feet touch the floor than a wave of nausea hit her. She was on her knees in front of the toilet bowl a moment later.

She hated throwing up. She hated even more what the nausea suggested.

It had been difficult to hide her symptoms from Konstantine. She was sure he'd noticed her irritation. There were clear moments when she looked at him and her desire to punch his face was so strong, she struggled to contain herself. It was an urge she hadn't had for a very long time. Worse still, there were times, when he was looking into her eyes, she had a sudden, violent urge to weep.

Her tits were sore, and her stomach was upset. She was tired. *Always* tired.

It was unbearable.

She flushed the toilet and rinsed her mouth at the sink. She gave herself a long hard look in the mirror. At least there were no visible changes in her body. But that was only a matter of time.

You can't run from this, a voice said. It was her aunt Lucy.

The woman had been dead for years, overtaken by bone cancer despite her best efforts to fight it. Yet that hadn't stopped her voice trailing through Lou's mind from time to time.

I'm not running, she thought. *I'm waiting.*

And she was.

Until this moment, Lou had hoped that maybe she would get shot. Maybe some drug lord or mafia king pin would kick her down a flight of stairs. She was—in essence—hoping chance or fate would take matters into its own hands. Then Lou wouldn't have to make a monumental decision.

But it had been two weeks and her symptoms were still present.

She wanted to take another pregnancy test.

She couldn't take the test here.

Even if she took every precaution to make sure Konstantine wouldn't discover packaging or a wayward test strip, there were the security cameras. He ran a program, worldwide, that identified and deleted her face from all public footage. She'd agreed to this in the name of her anonymity. She could walk into a hospital with gunshot wounds and a half-dead victim and walk out without being arrested or charged. She liked it that way.

But now it meant she also couldn't walk into a drug store and purchase a pregnancy test without the chance of him seeing her. And if she went to him and asked him to stop monitoring her for a day or two, that would look even more suspicious.

If Lou wanted to take another test, she would need help to do it.

4

Piper Genereux was stretched long on her bed. The curtains were drawn. The radiator clicked and hissed with heat in the corner of the room. She'd thought she'd be working right now, but when she'd arrived at the agency to find the doors locked and King gone, she'd climbed the back stairs to her apartment instead. When she texted King to ask if everything was all right, hoping there wasn't an emergency, he'd said they should reconvene after lunch.

That was fine with Piper. Her eyes were on fire and her head was pounding.

She'd stayed up too late cramming for her exam and had rushed to the eight o'clock class fueled only by her fear and six cups of coffee.

A nice long nap was needed. Or at least, she *would* be napping, if not for the growing ruckus outside her window.

"Mardi Gras isn't for two weeks," she moaned. "Can't I get a little peace around here?"

"Hey."

Piper jumped. Her eyes flew open to find Louie standing in the corner of her room. If anyone else had opened their eyes to discover a woman in leather and mirrored shades standing over them like this, they'd rightfully panic.

Piper, however, just pouted her lips. "You wanna go kill some tourists for me? They're early and they're loud."

"I need you to go to the store," Lou said.

"Oh man, I just laid down." Piper squeezed a pillow to her chest. "I was up all night. And unlike you, Ms. I-am-one-with-the-night, I can't *not* sleep. Sleep deprivation makes Piper a very, *very* sad girl. Come back in two hours."

Piper closed her eyes. After a few moments, she opened them again.

Lou had not left. She was still there, watching her.

"Is it really that important?"

"Yes," Lou said.

A pang of concern ran through her "What do you need from the store?"

"Just—" Lou shifted uncomfortably. "A pregnancy test?"

For a moment Piper didn't understand. Her exhausted brain heard the words, but they held no meaning. Then, slowly, recognition bloomed in her mind.

"A pregnancy test?" She sat up, throwing the pillow away. "Oh shit."

"Yeah," Lou said. "Oh *shit*."

It was ten minutes before Piper was properly disguised. She'd pulled on a black bob wig from her closet—one that Henry had left behind while modeling possible drag concepts for Piper. Then she put on Dani's bright pink coat and boots.

Lou explained that Konstantine didn't comb the world for her face like she did Lou's, but Piper wasn't taking any chances. This was serious.

Looking like a cross between Elizabeth Taylor and Marilyn Monroe, Piper turned to Lou and said, "I'm ready for my debut."

Two steps through Piper's dark hallway and she found herself outside a pharmacy.

Piper craned her neck up to look at the skyscrapers all around her. "Where the hell are we?"

"Denver," Lou said, hanging back, her face still cloaked in the thick shadows collecting on the side of the building. "Hurry up."

Lou pressed a hundred-dollar bill into Piper's hand.

"I doubt a pregnancy test is that expensive," she said, scoffing at the money before tucking it out of sight. "Or nobody would be buying them."

Holding her pink coat close, Piper sauntered through the automatic glass doors.

The pharmacy was well lit with those harsh fluorescents that Piper detested, but at least it was easy to find the pregnancy tests. The only problem was the number of choices.

There were so many different brands. Some had digital readouts. Others could only be deciphered by reading a number of lines. Overwhelmed, Piper picked one from each brand.

When she put all the boxes on the counter, the cashier looked up at her through long flashes.

"You know they're pretty accurate. You won't need this many to tell you if you're pregnant or not. If you're worried you won't understand it, just get these two."

The cashier pointed to ones with digital readouts that clearly said pregnant or not pregnant.

Piper's burning eyes and exhaustion were catching up to her. "Just put them in a bag, please."

She placed the hundred-dollar bill on the counter.

"You're right," the woman said. "It's none of my business. Maybe you're having a testing party for all I know. My cousin did that."

Piper thanked her, took the change and the plastic bag

full of pregnancy tests, and walked back out into the frosty morning.

She was halfway down the alleyway before Lou stepped out from behind a dumpster. Piper held up the bag. "Let's do this. But can we do coffee and donuts first or something."

Twenty minutes later, Piper and Lou were sitting on Piper's couch in the living room. Piper had gotten through half her coffee and two donuts, while Lou had only managed a single bite of hers. She wasn't even making good headway on her coffee.

Her attention kept sliding to the ten pregnancy tests lined up on the coffee table in front of them—all of which Lou had peed on.

Piper set her coffee down. "I've got to stop. I don't know if it's seeing you like this or the amount of caffeine I've had, but my anxiety is through the roof right now. I'm sweating. *Sweating*, in *February*."

Lou didn't even blink.

Piper ran her hand through her hair. "I'm sorry. I don't mean to make this about me. You must be freaking out right now. Are you freaking out?"

"Yes." The word was very different to the unreadable expression she wore.

Piper puffed up her cheeks and exhaled slowly. She checked her clock again. "It's been three minutes. Should we take a look?"

Together they bent over the coffee table and peered down at the tests.

Lou lifted one with a digital face, inspecting it more closely as if it said anything other than *Pregnant* printed clearly across its screen.

"I'm going to guess these aren't *all* false positives," Piper said. She couldn't tell by Lou's face if she was happy or upset by this news.

Piper was leaning toward upset. If she'd *wanted* to be pregnant, wouldn't she have bought the tests herself? Taken them at her place while her Italian stallion cheered her on?

"You're very pregnant. How do you feel about it?" Piper asked cautiously.

"I don't know," she said. "I guess I was hoping I wasn't still pregnant."

"Back up." Piper put down her donut and held up hand. "*Still* pregnant?"

"I found out two weeks ago, but it was early. And I've taken a good kick to the gut since then. I thought—maybe—"

"I'm going to guess that any baby you grow in that superwoman body of yours is going to be just as durable as you," Piper said. "The real question is why you were *hoping* you'd miscarry. You don't want kids? I thought you loved kids."

"I do."

Piper sucked donut glaze off her fingers. "But you don't want one?"

"It isn't a matter of *want*," Lou said.

"It's not like you don't have the money," Piper said. "Your baby daddy is, like, a billionaire, isn't he? Is he the problem? You don't want to have kids with him?"

"He's good with kids," Lou said.

Piper frowned. "He's rich. He's good with kids. So, I'm guessing he's not the problem. Though I know *I'd* have reservations about having a baby with the lord of the underworld. Considering his life expectancy with a job like that. And the fact that if anyone knew he had a kid they might do something stupid like try to kidnap her. Of course, I can't imagine anyone being so stupid as to come after *your* kid. All of this is assuming you want to keep it?"

"I don't think I would be a good mother," Lou said.

"What?" Piper choked. "Are you kidding me? You make kids feel super safe. I've seen the way they cling to you when you rescue them, man. You can't fake that. You're great with kids."

Lou still wouldn't look at her.

"Are you going to tell Konstantine? It's almost Valentine's Day. It might be romantic. I don't know. Whatever you heteros are into."

"I can't stop," Lou said quietly.

Her voice was so soft, Piper wasn't sure she'd heard it.

"Can't stop what? I don't think pregnancy means no sex," Piper said with a snort.

Lou laid her head against the back of the couch and covered her eyes with her arm.

"Seriously. Stop what?" Piper pressed.

"Hunting?"

Piper snorted. "Then don't. Who says you can't hunt and be a mother? Think about the lionesses on the nature channel, man. You'll be a working mom. Though I've got to say, I don't know how I feel about a baby Louie. Will it be cute? Terrifying? Probably both, right? Oh my god, I'm going to be the gay aunt!"

Lou pushed herself up from the couch and walked toward the corner of the room. "Thanks for your help."

Before Piper could say anything, she stepped through the dark and was gone.

"You're welcome," she said, more than a little put off by Lou's abrupt departure. How could she just walk out on a prime bonding opportunity like this? It wasn't every day that one of them was going to get pregnant.

Piper had the distinct impression she'd said something wrong. It wasn't that Lou had stood up and left without saying goodbye. She did that anyway. It was the *way* she'd left. The air of gloom about her.

Piper looked around her empty living room and at the

pregnancy tests still lined up on her coffee table beside the box of donuts and unfinished coffee.

She took another donut out of the box. "Good talk, I guess."

The apartment door opened and her live-in girlfriend, Dani, strode in. Her hair was windblown from the walk, her cheeks red from the cold. She plopped her Kate Spade bag in the armchair by the door and slipped out of her pumps before pushing the door shut behind her.

"I just wanted to grab lunch before I head over to the county jail. At two I've got an interview with Jay—"

Dani's words fell away as her eyes locked on the coffee table. Because Piper's mouth was full of donut, she was left trying to quickly choke it down as Dani approached.

She lifted one of the tests off the coffee table and arched a brow as she read the positive result. Then she peered at the others, her eyebrows only reaching higher.

"Do you have something to tell me?" she asked.

Her gaze slid from the pregnancy test back to Piper.

Piper wiped the donut glaze off her lips. "Maybe."

5

Lou stood between the two stone pillars which held up the arched sign for Bellefontaine Cemetery. She crossed beneath the arch and headed up the paved road, soft gravel shifting beneath her boots. She passed the well-manicured lawns and cleaned grave markers. It had been a long time since Lou had come here. She thought the last time might have been with Lucy, just before she'd died.

Lou casually noted some of the etched names as she passed, her hands loose in the pockets of her leather jacket, her mirrored shades pulled down to hide her eyes. Her gaze lingered on giant carved angels, and family crypts large enough to house the bones of generations.

But it was the grave at the top of the first hill, half hidden beneath the shade of a willow tree, that she was looking for. There were two plots there, side by side, nestled safely in the tangled roots of the ancient tree, looking just how she remembered them.

Lou searched the cemetery but found she was alone. In the distance, a runner in bright orange gear moved away from her, her ponytail swishing with each step.

Lou knelt and placed a hand on the cold granite marker in front of her.

Jacob Riley Thorne
1970–2004
Husband. Father. Hero.

HER FATHER, Jack, had been thirty-four when Konstantine's brother, Angelo Martinelli, shot him nine times behind the suburban Tudor house he'd shared in St. Louis with Lou and her mother. Even now, sixteen years later, she remembered everything. The way her father smelled. How it felt when he lifted her up, making her feel so small in his arms. He'd been a large man, well over six feet tall and built like someone who spent their days laboring on a farm from sunup to sundown.

The way his voice, a pleasing baritone, had sounded when he'd sang, *Louie Louiiiie. Oh baby*—

The way his beard scratched her palms when she cupped his face with her small hands.

Her father had been a hunter too, if in a more traditional sense, in his role as a DEA agent for the St. Louis division. It was his capture and arrest of Benito Martinelli that provoked the crime family. That's why they'd ordered the hit on him.

Jack was told to back off, but he hadn't.

And that inability to stop got his wife killed, got himself killed. And Louie would be dead too if he hadn't lifted her and thrown her into the pool the night Angelo busted through the back gate, gun raised.

Her father had thrown her into the pool knowing her dark gift would save her life—even as his was forfeited.

That level of parental sacrifice Lou understood. She could do the same—*would* do the same if the moment called for it.

But as she sat here on her father's grave, she also understood that self-sacrifice wasn't enough, not to the child left behind. Sacrifice wasn't enough to piece a shattered heart together again.

Jack Thorne hadn't been able to choose his family's safety over the hunt, and because he hadn't, this was what Lou's life had become.

Bloodthirsty. Vengeful. Insatiable.

"I'm no better than you," she said, her nails catching on the etching as she traced the letters of his name.

And what about me? an icy voice asked. *Are you any better than me?*

Lou looked to the second grave. The one she'd ignored until that moment.

The dead woman resting beside her father, Courtney Thorne, had been a cold mother to Lou. But she had been there day in and day out. She had been present in body, if not in heart and mind.

Were those Lou's choices?

To be warmhearted and loving like her father, but forever in harm's way?

Or ever-present like her mother, to the point that she was cold and resentful of the child that had changed her? Would her misery make everyone around her miserable as well?

Then there was Konstantine to consider.

Piper had been right.

He had more enemies than Lou. He was more visible than she was. Easier to track down. If Lou really decided to have her child, *his* child—the chances of that child losing one or both of its parents was a near certainty.

Wouldn't it be better to not be born at all than to be born into such a life?

Jack Thorne, to his credit, at least hadn't known what would happen. Like most men, he'd probably believed he'd live forever. That he would figure it all out, if such a time came.

What had been in his head when he first received the death threat from the Martinelli crime family? Obviously, he thought he was the only target. That's why he'd left a video behind, with instructions to deliver his last words to Lou when she turned eighteen.

Clearly it had not occurred to him that the Martinellis might kill his wife and child too.

Lou had no such illusions. She knew exactly the life she would be offering her child. She had been in this world for too long not to know what others could do when they were desperate.

If she were being honest with herself, Lou's worst fear wasn't even that she would die and leave behind an orphan, though it was certainly one of them. It was that she would make a fatal miscalculation, as her father had, and the *child* would die.

That there would come some terrible moment when Lou was face to face with her inadequacy as she held her dead child in her arms.

A wave of sympathy and compassion for her father washed over her.

"At least you didn't have to live with that," she whispered. If a person could live with such a thing. Lou knew there were some who'd have blown their brains out for less.

Her mind returned to Konstantine again. It had been circling back to him for weeks.

I'm pregnant.

Konstantine.

I'm pregnant.

Konstantine—

More than once Lou had done the math in her mind,

trying to calculate the moment of conception, and each time it brought her to Thanksgiving.

Unsurprising.

Konstantine had drunk nearly a bottle of wine by himself that night, but she hadn't been far behind him. He kept singing to her in Italian and peeling his clothes off, leaving a trail from the kitchen where they'd made dinner to the living room.

I am too hot, he'd purred. *Are you, by chance, also warm,* amore mio?

This was after they'd already made love on the balcony with the stars above them.

It had been his big green eyes, the hungry way he'd watched her. How handsome he was in the Christmas lights he'd hung with the help of Matteo, Gabriella, and the other children.

Swaying in the living room, he had brushed feather-soft kisses across her lips and cheek, before burying his face in the crook of her neck.

That had done it.

She'd been more than a little in love with him when they'd tumbled into bed together.

And look at what that had gotten her.

The warmth gathered from the happiness of the memory was cut short by a wave of nausea. A slap of reality.

I can't tell him, she thought. *Not yet.*

LOU FOUND the cabin buried under a foot of snow. It looked as if someone had simply dropped it in the middle of the woods and forgotten about it.

Not a footprint—save the rabbit tracks Lou spotted between two pines—marred the white powder. And the air held the silence that one often found in the dead of winter. A hush that pervaded everything. An atmosphere of hallowed reverence.

Lou knocked on the cabin's door, balancing the bags of food in her other hand.

Then she knocked again, waiting.

Not a sound came from inside the cabin.

Satisfied, she melted through the shadows and into its interior. She stepped from the dark bathroom into the main room. It had a high ceiling with crisscrossing wooden beams. A fire roared at the base of a stone hearth.

"You didn't answer the door," she called out by way of welcome.

"You told us not to," the boy said. Lou had learned that his name was Elijah, but she still often thought of him as *the boy*.

"Glad you listened," Lou said, and set down the two sacks of groceries and a new box of matches on the kitchen table. The girl had been on the sofa, writing something in her notebook. She snapped it shut when Lou's eyes turned in her direction.

"I don't know how being quiet protects us anyway. Anyone can see the smoke from the chimney, can't they?" the girl asked, though it didn't really feel like a question. Most of what she said, question or not, came across as an accusation.

Kaia was sharp. Lou had noticed on more than one occasion the way she immediately identified danger. Of course, that meant she'd had reason to develop such hypervigilance. And Lou wanted to know exactly what bastard had been responsible for that.

"As long as no one sees you, they'll think it's someone else. An old deaf man would be ideal."

"She has a point, Kaia," the boy said. "We could be anybody in here."

The girl shot him a pointed look.

"I brought more snacks but also a proper lunch." Lou handed the boy the bucket of fried chicken and then put the sides on the table. "Plates and napkins are in the bag."

The boy set the table and made the girl's plate first. While he did, Kaia poured their drinks.

"Are you eating with us?" Elijah asked, his hands holding a third paper plate.

"No, I've eaten. Thanks."

He put the extra plate back in the bag.

While they ate, Lou tended to the fire, building it up for them by adding wood and kindling. The cabin was warm, too warm in Lou's opinion, but if the children were comfortable, it didn't matter. The cabin had a proper heater, but it seemed they preferred the fire.

Lou felt better now that she'd seen them with her own eyes. She watched them eat, looking for any signs that they were not okay. But the color in their faces was improving. They were gaining a bit of weight. She gathered all of this by catching sidelong glances through her mirrored shades.

She'd been patient for two weeks.

They wouldn't tell her who they'd been running from or why they'd been running at all.

And Lou hadn't pushed them for several reasons. Firstly, because she'd been quite distracted with her own situation and the shocking possibility of motherhood looming on her horizon. But secondly, their silence hadn't stopped her from satisfying her blood lust. She'd found and killed four threats already, thanks to her dark gifts.

She'd only had to ask her compass for a target, anyone getting too close to their trail, and the compass had seemed all too happy to provide her with one.

But these hunts had brought her little resolution. They'd all been men, but otherwise the connection was unclear. She had no idea why her compass had considered them a threat.

Meanwhile she'd brought the children clothes, toiletries, books, and board games. She brought them anything they asked for—and it was always the boy who asked. The girl seemed to resent the fact that she had to ask Lou for anything at all.

Lou had never had anyone snatch a roll of toilet paper out of her hands so grumpily before.

The girl was sipping her soda when she caught Lou looking at her. "Is this where you ask us if there's anywhere we want to go again?"

Lou's lips quirked.

"I told you. There's nowhere for us to go."

"We can't stay in this cabin forever," the boy said. "It's not even hers. It's not yours, is it?"

"No," Lou said. "But the owners won't be back until summer."

Places like this were usually a warm-weather retreat for some city dweller who wanted to get away from it all.

"So we've got time," the girl said. "Months, maybe."

"If you tell me who you're hiding from—" Lou began.

"I'll tell you who we're hiding from when you tell me who you're working for," she replied, not for the first time.

"I work for myself."

"Doing what?"

"I kill very bad men. Sometimes women," Lou amended. Lou didn't think it was necessary to sugar-coat what she did for a child who had once shot her. Not to mention she was certain they'd seen what she'd done the night she'd come to save them—as failed as that attempt had been, they must have seen enough to know she wasn't exactly *normal*.

"How many people have you killed?" the girl said.

"I can't count that high," Lou said with a smirk.

She pulled her phone from her back pocket and scrolled

the photos. Finally, she found the shot she'd snapped of her last kill, shortly before blowing his brains out, that was.

Lou showed the girl the photo. "Do you know this one?"

The girl peered closer at the face before looking away. She said nothing.

The boy leaned across the table, trying to get a closer look. Lou noted Kaia's subtle movements. There was no mistaking that she was trying to block his view of the photo.

When he saw it, the color drained from his face. "You killed him?"

"I did. Did you know him?"

The boy didn't answer. He looked away.

"Put it away," Kaia said.

"He's dead."

She shoved Lou's hand away. "Turn it off, I said."

Lou darkened the phone's screen and slipped the phone back into her pocket. Elijah had begun to shake.

"He's dead," Lou promised. "Whatever he did to you, he's paid for it."

"Not enough," Kaia said, sounding disturbingly mature for such a little girl.

Lou stood. "I'm heading out. Do you need anything before I go?"

She looked from one face to the other.

Elijah pushed himself away from the table and went into the bedroom. Before closing the door behind him, he said, "Thanks for lunch."

Kaia was staring at Lou, her gaze unreadable. "Are you going to let us stay here or do we have to leave now?"

Lou wasn't sure how long their presence would remain undetected. Someone might get an electric bill and wonder just who had been using their cabin.

"I want you to stay," Lou said. "But you could make this

easier on yourselves if you told me what you knew. It's harder to keep you safe when I don't know who's after you."

She waited for an explanation, but the girl said nothing.

After a long, silent moment, Lou rose from the table and walked toward the dark bathroom full of shadows.

"How do you know?" Kaia called after her. Lou turned to find her leaning over the back of the sofa, the roaring fire at her back. "You came when we needed help and now you come when we're hungry. How do you know when we need you?"

Lou smiled, mischievous. She wasn't sure why she liked to tease this one so much. "I guess we both have our secrets."

Lou could have stepped through the dark to anywhere.

But she slipped through the bathroom to the crawlspace above the bedroom the children shared. The cabin had two bedrooms, but the kids had insisted on sharing the larger one. Lou could guess why they didn't want to sleep apart, given what they'd likely been through, and yet there was something about it that made her uneasy.

She had to wait for ten minutes in the tight, overheated space before she heard the bedroom door creak open on its hinges.

"Eli?" the girl whispered.

"Is she gone?" the boy asked.

"I think so."

"You're so mean to her. She's going to make us leave."

"Not if she works for Father. She might be keeping us here for him."

"You don't know that." He sniffed. "She killed all those people. Why would she kill Father's people if she worked for him?"

The girl didn't seem to have an answer to that. Instead, she said, "Maybe there are people worse than Father in the world."

Lou resisted the urge to shift her weight despite the

cramped conditions of the space. She was afraid they'd hear her if she did.

"Mr. Chris is dead," the girl whispered. "He won't ever touch you again."

"What if she was lying?"

"He's dead," the girl assured him.

For some reason Lou didn't fully understand, the boy cried all the harder, his tears falling in earnest now.

This was not the first time Lou had heard mention of *Father*, whoever the hell that was. But when she'd asked her compass to take her to the children's parents, nothing had happened. She'd recognized the cold silence on the other end of the line. She'd felt it before when trying to find someone who was already dead.

But if their parents were dead, then who was *Father*?

Who are they afraid of? she asked instead, but even as she did, Lou felt her compass's uncertainty. She'd experienced that once before, when hunting for Fernando Martinelli. It usually meant one of two things. Either that her target was well protected and not easy to reach, or that her target wasn't *one* target at all.

It could be many people, Lou realized. Many people who Elijah and Kaia feared.

What the hell is going on here?

Lou's irritation at being left in the dark nipped at the back of her neck.

She listened to the boy's soft crying and the girl's reassurances until her back couldn't tolerate the cramped space anymore.

Who should I take out next? she asked her compass. It found a target almost immediately.

She slipped through the darkness, allowing it to carry her hundreds of miles away in an instant. When the world reformed around her, she found herself in an art museum.

Odd.

Not the place she expected to find her next target.

It reminded her a little of a hunt she conducted in Paris about a year and a half ago. A serial killer couple had ties to an art museum there. She supposed someone could be a murderer and also have an interest in beautiful things.

And Lou had spent too many years following her instincts to start doubting them now. If a killer was here, a killer was here.

Lou stepped out from behind a large installation and into a room full of enormous painted panels.

They hung on the wall, spotlit in a way that featured the dramatic figures posed in bold colors. Contemporary in style, abstract and suggestive, rather than recognizable.

Lou's eyes locked on her target immediately. He wore a beige fisherman's hat, a nice button-up shirt and cargo khakis. He had white socks pulled up on his pale calves and thick glasses sitting on a very pointed nose.

He looked like someone's grandfather, a gold wedding band on his left hand. But there was something off about the ring. It sat on his finger loosely. Was it fake? A decoy? Sometimes killers liked to wear fake wedding rings, as it signaled safety to their targets. After all, why would someone's husband kill you?

But Lou knew a predatory stare when she saw one. She had her own.

Her target's eyes were fixed on a young mother. Early twenties, brunette, with a newborn cradled to her chest. She held its neck and bounced it gently as she moved from painting to painting. Lou would have thought she was enjoying herself—or at least trying to—if not for the dark circles under her eyes.

The baby was crying despite the mother's best efforts to soothe it.

Her target was across the room and holding the baby before Lou could decide what her response would be. Every muscle in her body was coiled tight. She was ready to pull her gun and blow the man's brains out here and now. Let Konstantine doctor the footage later—though he'd call her rash, she was sure.

But it was too late. He was already holding the baby, rocking it, cooing.

"How old is she?" he asked the mother in a kind voice.

"He," the young mother corrected. "One month tomorrow."

"Your first?"

"Yes," she said, almost embarrassed. "Isn't it obvious?"

"No. You were doing just fine." The man adjusted his grip on the baby, and it stopped crying immediately. Then it began to coo with pleasure.

The mother's face was overtaken by gratitude. "Oh, thank you. You have kids?"

"Oh yes," the man said. "My wife and I have six."

"Six," the young mother scoffed. "I can't imagine."

"It's easier if you have help," he said, his eyes fixed hungrily on the baby. "Do you have family nearby?"

"No, it's just me."

What are you? Lou wondered.

Because Lou knew the predator could be anything. Beyond a killer or kidnapper, he could be a pedophile, or even a cannibal—both of which Lou had recently encountered.

It was clear that the mother was pinned between her gratitude that her fussy baby had been appeased and her discomfort with the interaction.

Trust your instincts, Lou thought. *Take your baby back.*

"They grow up so fast," the predator said. "Before you know it he'll be hip high and talking back to you."

The mother was reaching for her child. "Thank you. But we should get going."

He handed over the baby without betraying an ounce of irritation. But Lou had seen the micromovements. The slight pivot in his back leg, a suppressed urge to take the baby and run.

You're good, Lou thought.

His ease and confidence, the way he'd simply taken the woman's baby from her arms in a gallery full of people—all of it gave Lou the distinct impression that this man was experienced. Seasoned. Whatever his interest in children, he'd pursued it for a long time.

He let the mother go with a kind smile and a little wave. Or at least that's what anyone else would have seen.

What Lou saw was his measured movements. The way he trailed the pair from gallery to gallery. How he kept his distance, sometimes letting them get far ahead and out of sight, only to end up in a room ahead of them. He stood in front of the paintings without really seeing them.

In the lobby, the mother strapped her infant into his stroller, bundled him against the cold, and pushed him out into the gray day.

Lou took one step beneath the coat check and a second out into the day, emerging from the shadows formed between two close buildings. She waited, knowing the man would pass her on the left.

She was right. Without thinking, she grabbed the back of his neck and yanked him through the shadows.

He was snarling when she released him on the banks of her Alaskan lake, her preferred dumping ground in winter when the sun never rose. It was dark now, even at this hour, as he spun on her, teeth bared in a snarl.

Not so grandfatherly now, she thought. "There you are. I was wondering what was beneath all that."

A light fog hung over the lake. Reeds and cattails framed the edge of the moonlit water and there was nothing but trees and uncultivated land as far as the eye could see.

Conifers loomed over them, the scent of Sitka spruce strong as he lunged for Lou, a blade glinting in his fist.

If she didn't move, if she remained fixed where she stood, she would take his blade to the gut, an inch below her navel. Certainly, *that* would end her pregnancy, wouldn't it?

She hesitated.

And she moved.

At the last moment, she pivoted, letting the blade pass her without making so much as a nick. Before the man could recover, her Beretta was in her hand, shoved into his temple. He dropped the knife without being asked.

"How clever. You read my mind," Lou said, kicking it out of reach. "Can you guess what I want from you next?"

He looked from Lou to the lake, back to Lou. She waited. She always found this part interesting, where their minds tried to work out what had happened, where they were.

"You're her then," he said, lowering his hands to his knees. He didn't try to get up, nor did he try to strike her.

Lou cocked her head. "*Her.* I'm guessing you had cameras that night then."

That was interesting because it meant the surveillance was hidden somehow. If it were accessible, Konstantine's program would have locked in on her, but it hadn't.

"Where are the kids?" he asked.

"Don't worry about them," Lou said, keeping her smile wolfish. "You were scouting for their replacements anyway, weren't you?"

He laughed, a genuine belly laugh.

"What can you tell me about this *Father* I've heard so much about?"

"It's me."

"No," she said. "It's not." Her compass was clear on that.

The humor evaporated even quicker than it had come.

"What have they told you?" he asked through gritted teeth.

Lou struck him hard across the mouth with the gun. She'd been wanting to do it since she'd gotten a good look at his real face. It was satisfying to finally have done it.

His lip split and bled. The swelling was immediate.

"I'm not sure someone like you deserves a swift death," Lou said, bending down to pick up the knife. "Do you?"

"It doesn't matter," he said, his eyes still cold. "Hurt me if you want, but I won't tell you anything."

Lou was annoyed to find he meant it.

On the embankment, she tried cutting him. She tried twisting the blade in non-essential organs—then in a few essential ones. She shot him in the shoulder, then in the thigh. But no amount of needling got her the answers that she wanted.

He screamed, certainly. He even lunged at her once, which cost him a finger. But he didn't spill his secrets or anyone else's.

The man wheezed, struggling to draw a breath. What did he expect? She'd punctured his lung.

She supposed she should be happy that she had something to look forward to. There was still someone out there—*someones*, perhaps—deserving of her retribution.

She would hunt and kill everyone responsible, without question. But this felt big. It felt like her first hunt in a lot of ways. All those years dedicated to extinguishing the family that had extinguished hers. But eliminating one of the oldest crime families in Italy had required a certain level of organization.

Lou needed to know more. About whom she was fighting.

About the size and shape of their operation. Or perhaps *operations*. Was it a large prostitution ring?

A pedophiliac network for trafficking children?

She'd hoped to be closer to these answers after wasting an hour on this guy, but he'd given her nothing.

"Am I losing my touch?" she murmured, her hands and forearms slick with blood all the way up to her elbows.

The man gurgled an incomprehensible reply.

Without ceremony, she sheathed the knife she'd been holding and pulled her Beretta. A single pull of the trigger spilled the man's brains across the embankment. Coyotes screamed in the distance.

As she dragged the lifeless mess of a body into the water, the smooth surface disturbed by her movements, Lou wondered if she was going about this the wrong way.

Gripping the man's cold calf, she dove, holding herself beneath the waters until her gift could work its magic.

As the black waters grew warmer, lightening to red, Lou realized she had been avoiding Konstantine. Not physically, as that would have created suspicion. But she had not asked for his help with this hunt, had not drawn on his skills or connections to discern the full extent of what she was up against.

And why?

Because some part of her worried her secret might be discovered. As if he might simply guess that she was pregnant if she spent too much time with him.

Was that why she had not lingered in his presence for weeks? Why she had struggled to look at him for any length of time?

At least he had not noticed.

Now her most promising lead was dead, and she was emerging from blood-red waters into the nightmare realm that had been her escape for years. Lou regarded the two moons in the sky, each a luminous white tonight, as they hung above the mountains in the distance.

I'm going to need his help on this, she thought, hauling the tortured remains of her kill onto the black shores of La Loon. Water dripped from her leather coat as she wiped the crimson droplets from her face. Ink-black foliage crowded the silent shore. Waves knocked against the heels of her boots as she dropped the body unceremoniously. The monster she called Jabbers would find it here when she was ready.

The fact that she wasn't here meant she was in the cave with her offspring. Lou didn't mind walking the mile to meet them, but she would *not* do it dragging a waterlogged corpse —no matter how fond she was of the beast.

After she dropped the body on the shore, she saw that she was bleeding. She spotted the cut on the back of her hand and bent to wash it in the water.

We know that the microbes in its waters heal you, and we find them in your blood. Will they cross the placenta?

Isadora had expressed concern over what these waters might do to Lou's unborn child.

They'd known for a long time that Lou's amazing ability to heal, to bring her body back from the brink of death again and again, was the result of the miraculous microbial life in these waters. She'd learned that only because of Konstantine's endless curiosity.

And as Lou washed her hand, she tried to count how many times she had crossed over to this place since becoming pregnant. Ten? Twenty times?

It was hard to say.

But even these musings were little more than casual chatter in the back of her mind as she walked away from the shore and headed in the direction of the distant rockface.

As she walked, her mind kept turning back to the moment her target had tried to stab her.

He'd had a good shot. Lou had been wide open, her stomach right there.

She could have let him strike her. Such a blow wouldn't have ended her life. She could have killed him easily—she'd been playing with him after all.

Then she would have crossed into the healing waters of La Loon and any remaining threat to her life would have evaporated.

Yet she'd turned at the last moment.

She hadn't allowed him to land the blow. More than that, she hadn't wanted the bastard to touch her.

The part that scared Lou wasn't that she'd simply refused to be stabbed by that asshole, it was the thought she'd had the moment she'd turned away.

She hadn't wanted him to stab *her*.

And the *her* hadn't been Lou. The *her* Lou had been thinking of was the baby.

A tornado of mixed emotions turned within her mind. Why had she been convinced in that moment that it *was* a *her*? Why had she felt protective of *her* if Lou didn't want a baby?

She was still trying to work out what she was thinking, what she was feeling, by the time she reached the mountain-side and followed the dark passage to the underwater cavern at its end.

Lou dove beneath the rock wall and swam the short passageway to the other side, hearing the ruckus of Jabbers' offspring as she hauled herself out of the shimmering blue pool onto a rock ledge.

Before Lou's eyes could adjust to the low light, Jabbers was there, pressing her large serpentine head into Lou's damp palm.

The beast was enormous with its six legs and pus-colored eyes. Every movement was a contraction of her entire body.

As she slid her torso along Lou's side in greeting, the force of it nearly knocked her off balance.

Chirping and trills echoed off the high walls, causing Lou's ears to ache from the ferocity of it. The six babies Jabbers had hatched five months ago had grown exponentially. At first it had been difficult to know how large they were. Since this first part of their life cycle was spent in the water, Lou had not been able to gauge their full size. They poked their heads above the surface from time to time, giving Lou the impression of tadpoles blinking large, uncomprehending eyes.

They would slide by and let her stroke their scales on occasion, and she'd estimated that the longest was perhaps close to ten or twelve feet long, though she hadn't touched it all the way to the tip of its tail.

If they grew up to be like their mother, they would eventually escape this cavern for the world outside. Then what? Would Lou have to worry about being their next meal, or would they be used to her?

She supposed only time would tell.

Jabbers didn't seem concerned either way. She dove into the dark pool in the center of the cavern and disappeared.

The bulbous head of one of Jabbers's offspring emerged from the water at Lou's feet, and she reached out to touch it.

The creature pulled back, but only enough to flare its nostrils and take in Lou's scent.

Yes, get a good whiff, Lou thought. *Commit me to memory. One day my life may depend on it.*

6

Konstantine had always enjoyed cooking, but he enjoyed it most when it was for both of them. Tonight he'd made a plate of pasta with an amatriciana sauce. The second course was braised beef. He'd just opened a bottle of red wine and poured himself a glass when Lou, soaking wet, stepped from the hallway closet.

"Get ready for dinner, *amore mio*," he called. "I'm almost finished."

If she'd heard him, he couldn't be sure. He listened to the shower run, the opening and closing of drawers. Then she was in front of him. Her wet hair brushed back from her face, her cheeks red from either the shower's steam or the exertion of a hunt.

He went to her, putting a glass of wine in her hand. "I missed you."

Her lips quirked. "I saw you this morning."

He placed a kiss behind her ear, then lower on her throat. She slid her free arm around him, and this reciprocation, as small as it was, cheered him.

We are all right, he told himself. *We will be all right.*

Yet he couldn't stop himself from watching her every move at dinner. He watched how much she ate, how much she drank—little more than a few sips. Her eyes followed him. She responded to all of his inquiries about the events of the day. On the surface, everything was normal, but beneath —something was missing.

He wanted to ask what preoccupied her, what was on her mind. But he was afraid she would only retreat further from him if he did.

His own cheeks were warm from the wine when he reached across the table and pulled her seat to his. "You're too far away. Did you get enough to eat?"

"Yes, thanks," she said. "I'll clean up."

"Later," he said. "I want to hold you, *amore mio*. Can we go to bed?"

By way of answering him, she began pulling off his clothes. No sooner did she remove his shirt, revealing his bare chest and abs, than she started on his belt. She held on to the leather loosely with one hand as she pulled him toward the bed.

This was not what he'd meant. But seeing that look in her eyes, he could hardly bring himself to stop her.

He fell onto the flat of his back, her weight collapsing onto him.

"Wait, *amore mio*. One minute."

It was as if she didn't hear him. She removed her shirt and revealed she wore no bra.

He took in the view, certainly, but he didn't like the look of the bruise forming on her collarbone, or the cut on her hip.

"When did this happen?" he asked, trailing his fingers over the skin.

"Today," she said. She pressed his wrists together, cinching them tight with the belt.

She means to distract me. She knows I won't ask questions when she has me like this.

"Look at me, Louie."

She did as she unfastened his pants and pulled them free. He lay there exposed, and the hungry look in her eye was enough to end all his attempts at making conversation. He warmed from head to toe, even as he lay naked on their sheets. She traced kisses from his chest over his stomach, down one thigh.

He was already hard when she took him into her mouth, drawing a moan from him.

He was almost lost in the delicious pleasure of it when a dark thought occurred to him.

He fisted her hair as her suction intensified and her tongue massaged the base of him.

"Wait," he begged. Already the edge of his mind was soft.

She sucked harder.

"*Per favore. Ti prego.*"

She lifted her head, her lips wet. "Yes?"

"Valentine's Day," he said.

"What about it?" Her eyes were dark as she placed one kiss on his shaft, pillow soft. Then another.

"Spend it with me," he said, his fingers softening in her hair. "*Per favore.*"

She slid her mouth down to the hilt again before answering.

The vibration almost sent him over the edge. "*Amore.*"

She released him, lifting her head and smiling. "I said 'fine.' Anything else?"

Yes, he thought. *Tell me what's wrong.*

But he said nothing. He let her take him first with her mouth before he did the same, though before she was finished, she pulled him up between her legs and guided him inside her. Still he came before she did.

And despite his best efforts—he found his treacherous thoughts overtaking him.

He imagined her doing this with any other man.

Imagined him placing his hands on her hips like this.

Listening to the soft purr of her moans like this.

Feeling her tight around him like this.

As he started to lose his erection, she simply rolled him onto his back and finished, keeping him pinned inside her until her body convulsed with her release.

I can't, he thought, and held her close. *Ti amo.*

He wouldn't say it. She'd asked him not to, but she could not stop him from thinking it.

I love you.

He was surprised to find that she let him hold her for a moment after, but even this did not last. He'd only just inched toward sleep before she was slipping out of the bed.

He tried to quell the fear welling up within him and keep all signs of his distress and desperation suppressed.

Don't go, he wanted to say. *Stay with me.*

But he could no sooner command her than he could the ocean, or the wind sliding along its waves.

"You have a hunt?" he asked, forcing his voice to remain calm, unreadable.

"Yes," she said. "I shouldn't be gone long."

And that was it. She dressed, pulling on her holster and guns. Then her leather jacket.

He thought she would leave without another word. But she surprised him.

"I need your help," she said.

He came up onto his elbows. "With what?"

"I haven't been able to find who's responsible for hurting the kids. I've killed a lot of people. It can only mean this must be a huge operation."

"Do you think it's trafficking?" he asked. He hoped she

would not mistake his excitement. He wasn't thrilled that there were people in the world who would hurt precious children. He was only excited that she was confiding in him at long last, giving him a chance to prove that they were still better together, as a team.

"Maybe. I want to search someone's place tonight. I think I can get his ID, and if I do, maybe we'll have a name. Tomorrow or the day after we can go to the cabin together. If there's a way for you to take pictures of the kids without them knowing, let's do that. I want to know who they are. I can't even be sure Kaia and Elijah are their real names."

"Of course. I have a pair of glasses that can do it," he said.

"The girl is sharp. The sneakier you can be, the better. How long do you need to get ready?"

"Hours. I'm happy to help you," he added. And he was. This was the most she'd said to him in weeks.

DANI SIPPED her whiskey sour and grimaced. "*Pregnant.* Like *pregnant* pregnant?"

"You saw the tests," Piper said, and threw back her Jäger Bomb. "Besides, she said that she's known for weeks. Apparently, a doctor already told her after digging out a bullet or something."

"Yeah, but *pregnant.*" Dani's eyes were wider than Piper had ever seen them. "That's a huge responsibility. What if she loses it because she gets shot or stabbed? What if she blames herself? Or what if she loses it and then she feels relieved? A woman can find herself in a guilt spiral over something like that."

"Do you think it's that or the idea of being a mom? Or maybe the idea of having a baby with Konstantine, of all people?"

Dani tilted her head. "You're still looking for a reason not to like him."

"*No*," Piper protested, though that had certainly been true in the past. She had, over time, begrudgingly accepted the mob boss into their lives. Even if there were things about him that rubbed Piper the wrong way, she couldn't deny that the man was in love with Lou. He'd showed his devotion to her happiness and safety too many times for Piper to doubt him. "No, I'm just trying to understand how she's feeling right now. She's a hard read, you know? I could tell she was freaking out even though she looked like this." Piper did her best impression of Lou's flat expression.

"Of course she's freaking out. She's pregnant!" Dani said.

"Who's pregnant?" someone asked.

Piper turned to find King standing beside her, his hands in the pockets of his coat.

"Oh shit—" Piper muttered, her heart dropping into her stomach.

"My friend from school," Dani said without missing a beat. "She's not sure what she wants to do about it. Her life is complicated."

"Does she like the guy?" King asked. "Will he stick around?"

"I think so," Dani said. "He seems pretty into her. And they've got the money."

"Then they'll be fine," King said, motioning for the bartender.

Piper was hella impressed. Dani hadn't given the game away with even the smallest tell. Not a bat of the eyelash or flash of the brow. It seemed like every muscle in her face had been made of stone. No wonder she'd had such luck with her interrogation at the jail today.

Piper realized King was looking at her.

"You don't think it's a good idea?" King asked.

"Motherhood is just so final," Piper said. "You know what I mean?"

"But such a joy." Piper turned to see the DA, Beth Miller, sliding up on her right side. "I'm with Robbie. Your friend is going to be just fine once she gets into it."

"What are you guys doing here?" Piper asked. She wanted to steer the conversation away from pregnancy.

"Well, this man here missed our lunch date today, and so he's making it up to me with a couple of cocktails and a little live music, aren't you?"

"Aww, that's sweet," Dani said. "No drink for you?"

Dani nodded toward King's empty hands.

"No." He shook his head. "I'm just here for the music."

"And because Mel hates it if you smell like alcohol," Piper said.

"Does she?" Beth said, arching a brow. "And do you come home smelling like alcohol often, Robbie?"

"Not in a long time," he said with a good-natured smile.

Beth pointed at a table closer to the stage. A couple was clearing out, leaving the seats behind. "I'm gonna grab that. You can join me once you get my drink. A gin and tonic, please."

King watched her make her way through the crowd and settle down at the table before passing along her order to the bartender.

"Have you heard from Lou?" King asked.

"Nope," Piper lied. "She's hunting those kidnappers, isn't she?"

"I need her help. We had a case come in today. I want to prioritize it."

Piper frowned. "Must be serious if you're going to bump the Mendoza and Platt cases for it."

"There's a missing girl. *Woman*," he corrected. "She's nineteen. Her mom thinks she's caught up in a satanic cult."

"There's a cult that meets regularly over at Mabel's." Dani finished off her whiskey sour and motioned for the bartender to come back.

King snorted. "You're kidding."

"No, really. We've known about them for a while. I don't know how much Satan is actually involved. They do séances in the cemeteries and full moon rituals in abandoned haunted houses. We got a tip saying they were responsible for about a dozen missing cats in the area. Someone thought they were using them for sacrifice. We did a piece on it a few Halloweens ago."

"And were they?" Piper asked, because this was the first she'd heard about it. Dani investigated some weird stories from time to time. But Piper had lived in New Orleans all her life. She felt like she should know if there was a satanic cult in the area.

"I don't think they were responsible for the missing cats," Dani said. "But they have a standing reservation on Tuesday nights at Mabel's for new recruits. You should go if you want to talk to them. They'll be friendlier than you expect."

Piper snorted. "Reminds me of the joke about the interview to Hell. Hell is fun until you actually sign up for it."

The bartender put Beth's drink on the bar.

King half turned, watching Beth fight off a couple, insisting that she needed the other chair. "I better go over there. But thanks for the tip." To Piper, he added, "See you tomorrow."

"Sure thing, boss." She gave him a little salute, hoping that her nerves weren't showing.

"You better pull it together before tomorrow," Dani said, accepting her new drink from the bartender. "You've got no chill."

"He just surprised me. I didn't expect to see him in the

bar. This is what we get for venturing outside of the gay zone," Piper said.

"I'm serious," Dani said. "You're bad at secrets but pregnancy is a big deal. You can't let that slip to King of all people unless Lou is ready."

"I won't! I could never do that," Piper said.

THE PROMISE PROVED HARDER to keep the next morning when all three of them—King, Lou, and Piper herself—were together in the agency. Piper kept dragging her eyes back to her computer, trying to appear nonchalant, and yet for some strange reason, her gaze kept sliding back to Lou.

She wasn't sure why she felt compelled to stare at Lou in the daylight. *Why* it was so weird to think that she was pregnant right now. No one would look at her and think *pregnant*. She had the same muscular, badass body that she'd always had. Maybe that's why Piper's brain kept struggling to reconcile its appearance with the fact she knew there was a baby in there.

Her mind just kept saying it: *There's a baby in there.*

"Pull yourself together, Genereux," she muttered.

"What's that?" King said. He'd been leaning back in his desk chair, squeezing his stress penguin, forcing its little eyes to bulge in and out with each compression while he explained the possible satanic cult case to them.

But now his eyes were on Piper.

"Just mad at my computer," Piper said, forcing a smile. "It's glitching on me. So, what did you decide?"

Lou was looking at her—or at least Piper thought she was looking at her. It was hard to be sure with her mirrored shades covering her eyes.

"I think the best course of action is to first check and see if the girl is alive," he said.

"And if she is?" Lou asked.

"Then we tell her mother, but also keep an eye on her. It's possible that, as was the case with Zoey Peterson, we're ahead of this. Just because she's alive now, it doesn't mean she isn't in danger."

"That's what we learned from Zoey, yes." Piper strove for an air of professionalism and focus. She kept her eyes glued on King's. *Don't look at her again. Just don't look at her.*

But Lou's presence loomed, a black smudge in the corner of Piper's eye.

"I think I found her," Lou said.

"You've got a lock?" King sat forward. "Great. Get a clear picture that I can share with her mother. You've got your phone on you?"

Lou held her phone up for him to see.

"Off you go then," he said, placing the penguin back on the fake iceberg occupying the corner of his desk.

Without another word, Lou left. She went into the storage closet and closed the door behind her as if it were a real exit. Piper supposed it was. For her.

As soon as the door shut, King said, "What's up with you today?"

"What do you mean?" Piper's heart skipped a beat. "Do I have something on my face?"

"No, what's up with you and Lou? Did you two have a fight?"

"No." Piper was genuinely hurt by the idea that she and Lou wouldn't be the best of friends every minute of their lives until one—or both—of them died.

"Did it look like she was mad at me?" Piper whined.

"You couldn't stop looking at her, and she didn't take her shades off. I thought she only did that when she was upset."

Piper supposed that this was what she got for working with a detective. Of course King was going to read the room, even if Piper did her best to hide her true feelings. Damn him.

"We're fine," Piper said firmly. "Nothing is wrong."

"Might something be *right* then?" His smile grew mischievous. "Would you let me guess?"

"Don't you dare," she said. "Act like you're the boss here. Work on your cases."

But it was too late. Piper had the feeling that King already knew. It was the way he was smiling as he turned back to his computer, humming a tune.

7

L ou stepped from the agency's storage closet out onto a busy street. For a moment, she wasn't sure where she was. She looked up and down the road, trying to get a sense of her surroundings. On her left stood one of the large cemeteries with its sun-bleached tombs. That told Lou she was still in New Orleans at least. She'd not yet seen a cemetery anywhere else that looked quite the same.

But the rest of the road was nondescript. A sandwich shop. A small clothing boutique. A grocer that still had its sign turned to *Closed*. These things could have been anywhere.

They weren't on the main strip, or in the Quarter, that was for sure.

And she didn't see the girl, at least not right away.

Lou quieted her mind until she felt that tug in her gut. It guided her east, up the road in the direction of the intersection.

As Lou walked, she pulled her phone from her pocket and dropped a pin, marking her location. She'd been doing it a lot lately. She'd gotten tired of Konstantine asking her where she'd been, and her not knowing what to tell him. Often her hunts were target based, not location based. And it wasn't like there was a sign that said *Welcome to Glendale* or anything when she snatched a person.

The cemetery ended at the intersection. Cars slid by, most of them going far too fast. But despite the dizzying flow of traffic, Lou's compass locked on its target.

The girl was sitting on the edge of a fountain. This small park was sandwiched between two monstrous rivers of traffic, but the girl didn't seem to mind the frenzy of it. Her hand trailed through the fountain's waters.

When the light turned red, Lou crossed, annoyed by the sun on the back of her neck, her cheeks.

She didn't go straight to the girl, of course. She went to the fountain and walked around it, pretending to enjoy the view.

The girl hardly noticed her. Her hand was still trailing in the water. Her expression downcast and sad.

Lou took a few pictures from different angles. It helped that the girl's thoughts were elsewhere and that there was the fountain. If she asked, Lou could say she was taking photos of it, not her.

After getting four or five decent shots, Lou lingered. With her eyes hidden behind her shades, she could inspect the girl more closely. She didn't seem drunk or strung out on drugs, both of which Lou felt confident she could recognize on sight.

But she did seem thin. Exhausted. And very lost.

Lou stopped in front of her.

"Are you okay?" she asked.

The girl was startled. Her eyes went wide. "Oh, yes. I'm fine."

Then, as if she realized the inadequacy of this answer, she added, "I'm just waiting for somebody."

"Okay," Lou said. "Can you tell me which direction is the French Quarter?"

The girl smiled. It was halfhearted at best. "It's that way. But you're a bit far. If you walk two blocks up that way instead, you can grab the streetcar."

"Thanks," Lou said, and started walking in the direction of the streetcar stop.

Except Lou never reached it. She stepped into the first shadow she found and was gone.

LOU'S inner compass tugged at her attention until she had no choice but to answer the call. But it wasn't the children in the Canadian woods that needed her, nor was it Konstantine, King, or even Piper. It didn't feel like an emergency, but it was incessant nonetheless. Curious, Lou forwarded the photos of the girl to King's cell phone, then took two steps through the nearest shadow, only to find herself at the back of a large lecture hall. Lou had never been to a college lecture in her life—her education had been acquired by other means.

Yet she recognized the scene all the same. The stadium seating. The students sprawled out with their computers, notes, and books spread in front of them. Many of the hands were furiously writing. But the boy Lou chose to sit behind was playing some sort of computer game. It was a first-person shooter, and his character was running through what appeared to be an abandoned warehouse, only to be attacked by a zombie every few hundred feet.

It wasn't the boy or the game that her compass had been drawn to.

It was the professor.

As soon as Lou locked eyes with him, she knew. Her compass snagged almost violently.

His appearance certainly didn't scream *killer*. He was of

medium height and medium build. He wore dress pants and a button-up dress shirt beneath a burgundy sweater vest.

Lou thought of at least two serial killers who'd been wearing sweater vests before she'd killed them.

What's up with the sweater vests?

But already her attention was sliding away from his appearance to his voice.

It was soothing, pleasant.

He could have a lucrative career calming wild animals, or perhaps narrating those sleep stories that Dani liked to listen to before going to bed. But for all its pleasantness, it didn't match his eyes.

Lou could see the coldness in them, even from this distance.

"And here," he was saying, motioning to the image projected on the large screen over his shoulder, "here we have Ted Bundy's work."

He pointed to the bloody, carved remains of a dead body.

His work? Lou almost snorted. To imagine that one day someone might look at all she'd done and refer to it as her *work*.

"We could call it his *body* of work," the professor said, and laughed. "Get it? *Body*."

A few students laughed. More than a few shifted uncomfortably.

"When we study the abnormalities of a mind like Bundy's, we have to ask ourselves if it is nature or nurture. Presently, it's the opinion that sociopathy is a mixture of environmental and genetic factors. A person might be born with a predisposition to sociopathy. But if they are also placed in an environment where love and praise are withheld, where trauma is inflicted and no opportunities to develop resiliency are offered, we are much more likely to see that sociopathy developed fully into *psychopathy*. Can anyone tell me the difference between sociopathy and psychopathy?"

Lou tapped the boy playing the computer game on the shoulder.

He turned toward her, his eyes wide. Clearly he thought he'd been caught.

"Do you have a copy of the syllabus?" she asked him. She wasn't sure he would. After all, how much interest could he have in the course if he spent the entire lecture shooting zombies?

But he surprised her. He reached into his bag, pulled out a folder, and after a short search, produced a thick bundle of papers.

"Thanks," she said, and took the pages.

She scanned the first.

DR. JOHN W. Gein

Psychology 3310: Psychopaths and Psychopathy
Mondays, Wednesdays, Fridays, 12:10 – 2:00

THAT WAS ALL SHE WANTED. She wasn't actually interested in the details of the course or its proposed topics. She wanted only to know the name of her target.

Dr. John W. Gein.

She had a feeling he was connected to the children some-how. This was little more than an inkling, but Lou would take any lead, however small, that she could. Her search thus far had been infuriatingly fruitless.

"You in the back?" the professor said. "Do you know the difference between psychopathy and sociopathy?"

The gamer in front of Lou pointed at his chest. "Are you asking me, Professor?"

"No," the professor said. "The young woman behind you."

Many of the students turned in that direction, craning their necks so they could listen to the response.

But one girl further up was frowning. "There's no one behind him, Professor Gein."

"Oh. My mistake," the professor said, frowning. "My eyes must be playing tricks on me."

LOU WALKED through the glass door of the *The Herald*'s offices, pausing in front of the receptionist stationed there. It was the perky redhead again today. She straightened when she saw Lou, her face lighting up.

"Ms. Allendale is in her office," she said with far too much enthusiasm.

"Thanks." Lou had gone through this exchange many times before. Dani once explained that the girl was infinitely curious about Lou, having assumed that she was her source for top-secret information.

Every time I publish a big story after you come in here, Dani had explained, *she assumes it's you. Should I be insulted that she thinks my investigative skills won't hold on their own? Or jealous because she thinks you're so cool?*

Lou knocked on the open office door. Dani turned, her shoulder pinning her phone to one ear while she typed something furiously on her laptop. There was a discernible jerk of her chin upon seeing Lou, which Lou took to mean, *Sit down, I'll be right with you.*

So Lou did take a seat in one of the chairs opposite her desk, crossing her legs and letting one of her leather boots rest on the opposite side, gentleman style.

Five minutes later, a breathless Dani ended her call. "Sorry about that. I had the most amazing interview yesterday that would have really sold this story I'm working on, and now the guy is backtracking, saying he doesn't want to be on record. I hate it when they get cold feet."

Lou gave her a wolfish grin. "Want me to talk to him?"

"Ha!" Dani barked a laugh. "First of all, he's in jail—"

"I can get into a jail," Lou said. "Those cells are pretty dark at night."

"—*Second*, I don't know if his story will be as valuable if it seems like he was coerced into giving it. Which he absolutely will be if you rough him up for me."

Lou shrugged. "Let me know if you change your mind."

The humor on Dani's face tightened. "How are you feeling?"

"Piper told you."

"Yes, but she didn't have to. I came home to find *ten* pregnancy tests on our coffee table. And unless I've developed some amazing powers of procreation, of which I was *not* aware, I don't think it's possible for me to impregnate my girlfriend. I'm curious though. Why so many tests?"

"I wanted to be sure," Lou said.

"Are you sure?"

"Very."

"Which brings me back to 'How are you feeling?'"

Lou pushed her shades up onto her head. "My boobs are always sore. I can feel them even when I draw a gun and—"

"I will fire you for eavesdropping!" Dani shot a fierce look into the hallway beyond Lou's head. Lou half turned to find the receptionist had been lingering outside the office door, listening. "Get back to work."

"Sorry, Ms. Allendale!" The girl scurried out of sight.

Dani shut the door hard. "I swear to God, if she wasn't so organized and punctual, I'd get rid of her. I'm sorry. You were saying about your boobs?"

"It's less pleasant to pull a gun than it was," Lou said

simply. "And I'm nauseated a lot of the time, but that seems to be going away."

"I think the nausea only lasts for the first trimester. You must be nearing the end of yours. I didn't just mean physically though." Dani gestured at her head, then her heart. "How are you feeling up here? I'd be freaking out."

Lou wasn't sure what to say. Some rational part of her could see that she was in denial. Some sort of shock that this had happened. The other part of her brain thought, *Of course it happened. You can't take a birth control pill regularly when sometimes you end up in a hospital for a day or two at a time. And you keep the most erratic schedule.*

But this was an intellectual war. Her mind was trying to puzzle out what was happening and why. Dani was asking about *feelings*, a very different consideration.

The only feeling that Lou seemed to recognize in herself now was fear.

It was hard to overlook. She hadn't been this afraid in a long time.

"We don't have to talk about this," Dani said, her face soft and sympathetic. "What did you bring me?"

Her eyes were on the syllabus in Lou's hands.

Lou handed the pages over, pointing at the name in the top corner. "I want to know everything there is about this guy."

Dani's brows rose. "A professor of psychopathy who is secretly a killer? That's juicy."

"I *think* he's a killer, and connected to the kids somehow. That's all I know."

Dani glanced from the syllabus to her screen and back again as she typed his name into her computer.

"A short initial search tells us that he's a tenured professor of psychology. He's been at that school for almost twenty years. Oh, and it seems like the two of you have something in common."

"What?" Lou asked, leaning forward and resting her elbows on the desk. But she still couldn't see the computer screen from this angle.

"You're both obsessed with killers. It looks like he's a pretty big expert in his field. He's even headlining a conference in two months as the keynote speaker."

Dani's fingers flew across the keys again. After a few minutes, she frowned. "I don't immediately see what connection he would have to the kids though. I'm not saying he doesn't. I'm just saying I can't spot it from here."

"What do you mean?"

"He doesn't work with children. He co-owns a private practice, but it says in his website's bio that he only accepts adult clients. I don't know where he'd have access to these kids he's taking. He's got the college courses, but those students would be too old. Unless he just snatched those kids off the street—which of course he could have. There's no mention of missing kids in his town or the surrounding area. At least nothing that fits the descriptions you gave me before."

Dani closed her laptop. "I'll do a proper search on him later. You could give his name to Konstantine too. I'm sure he can turn up some things that I can't. Assuming you're talking to him."

Dani tilted her head teasingly. She wrote the professor's name down on a pad of paper.

"I'm talking to him," Lou said. "At least about this."

8

King found the restaurant without much trouble. It had been a twenty-minute walk from the agency, out of the Quarter and then down Canal Street a few blocks. It was an easy walk on a mild day, so he was silently counting his blessings that the weather had turned and the icy wind rolling off the Mississippi had deigned to spare him. He only wished now that the sky wasn't so gray, but he couldn't have everything he wanted.

Life had taught him that much at least.

The store was warm, a short line forming at the counter. He spotted Ms. Bright behind the register almost immediately. Even with the uniform and the little paper hat on her head, she was recognizable.

When it was his turn, he ordered a two-piece meal, dark meat and mashed potatoes. Extra gravy on the side. He also asked for honey for his biscuit, all before she looked up from her register and realized it was him.

"Oh," she said, her eyes widening at the sight of him. "Mr. King."

"I've got an update," he said, keeping his voice low. "I'm in no hurry. I'll be over at that little table if you can step away for a bit."

"Is it bad?" she asked, her fingers turning white as she gripped the counter.

"No," King said.

Had it been bad news, he would have never come to her workplace. No one wants to be told that their daughter is dead, but hearing such news in the middle of an eight-hour shift would be even worse.

"Oh, okay. I'll be right out with your order."

King paid for his meal and stuck an extra five dollars in the tip jar before accepting the paper cup for his fountain drink.

He filled it with unsweet tea—blasphemous, this far south. He enjoyed sweet tea from time to time, but King had spent too much of his life in St. Louis. His taste reflected that.

While he waited, he gazed out the big glass window. Traffic rolled by. Pedestrians began opening their umbrellas—those who had them anyway—and the sidewalk darkened as a light drizzle began to fall.

He was almost through his first tea by the time Ms. Bright sat down in front of him, placing the tray holding his order between them.

"I'm sorry it took me a minute," she said. "But I'm on break now. I've got fifteen minutes."

"Not a problem," King said. "I'm in no hurry. Do you want to get yourself a drink or something to eat?"

"No, no. I had lunch. But maybe a Coke. Do you really have time?"

"I do," he said.

That was mostly true. It wasn't that there weren't many demands on his time. It was simply that he had a space of an hour or two before they would overtake him again.

Once she returned with her own fountain cup, King slid his phone across the table to her, pointing at the woman whose photo was centered there.

"That's her, isn't it?" King asked. "Your daughter?"

The woman's shoulders sagged visibly with relief. "Yes. My god. So, she's okay?"

"That was taken this morning," he told her.

"Did you talk to her? Did you ask her if she's been in touch with Tommy?"

"No," King confessed. "My first objective was to make sure she was alive and well and we did that."

"So my dream—" she began. Then she shook her head. "But it had seemed so real."

"If you like, I can keep an eye on her for a little while longer," King promised. "If she runs into trouble, we'll step in."

The woman's face visibly lit. "Really? You can do that?"

"I can. If you hear anything or have any more dreams, you can always let us know," King added. "But in the meantime, assume that everything is all right. It won't do you any good to worry about her."

Carrie scoffed. "I'm a mother. Mothers always worry about their children."

KING KNOCKED on Mel's door just past ten that evening. Lady barked even before he heard Mel's footsteps crossing the kitchen floor. She opened the door and his breath hitched. She wasn't wearing her fortune teller outfit tonight. Or her pajamas and house coat, which he also saw her in often enough.

She wore head-to-toe black. A black turtleneck and a tight pair of black jeans. Her shoes were snug black boots, which he wasn't sure he'd seen before, though it was possible they'd been overlooked given the length of her skirts.

Around her neck hung a large necklace. An Egyptian cat head was centered on either side by an ankh.

She caught King staring at it. "I know. It's not satanic, but I wasn't sure what else to wear. I don't have a pentagram, even in the shop. I checked my inventory twice. But one of the shopgirls said that Mabel's has an Egyptian theme, so I went with that."

When he didn't say anything, she tugged at her blood-red headscarf self-consciously.

"What is it? Do I look ridiculous? Don't you just stare at me like that. I'm already overdue to get my braids done."

"No, no. You look great. I'm sorry," King said, pulling himself together. "I just didn't expect you to look so nice. I feel like I'm underdressed."

She frowned at him. "What do you mean you didn't expect me to look so nice? Don't I usually look nice?"

"Of course," he said, feeling the ground fall away beneath him. "Of course, but considering this is a *satanic cult* meeting, I don't know. I thought you'd look—"

He didn't even know how to finish.

"Because satanists don't care about their appearance?" Mel asked sternly. Then, fortunately for King, her face broke open in a grin. "I'm kidding. You look fine. A bit like a cop, but I think we can fix that if you take off your duster and put on a leather jacket. Don't you have one?"

He did, though it almost didn't fit him.

He went back to his apartment to exchange it and came back five minutes later. Lady was still standing in the doorway, tail swishing as he approached.

King gave her a scratch on the head as Mel came out of the bedroom. "Here, you can wear this tonight, but give it back to me."

King looked at the collar she held incredulously. "A *spiked* collar?"

"I'm guessing you've never taken a good look at the jewelry I keep in the cases downstairs," she said, and helped him fasten it around his throat. He was very aware of the warmth radiating from her body as her arms were around him.

She stepped back to inspect her work and frowned. "It's the hair. You're too clean-cut. Hold on."

She returned a moment later with a bottle of gel, squeezing one pump into her palm. Before King could protest, her fingers scraped his scalp, pushing the hair this way and that.

He went very still, concentrating on the wall behind her and not on the sensation of her fingers running through his hair.

Then it was over.

"Much better," she declared. "Now let's go. I don't know why these things have to start so late. Don't they know that old people have to sleep?"

"I suspect we'll be the oldest ones there," he said, grateful to have a conversation to escape into, away from the heat that had built in his cheeks.

KING WASN'T sure what he'd find at the lounge just off Jackson Square, but this was not it.

The lights were low. For some reason, someone had replaced the perfectly good bulbs in the chandelier with red ones, so everything was crimson. And there were more people than he'd imagined. Most people stood in threes and fours, chatting with one another. Everyone seemed to have a cocktail that smoked, resembling a magic potion in their hands. Even up close, King couldn't be sure what it was.

There was no punchbowl, no bartender. He wasn't even sure where they'd gotten it.

There was no clear structure to the event either. People were just standing around, nestled between the Egyptian sarcophagi taller than even King himself. Someone had propped a skeleton up on the sofa with its arm stretched over the back, and the *satanists*—if that's what they were—shared the couch with it as if it were a longtime friend and not a heap of bones.

"Is this what you expected?" Mel asked him.

He snorted. "No. This looks more like a college Halloween party than a cult. Are you sure we're in the right place?"

"Yes," Mel said. "Unless Dani got it wrong. I don't think she did."

"Maybe this is one of those counterculture meetings you were talking about," King said, nodding first at her necklace, then at the decor. "At least you blend in."

A woman slid past Mel and she reached out an arm. "Excuse me, is this the meeting place for the—"

King understood her hesitation. It seemed odd to just say the words *satanic cult* at full volume.

"—gathering?" she finished.

"Yes," the girl said with a bright smile. King saw that she had vampire fangs. "It will start in about twenty minutes. You can get yourself a drink downstairs while you wait if you want. Or if you have questions, you can talk to Aleister."

The girl pointed at the guy sitting on the sofa beside the skeleton as if it didn't bother him one bit that its arm was stretched around him.

"Aleister?" Melandra repeated. "Thanks."

Once she was out of earshot, Mel rolled her eyes at King. "What?" he asked.

"Aleister as in Aleister Crowley. If that's his real name, I'll eat my shirt."

King didn't know who Aleister Crowley was. He made his best guess. "A rock star?"

Mel laughed. "No. He was an occultist. He died in the forties."

Someone shrieked and King turned, bewildered.

"Is that Taylor Swift?" It was Aleister. He sucked in a deep breath. "Oh my god, I love this song. Turn it up."

The music, which King had barely been able to hear before, was now thumping his chest. To his surprise, it was in fact Taylor Swift. He'd thought it was some sort of moody ambient music when its volume had been low.

The guy beside the skeleton—Aleister—placed a hand on his chest. "One of the best artists of the twenty-first century. She is *so* underrated. I do a spell every full moon that she'll get the respect she deserves. Do you remember what Kanye did to her? Now there's one that hell would send back."

King didn't comprehend most of this conversation. He understood they were talking about music, and that was the extent of it.

The couple on the sofa beside Aleister rose and excused themselves. As he bid them goodbye, King saw his chance. He went straight to the sofa and took a seat before anyone else could.

"Are you Aleister?" he asked.

Aleister took a sip of his smoking drink. "That's me."

"I was told to speak to you if I had questions."

Aleister's face lit up. "Oh! Are you new? Are you looking to join us?"

"Maybe," King said. He wasn't above lying if undercover work required it. Hell, he was wearing a spiked collar and he had gel in his hair.

He felt someone settling down on the sofa behind him and turned. It was only Mel. He relaxed at that.

"Well, what we do is pretty simple. We believe that people and animals live in an amoral universe. We reject all forms of guilt and self-deprivation. We'd rather indulge ourselves and enjoy our time here on Earth before we blink out of existence."

"You don't believe in Hell?" Mel asked.

"Some of us do. Some of us don't. You've got the *literal* satanists who hold a love of ritual magic in their hearts, and then you have satanists who are more philosophical. They view Satan as the ultimate representative for all things anti-authority."

There. He'd said *satanist*. It was the first time King was hearing the word coming out of someone's mouth. At least he knew for sure he was in the right place.

"I personally view satanism as a chance to see human nature for what it really is and to *appreciate* it for what it is."

"What about sacrifices?" King asked.

"No," Aleister laughed. "I'm *vegan*."

"Oh. My friends told me that was a thing. They're the reason we're here tonight."

Aleister sipped his smoking drink again. "Are they here?"

"No, but maybe you know them. Jenny Bright? And her cousin Tommy."

Aleister shook his head. "Sorry, no. Doesn't ring a bell."

"Maybe I'm mistaken," King said. "It's not possible that I'm confusing you with another group of satanists, am I?"

Aleister laughed. "Probably not. There are a few loners out there, but you gotta watch out for those. Even Satan had his friends when he—*Trinity!*"

King followed his gaze to a woman across the room, bewildered by the interruption.

"Change the music *back*," Aleister commanded. His

expression was far more sinister now than it had been a moment before. "And if you turn off Taylor again, I will *murder* you."

"I'm here!" A tall man covered in glitter wearing horns burst into the room. "Let's eat while the quiche is still warm."

"Oh, you *have* to try Dan's quiche," Aleister said, rising from the sofa. "It's to die for."

Five minutes later King and Mel stood in Jackson Square, just outside Mabel's. They were laughing so hard they cried.

"They could still be a cult," Melandra said, dabbing at her eyes. "But I think Aleister worships Taylor Swift more than he does Satan."

They burst out laughing again and began walking in the direction of home.

They passed the tarot card readers and palmists cluttering the square. They caught snippets of conversation as they passed, promises made of future success in love and wealth.

"I wonder if she misses it," King said, remembering how Piper used to do readings in the square. She had rented one of Jim's card tables for five dollars a night and set it up outside of his jambalaya restaurant.

"She told me she does," Mel said. "But she likes what she's doing for you."

"She's good at it. She'll be a great agent one day if that's where she decides to go with it."

"And if she doesn't? What if she wants to stay in the PI business with you?"

King shrugged. It tugged at his heartstrings to know that one day Piper might move on. He'd grown very fond of the kid and her company. She was smart, brave, and loyal. Three traits he really admired.

"I'll support her no matter what path she takes," he said finally, his throat a little tight.

They walked down Royal Street in silence. Once they

reached her shop, King waited for Mel to open the locked door before they stepped inside. They kept the lights off. In New Orleans, a light was an invitation. The Quarter rarely slept and expected everyone to keep indecent hours. So, they remained in the dark as they locked up and crept up the stairs to their waiting apartments.

Lady started barking as soon she heard the first footstep on the stairs.

King walked Mel to her door first, waiting at the threshold until she was inside. Lady licked his hand good-night before he turned to go.

"Sleep tight," he said. "Thanks for your help tonight."

Mel was looking at him funny.

"What?" He touched his face self-consciously.

"You going to give me back that collar? It looks good on you, but the girls might have some questions."

They burst out laughing again. He struggled to unfasten it from his throat, and she had to help him.

And he kept thinking about the way her fingers felt on the back of his neck, and earlier in his hair.

Even after he was alone in his apartment, with the sounds of Bourbon Street filtering through his windows. Even after he'd closed his eyes.

He kept thinking about her.

9

W hen they woke on Valentine's Day, Konstantine was ready. He'd already made their breakfast by the time Lou came into the kitchen.

"What's this?" she asked.

She picked up the box of chocolate-covered hazelnuts he'd left beside her plate. "It's for La Festa Degli Innamorati. There's a poem inside."

Lou opened the box, slipped a chocolate between her teeth, and read the poem. "It's in Italian."

"You can practice translating it. I'll help you," he said, and placed a slice of frittata on her plate.

He was pleased that she ate well. He didn't like American breakfast himself. It was far too much for his Italian stomach, which required little more than coffee and perhaps fette biscottate or toasted bread with butter and jam.

But since Lou often didn't eat during the day, it felt necessary to feed her well at breakfast and again at dinner—the only times he could be sure she'd eaten at all.

So an American breakfast it was. He watched her

consume a generous slice of the frittata and two ricotta pancakes.

He quickly turned his attention to clearing the dishes.

"What is it?" she said. "Why were you looking at me like that?"

"I like to see you eat," he said. "That's it, *amore mio*."

"I need a shower." She closed the chocolate box and pushed it away from her. "Are we in a hurry?"

"No," he said. "They will be ready for us whenever we arrive."

"Who?"

He grinned. "You'll see."

It was nearly noon before they arrived at the leather goods store overlooking the Piazza Strozzi.

She snorted when she saw the mannequins in the glass storefront. "I should have guessed we'd be shopping for clothes. It's your favorite thing."

Her words made him reconsider his decision. Should he have gone for the guns instead? Did she think this trip was for himself and not for her?

"I thought we could look at their jackets, gloves, and boots," he said. "Yours need replacing."

"You're wasting your money," she said.

He opened the door for her. "I like wasting money on you."

Konstantine had worried that perhaps her impatience would make it impossible to truly enjoy the experience. But she indulged him, trying on more than eight jackets before deciding on two—one for play, one for hunting. She also selected a new pair of boots and a set of fingerless gloves. He even persuaded her to try on two pairs of leather pants, but though they looked nothing less than divine on her body, she didn't want them.

"They're impractical," she declared. "Now your turn."

"No, *amore mio*. This is for you. I want to make you happy."

"Then let me buy you something," she said. "That will make me happy."

Her eyes were fixed on him in a silent challenge. The girl who'd been helping them took a step back. That more than anything caused Konstantine to fold. "All right. If that will make you happy."

"It will," she said, without blinking.

But even as he tried on the clothes, selecting items that he thought complemented hers, he couldn't help but feel like she was only trying to stay on even footing with him. That perhaps she didn't want to owe him anything.

Because she wants to leave, his dark mind said. *She wants to owe me nothing when she leaves me.*

It was the shopgirl's small voice that pulled him back to his senses. "Will that be all, signore?"

"Yes. Wrap it all and send it all to this address, *per favore*."

Then they were standing outside the store, piazza bustling around them. Foot traffic and mopeds heading in all directions.

"Was there something else you wanted to do?" she asked. "You made me promise to give you the whole day."

Made.

Was she not having a good time?

"I had one other thing in mind," he said. "But if you're tired or bored—"

"I'm not," she said simply.

"It will require the use of your special gift. I would drive us, but it is more than five hours away. I don't suspect you'd tolerate such a delay."

"I'll take us," Lou said simply. She pulled him into the shadows between the two buildings.

"Are you thinking of where you want to go?"

"Yes." He enjoyed her warmth and weight against him.

Before he could take a steadying breath, they were through.

When the world reformed, he could smell the sea. And as they stepped away from the protection of the building, he could see and hear it too. An endless view of deep blue stretched infinite before them. From the cliff where they stood, the waves looked like little more than swaths of froth on the surface.

For a moment neither of them could move or speak. They were so struck by the beauty.

"I don't know if I've ever seen so much ocean before," Lou said. "Where are we?"

"Sorrento."

"You've been here before?" she asked, trying to smooth her hair back from her face. The wind was assaulting it, sending her dark strands flying in all directions.

"A few times. The first was when my mother brought me as a boy."

"I've never seen water so blue," Lou said.

Together they sank down onto the sole bench at the top of the cliff and watched the vast ocean.

They were silent for almost an hour, when Konstantine saw the goosebumps on her arms.

"This is all I had planned," he said finally. "You can go whenever you want."

"Come with me," she said.

His heart lifted. "Anywhere."

LOU FOUND IT JARRING. To go from the beautiful seaside view off the Italian coast to the snowy Canadian woods. Sometimes it didn't bother her, to go all over the world in a single day. Other times, her mind seemed very aware of the impermanence of her hours. This morning she was having breakfast, eating chocolates while Konstantine poured her a cup of coffee.

Now that morning seemed like a lifetime ago.

Perhaps it was a lack of sleep that gave her life this strange, dazed quality.

Her night had been stressful. She couldn't recall exactly what she'd dreamed of, only the theme. She'd been looking for something. Looking again and again, but no matter how hard she tried, she couldn't reach it.

But at least the nausea was gone. Now, in its place seemed to be a ravenous appetite. She'd had to control herself at breakfast.

And now Konstantine stood outside the cabin holding two Florentine pizzas. They smelled amazing.

"Are you ready?" she asked.

He adjusted the glasses on the bridge of his nose. "Yes."

He looked very handsome in glasses. She wondered if he knew. "Is there any way for someone to hack your glasses and see the children?"

"No," he said. "I have them linked to my network only. No one has penetrated my defenses before."

"There's a first time for everything," she said, and pulled them into the cabin's bathroom.

There was no point in knocking on the door to announce her arrival. She was already anticipating chaos. If they weren't suspicious of her before, they certainly would be now that she'd brought a stranger to their secret hideout.

And she was right. As soon as they stepped into the living room, they both leapt up from the sofa by the fire and sprinted for the bedroom.

Lou shifted through the dark into the bedroom before they even got the door closed.

"That's rude," she said.

They screamed, the girl launching herself at Lou.

Lou caught her easily, holding Kaia at arm's length so she couldn't land a blow.

"Why are you upset?" she said plainly. "You don't even know him."

"You're going to take us back!" Elijah screamed.

"The hell I am," Lou said. "We brought pizza."

Kaia stopped twisting in Lou's arms at least, but her gaze remained murderous.

"Pizza?" she asked through clenched teeth.

"Yes," Lou said. "Aren't you running low on snacks?"

"But why did you bring him?" Elijah asked.

"Because I trust him. And because I want someone to know where you are if something happens to me."

This got their attention.

It was a bald-faced lie, of course, but Lou was hardly a saint. And it worked as she'd intended.

"If something happens to you?" Kaia said, taking a step back. She rubbed her red wrist. "Why would something happen to you?"

"Because I've been hunting the people who hurt you," Lou said. "They're dangerous people. Things happen."

Again, Lou had zero intention of letting herself get killed by whoever *Father* and his people were. But she was willing to play to Kaia's fears to get her to comply with her plan. If Kaia was willing to come out into the living room, then Elijah would follow her lead.

"Won't you come meet him?" Lou pressed. "His name is Konstantine."

Lou opened the door, holding it open for them. As she'd expected, Kaia went out first with Elijah close on her heels.

"Hello," Konstantine said. He'd set the pizzas on the wooden coffee table in front of the fire. Now he was on the sofa, his body relaxed. "I realize we didn't bring drinks, *amore mio*."

"You have a funny accent," Elijah said.

"Where are you from?" Kaia demanded, wringing her little hands as if she wasn't sure what to do with them.

"Italy," Konstantine said. "This pizza is from Italy too. Have you ever had authentic Italian pizza?"

That was all that needed to be said before Elijah took a slice and shoveled it into his mouth.

"It's good," Elijah said.

"You're hungry," Kaia said grumpily. "Everything tastes good when you're hungry."

Konstantine looked like he was on the verge of laughing.

Reluctantly, Kaia took a slice. Lou could tell by the speed at which she ate that she'd been hungry too. Lou walked to the kitchen and pulled two glasses from the cabinet and filled them with water from the jug in the fridge. They were down to one. She'd have to remember to bring more tomorrow.

"Do you have green eyes?" Elijah asked.

"I do," Konstantine said. "See?"

The boy came quite close to Konstantine's face, and Konstantine grabbed the side of his glasses, sliding them down so the boy could look into his eyes.

Smooth, Lou thought as she put a glass of water in front of each of the children.

"They're really green like yours, Kaia. I thought green eyes were really rare."

"No one has green eyes like mine," Kaia said, finishing off her pizza slice. She took the paper towel Lou offered and meticulously cleaned her hands.

"Are you sure?" Konstantine asked. "Take a look."

Kaia didn't come as close as the boy, but she did look him square in the eyes. Lou hoped that would be enough to get a good photo of her face.

"Yours are darker than mine," Kaia said, triumphant.

"In this light, yes," Konstantine conceded, his smile bright. He turned to Lou and gave her a wink. Lou took that to mean that they had what they needed.

"If anything happens to me, Konstantine will come for you," Lou said. "He'll take care of you. Keep you safe."

"Why wait? We could bring them to Italy now, *amore mio*."

Eli's face lit up. "Italy!"

"No!" Kaia cried.

Konstantine pouted his lips. "Why don't you want to come to Italy? You know, there are other children there that I look after."

"Really?" Elijah asked, clearly half in love with the idea.

"Matteo is your age," Konstantine said to Eli. To Kaia he added, "It's mostly boys, but there is another girl. Gabriella. They do not speak English well, but they will be very kind to you. You can even go to school if you want to. And you can play football in the piazza with the others after school. Or soccer. You call it soccer."

Lou thought she saw something in Kaia's face before it hardened again.

"We want to stay together," she said, her voice quavering a little at the end.

"No one said anything about separating you," Konstantine said, holding open his hands. "Do you mean at night? Gabriella sleeps in her own room, that's true."

"Anytime," Kaia said. "We're not going to be separated *ever*."

Konstantine looked to Lou. Lou shrugged. It hadn't occurred to her to bring them to Italy. But he was right. They might be safer there. With an ocean between them and those who hunted them, deep in Konstantine's stronghold. She could think of no safer place. He already had twenty-four-seven surveillance on the orphans he cared for.

"Think about it," Lou told them. "If you change your mind, I'll take you."

Eli's shoulders sagged. It was clear he was far more excited by the idea of living with boys his age, in some mystical land of delicious pizza and football after school.

But Kaia was in charge here, and everyone in the room seemed to know it.

"We should get going," Lou said, giving Konstantine's shoulder a squeeze. "You've marked the place on your watch?"

Konstantine looked at the watch on his wrist.

"Yes. But I do not travel as quickly as you." He turned to the kids. "I don't think anything will happen—Lou is very strong, very powerful—but if it does, it will take me longer to reach you. Can you be patient with me if that happens?"

They had agreed on this dialogue before they came to the cabin. Lou had hoped by planting the seed in their minds that Lou's life was at risk, that they were running out of time to help *her* help *them*, maybe they would finally tell her the truth of their situation.

But Kaia wasn't so easily manipulated. "We don't need anyone to save us."

Konstantine only gave her a pitying smile. "You know, you remind me of Gabriella. She also didn't want to be saved."

Konstantine placed his hands on his knees and stood. "Shall we, *amore mio?*"

"Do you need anything before I go?" Lou asked them.

Lou saw Elijah's fingers were still greasy with pizza oil, and handed him another napkin.

"No," Elijah said.

Kaia said nothing. She was only staring moodily at the pizza, seemingly lost in her own thoughts.

"It was nice to meet you both," Konstantine said. And then they were through the dark bathroom and back out in the snowy day.

They hid amongst the snow-laden pines while Konstantine snapped a few more photos of the cabin and recorded its coordinates.

"I can also consider other possible surveillance options for this place, if I have a sense of the landscape."

"You're full of good ideas today," she said. "The ocean. Pizza."

Konstantine beamed. "I'm always happy to help you, *amore mio*. I am with you, in all things."

Without realizing its significance, he placed a hand on her stomach.

Her chest compressed.

I am with you in all things.

All things.

But would he be with her in this?

10

K ing was on his third cup of coffee for the day when he got the email he'd been waiting for. He read the report twice, printing two copies. Then he highlighted what he thought was essential.

Once he was satisfied and felt ready to begin, he looked across the room to Piper, who had been typing furiously, frowning at the screen.

"Can you spare me a couple of hours?" he asked her.

"God, please yes." She almost slammed her laptop closed. "I'm going blind looking at these statements. I need a break."

"I've got addresses for both Jenny and Tommy. Let's drive around and see if we can catch them."

"Let me just put this stuff upstairs." Piper gathered up her things, before carrying them to the door at the end of the room, the one leading up to her apartment.

King listened to her footsteps above while he locked his own belongings into his desk and poured the remainder of the coffee into two travel cups and turned off the pot. He'd wash it later. As he added a splash of cream to his—he was still trying to watch his sugar intake—the sun came out, brightening the street outside.

Five minutes later they were walking down Royal Street in the direction of his Buick, parked in the alley beside Melandra's Fortunes and Fixes. The sun on the back of his neck was so pleasant, it almost felt like spring.

Yes, it was best not to spend afternoons like this locked up in an office.

Once they'd climbed into the Buick and fastened their seatbelts, Piper took a sip of her coffee. Hers was a caramel color, having added much more cream and sugar than King had.

"Where's her place?" Piper asked.

"Black Pearl," King said. "There's an apartment building a couple of blocks from the last St. Charles streetcar stop."

"Short trip then," she said, and took a bigger drink of her coffee.

"You look professional," King said, noting the file and materials on her lap. "You're getting very good at this."

"Thanks." Piper brightened as he knew she would.

"Have you thought any more about the path you want to take?"

"After your horrible stories about Quantico, it's not my first pick," she admitted. "But I can't help but think it would be really cool to be an FBI agent."

King didn't want to deflate her opinions with facts. He said simply, "It's not always as exciting as they portray it on television. The work you do with Lou and I might be about as adventurous as it gets."

"Especially Lou," Piper moaned. "With her I can see Europe and a Hawaiian beach in the same night. But you know, I was thinking about that. Even if I don't end up being an agent full-time, I think it would be cool to go through the training and learn all the cool agent stuff. Then I'd be of more use to you guys."

King waved at the car ahead of him. It was slowly—far too slowly—trying to merge. The driver held up his hand in thanks.

"What do you mean?" King said. "You're already useful."

"Yeah, but I don't have your investigative skills—"

"You're getting there."

Piper rolled her eyes. "Dani's the badass investigative journalist. Lou's the ninja. The Italian stallion is the eyes-everywhere tech guy. And nobody detectives like you. I can't even shoot a gun well. I just feel like I need to bring something to the table if I'm going to be part of the team. Maybe if I got some formal training, I'd be more useful."

"You're already essential to the team. You don't need the training to prove that."

Piper took a sip of her coffee and looked out the window.

She seemed embarrassed to have said this out loud. Her cheeks turned red.

A car was coming the wrong way down a one-way. King laid on the horn. "People."

"Mardi Gras," Piper corrected. "It'll be nuts for the next few weeks. I thought you'd be used to that by now."

Despite the traffic and the tourists who couldn't navigate New Orleans's intricate system of one-way streets, they pulled up outside Jenny's apartment building fifteen minutes later.

The sky had darkened again. The brief splash of sunshine King had been soaking up was now behind dark storm clouds once more. And the wind had kicked up ominously as he craned his neck up at the sky to regard the building.

It was unremarkable red brick, featureless. The windows ran in ten rows on each side. King knew that one of those windows on the ninth floor belonged to Jenny. He half expected to see someone peel back the blinds and look down at him suspiciously.

But nothing moved.

King double-checked that he'd locked the Buick and opened the lobby door for Piper.

The lobby smelled, oddly, like a mix of bleach and stale food. On one side were metal mailboxes and on the other an empty desk. If this place did have a doorperson, they were out.

"Not a very secure building," King noted. "If someone can just come in off the street. No one watching the door. No need for a resident to buzz you in."

"Home not secure. Doesn't bode well for our girl." Piper gestured at the elevator at the end of the entryway. "Should we risk it or take the stairs? This feels like the kind of building where maybe they don't keep the elevator maintenance up to date."

King's knees protested at the very idea of nine flights of stairs. "I'll take my chances with the elevator."

Piper stepped in after him without complaint.

He pushed the floor button marked nine and the doors creaked closed. Then the elevator shuddered.

Piper grabbed his arm. "It's not tall enough of a building for us to die if the elevator cables snap and we go crashing to the ground, is it?"

"Control that imagination of yours," he said as the floor began to rise. "See. We're fine."

He wouldn't admit to her that he was also nervous about the way the wheels or belts or whatever made this box move screeched horribly out of sight. It sounded like it needed a whole can of WD-40.

When the elevator shuddered to a stop, Piper shot out before the doors even fully opened. She visibly exhaled with relief once her feet were on solid ground again.

"I'll be taking the stairs on the way down. Nothing personal," she said.

King glanced at his notes. "It's apartment 910."

They found apartment 910 at the end of the hallway. Except the door didn't say 910. It read 91. The zero, wherever it was, had escaped. King knocked.

There was no answer on the first try.

He knocked again, more loudly this time, and was answered by a yappy dog. King guessed it was a pint-sized hell beast even before the door opened.

"Shut it, Sugar," someone groaned out of sight. "You're killing me."

King knocked a third time, and someone yelled, "I'm coming, for Christ's sake!"

Feet pounded in their direction and the door flew open.

"*What?*" a woman hissed. She scowled up at King. She was no taller than five-two and wore an oversized t-shirt and fuzzy purple slippers.

"*What?*" she said again. "Say something or I'm closing the door."

"We're looking for Jenny Bright," King said. "You're not her."

"Brilliant," the girl said. "You must've gotten great grades in school."

"Her mother is looking for her," King added.

"Sure," the girl said, looking him up and down. It was a thrashing Pomeranian that was wiggling in her arms, its murderous eyes fixed on King.

"We just want to talk to her if she's home. Once I know she's okay, I can let her mother know."

In truth, King wanted to see the girl with his own eyes. The photos Lou took had satisfied the mother, but not King. Every time his mind returned to Jenny, his heart sank a little.

The woman turned her sinister gaze to Piper and the eyes widened. "P? Holy shit. Is that you?"

"Hey, Dom," Piper said. "It's been a minute."

Dom scoffed. "About ten years. What the hell you doing here with a cop?"

King looked at his clothes. Why did everyone keep saying he looked like a cop? He was only wearing a button-down. Plenty of people wore button-downs.

"He's a private detective, actually," Piper said. "I'm his co-investigator. I've even got my own cases."

Her eyes widened. "Oh shit. Like *CSI* or something. That's cool. Wait. Then what are you doing here?" she asked. "Jenny's not home. I haven't seen her in weeks."

Weeks. King's heart skipped a beat.

Dom's face lit up. "Oh my god. Are you telling me she's dead? Is this some true crime shit?"

She looked far too excited given the topic at hand.

"Can we come in?" he asked.

She looked ready to refuse him on principle. Then Piper added, "Please."

"Whatever. Get in here. But if Sugar bites you or pisses on your leg, I'm not responsible."

"I thought you hated dogs," Piper said.

Dom held Sugar up. "I do. This is Jenny's dog, but since she hasn't come back, what was I going to do? Let it starve? Besides, it's hard to dislike something as hateful as I am."

She laughed at her own joke. But it didn't stay. Her face was serious again by the time King and Piper took a seat on one of the two plaid sofas.

"What's going on with Jenny? She in serious trouble?"

King flipped through his files and produced a picture of Tommy. "Have you seen this guy hanging around? Maybe he came over with Jenny."

"Yeah," she said. "That bastard has been here a few times. He's creepy as hell. I don't think he blinks. Did *he* kill her?"

"We don't know if she's dead," Piper said frankly. "That's what we're trying to figure out."

Dom touched her throat. "Oh my god, they're going to make a movie about this. I'm gonna be one of those shadow people, you know? You just see their silhouette and hear their voice while they tell you about their roommate who was hacked up and thrown in a dumpster by a creep."

King wasn't sure if he should write any of that down. "Did Jenny ever talk about him?"

"No, not really," Dom said. "She said he was her cousin and that they had a crazy family. But that's all I remember. The last time I saw her, he was here though. Then the other guy came."

King's hand stopped scribbling and he looked up. "The other guy?"

"Yeah, the guy who's always giving her money. He's older. Strong jaw. Gray in his hair, but like the sexy gray. With the black mixed in. My *god*." Dom said this to Piper as if she would appreciate it.

Piper forced a smile. It was that expression alone that told King that Dom had been a casual high school acquaintance at best. Had it not been safe to tell people she was gay in high school? Or maybe Dom just wasn't the kind of person one could confide in.

"Do you remember when this older guy came by?" Piper asked.

"Three days ago. I got the light bill that day and I asked him if he was going to pay it. At first he acted like he was pissed off, but I was like, 'Look, buddy, Jenny hasn't even paid her half of the rent this month, and I can't cover that *and* all the utilities.'"

Piper was jotting down her own notes. "What did he say?"

"He wrote me a check for five hundred bucks and left."

"Do you still have the check?" King asked.

"Yeah. Hold on."

Dom put the Pomeranian down on the sofa, and before she even disappeared from the living room, it had bounded across onto King's lap. It pounced on his notes, its untrimmed nails carving up King's thighs as he tried to keep the dog from tearing the paper. He prevented most of the damage, in part because the dog was so light, but its frenetic energy gave him a speed that was hard to contain.

No sooner had King got his papers out of harm's way did the dog start attacking his face, trying to lick it.

"Wow," Piper said. "You've got a serious fan."

Dom returned with the check.

"For Christ's sake, Sugar. Pull yourself together."

When she picked the dog up off King's lap, it began to pee. King escaped most of it by leaning sharply to one side, but a small splash struck his shoes.

Piper was trying not to laugh as she said, "You have a towel or something?"

King focused on the check instead of his annoyance. He managed to get a picture of the check, including the name and address in the top left corner, before Dom came back into the room.

She handed him a damp paper towel, which he used to wipe his shoe.

When he was finished, he handed it back to her. "Why haven't you cashed the check?"

"I tried!" Dom exclaimed. "But it bounced. I kept the check so that I could try and contact the guy again. The bank almost didn't let me keep it though. They said something about destroying bounced checks. Sounds like a bunch of government bullshit to me."

"The stranger's check bounced. Jenny hasn't been back to

pay rent, you haven't even seen her in weeks. What about Tommy? Have you seen Tommy since?"

"Tommy?" she asked.

"The creepy cousin who doesn't blink," Piper clarified.

"Oh, right. No, the last time I saw him was a few days before she left." The Pomeranian thrashed around in her arms. "Didn't know that was the last time I'd see her, did I?"

"Did she say anything when she left? Like where she was going? Headed to work or to a friend's house?"

"No," Dom said. "I told her goodnight, and I went to bed because I had to work at the buttcrack of dawn. And she's usually pretty quiet. It's the only reason I've put up with her so long—it's really hard to find a quiet roommate. You've no idea. Do you need a roommate?"

It took Piper a minute to realize that the girl was talking to her. She looked up from her notes, surprised.

"Oh, no. I'm already living with someone," she said. Then, as if this might be devastating news, she added, "Sorry."

Dom shrugged. "Anyway, like I said, she's usually quiet, but that night she was banging around in her room. I got mad and knocked on the wall and she apologized. This was probably three in the morning. That's the last I heard from her."

"The last you heard from her was when you knocked on the bedroom wall?" King asked, writing all of this down. But it was hard to focus with a dog trying to lunge for him in the corner of his vision.

"Yeah. That's it."

"Can we have a look in her room?" Piper asked.

King was glad that she was the one to broach the subject.

"Sure. But it's a mess in there. And before you ask, *no*, I wasn't the one who tore it up like that. Though I did go snooping around in there when the first of the month rolled by and I was out half the rent money. I was hoping I'd find some cash that I could put toward her part of it."

"But you didn't find anything?" King asked.

"Nope. And I didn't take anything either," she said defensively.

"Which room is hers?" King pointed at the three closed doors off to the left. Since the kitchen was on the right side of the living room, King had to assume that one of these was the way through.

"Hers is on the right. Mine on the left."

"Do you mind if I keep her door shut while we look around? I don't want the dog getting in."

"Fine by me." Dom shrugged. "I'm tired of holding him. Look, he's scratched my arms all up."

But even with the bedroom door shut, it was hard for King to breathe easy. It was all that frantic scratching by tiny little paws that made it impossible for him to relax.

"Do you think he's begging for us to rescue him?" Piper whispered. "Because those are pretty desperate pleas."

"I can't bring a dog like that around Lady," King said. "She's got a high prey drive."

Piper whistled. "And I thought I was messy."

The bedroom did look like it had been ransacked. The covers were rumpled and thrown to one side. Drawers had been left half open. The closet was still full of clothes, which King thought was interesting. If Jenny had packed a bag, it had been a small one. And given that her box of jewelry was still here—*and let's not forget the dog*—she hadn't expected to be gone for so long.

So why hadn't she come back to the apartment?

Why had she missed a rent payment?

And who was the guy that had come by and written Dom a bad check?

"Does this look like the room of someone in trouble?" King asked.

"Yes," Piper said plainly, leaning against the door even as

the scratching continued. "I mean, maybe she's this messy, but I wouldn't leave all my stuff behind like this if I wasn't planning to come back. Even when I was trying to stay away from my mom's place, I came back every few days or so to get clothes."

"Right," King said, opening one of the drawers and looking through its contents.

No diary or journal. Nothing that might alert King to the secret workings of Jenny Bright's life.

Piper cracked the door just enough to yell out, keeping her foot braced against it, "Hey, Dom. Is Jenny's room usually this messy?"

"No, she's a neat freak. I was really surprised that it looked like that too."

Piper shut the door, much to the Pomeranian's dismay.

"She leaves in a hurry and doesn't come back. Sounds like she's in trouble to me."

"What did Lou say?" Piper rubbed her forehead. King had noticed it was something she often did when she was trying to remember details. "That she'd been waiting for someone by the fountain. Do you think she was waiting for the guy who brought the money? Or the creepy cousin? Or maybe she got into some kind of trouble with the creepy cousin and she called the mysterious stranger to help her out."

"Anything is possible." King pulled up the photo of the check on his phone again.

He zoomed in on the name. Ashley Wexler.

"If that's the case, then we need to find out who this is."

Konstantine listened to the rain fall outside their bedroom window. It struck the iron railings, the patio furniture, the little plastic bird feeder, and the glass bath musically. Normally this would have soothed him. A hush fell over Florence on days like this, and often brought a calm he enjoyed.

But tonight he was troubled.

For the first time in weeks, Louie was not the cause of his concern.

He moved the images around on his computer, comparing the photos side by side, still frowning.

This isn't good, he thought. He shuffled the photos to one side of his screen and opened the news articles again.

It wasn't only the content of the story: *Whole family brutally murdered, infant missing.*

That would be enough to upset anyone.

It was where he'd found the article. Even though it was only seven years old, long after the advent of the digital world, he'd found a digitized copy only in a small community library. Someone had scanned an original print edition of the article and saved it to the catalog.

Furthermore, it was the only one he could find.

The murder had occurred in a funny little town called Kalamazoo. Konstantine had never heard such a name before and was half convinced that it couldn't even be English.

But it existed. And once there had been a family there. A mother, a father, and two children. There had been a large age gap between the children. A boy who was nearly fifteen. An infant who was only four months old.

One night in July, the family went to bed unaware of the horror that would find them between the hours of midnight and four.

The infant girl was never recovered. They had only a photograph of a suspected age progression, but age progressions on infants were unreliable.

Still, Konstantine could see the similarities in her features. Not just the features between the girl and the infant, but between the girl and her three slaughtered family members.

Especially the brother. She looked just like him.

But if this was her, if Kaia was the child who had been stolen from the crib the night her family was murdered, it begged the question, who took her? And for what nefarious purpose?

If he was being honest with himself, it wasn't even the murder or the abduction that made him uneasy. He wasn't naïve, after all. He'd lived in the underbelly of the world all his life. He knew what darkness lay in the human heart.

No. What concerned him were the obvious lengths that someone had gone to to suppress the story. Something this sensational would have been all over the national news. Manhunts would have been launched. No one would have been able to escape the American media frenzy of a missing baby.

And yet all he had been able to find was this one news article.

Who had suppressed the story? Who would have the *power* to suppress such a story?

His first thought was someone like him. Someone with resources and a penchant for using technology to bend the world to his will.

But Konstantine also knew he was a rarity. Crime lords rarely targeted families purely for the chance to steal an infant. Babies, sadly, were easy to come by. If a child was what someone wanted, for whatever the reason, it could easily have been taken from anywhere in the world with far less effort than would have been required to extract a child from white suburbia.

He was willing to believe that it was simply chance. That perhaps the family had had the misfortune to be targeted by a killer. Someone who saw the baby, wanted it, and wasn't afraid to kill a whole family to obtain her.

Except that Kaia wasn't the only one.

Konstantine, in his desperate search to find more news articles on Kaia's family, had found *eighteen* other such families in the span of five years.

The families had been spread all across the country, including one across the border in Ontario, but their stories were the same. A family had been murdered and a baby was stolen. Except for one case, where twins were taken.

The babies were always younger than a year old, and if there were older children in the house, they were killed along with the parents.

The closet door opened and Lou stepped into their bedroom. She was shrugging out of her wet clothes, suggesting that she'd had a successful hunt. She only ever came home wet if she'd had reason to drag a body through the lake, to that otherworldly place where she left the remains for her monstrous pet.

"What is it?" she asked, pulling her wet shirt over her head. "You look unhappy."

"I've found something on the children," he said. "Shower and I'll show you."

While steam rolled out of the bathroom, his ear half turned toward the sounds of her progress, Konstantine tried to organize his findings. He didn't want to take her step by step through his whole process.

She would want only the facts and his conclusions.

But Konstantine wasn't sure what his conclusion was. True, it wasn't unique for a serial killer to specialize in murdering families. What made this situation exceptional was the lack of media coverage. Konstantine just could not imagine a world that would not have been half mad with the idea of a murdering baby-snatcher.

These murderer-kidnappers—and yes, Konstantine was sure there had to be more than one—had to be professionals.

Lou was wearing her pajamas when she finally came to the bed and slipped in beside him.

Her skin was cold against his arm, causing him to shiver.

"You're freezing." He tucked the comforter between them.

"I was going to tell you to warm me up."

"I need my hands to show you this," he said.

He pulled up the age progression photo for the girl known as Kaia, the photo of her family, and the photo he himself took. He put them side by side on his computer screen, turning it ever so slightly so she could get a good look.

"Would you say that's her?" he asked.

"The progression is a little off. But she looks just like her mother and her brother," Lou said.

"That's what I thought. Now..." He pulled up the family portrait of the gay fathers from Canada. "Does Elijah look like the one on the left?"

Lou leaned closer to the screen. "It's the eyes."

"That's what I thought, too. Here is where it gets interesting."

He explained the best he could about the murders. About the lack of connection between the families, at least as far as he could tell. That it would have been impossible, unless the killer had a gift like Lou's, to be in so many places at once.

"It can't be a single person," he insisted. "Two of the children were taken on the same night, even though they were hundreds of miles apart. And three others were taken the same week, and it would be nearly impossible to cross that distance in such a short time."

"I don't remember this story ever being in the news," she said.

"That's the other incredible part of this. Someone is doing what I do. Wiping all the records clean. Suppressing the coverage."

"Who could do that?"

"Someone with the skills. Or a very rich person who can hire someone with the skills. Or someone with a great deal of power. A state. An agency."

She arched a brow. "A state? You think the *government* is collecting babies? Which government? For what purpose?"

Konstantine held up his hands. "I can't tell you. Maybe we could figure it out if the children explained to us what they were forced to do when they were with their captives. If they could describe for us where they were kept. Who they interacted with. What was done to them."

"They don't want to talk about any of it," she said.

Konstantine closed his laptop. "I don't know, *amore mio*. I will keep searching."

Her gaze was distant. Konstantine could have made the mistake of thinking she was watching the rain fall gently on the balcony, if not for the unfocused gaze.

"That explains what I was feeling," she said finally.

"What were you feeling?" He pushed the computer away now and drew her to him, ready to offer up his own warmth for her comfort.

"Because they'd mentioned 'Father,' I kept asking the compass to take me to their parents. But I got the feeling I usually get when the person is dead. When there's no one on the other side."

"So this Father is not related to them," he said.

"I also think Father might be more than one person. Maybe it's several people who pretend to be the same person when interacting with the children. Otherwise, why does my compass struggle to get a lock? I need to ask them if they've ever actually seen Father's face. Or if he hid his face. It's possible Father took precautions so the children couldn't identify him."

Konstantine remembered the last time that Lou struggled with locating her target. There had been a pair of pedophiles running a pornography ring under a shared alias. *Winter*, he believed it was.

"You will figure it out, *amore mio*," he promised, and placed a kiss against her forehead. "You had a good hunt tonight?"

"Yes, at least there's that. If I keep up the pace, I'll find this so-called Father sooner or later. Maybe it's the professor."

Konstantine turned to look at her. "What professor?"

"Dr. John W. Gein. He studies psychopathy, but I think he's the killer. I just don't know if he's Father or if he's one of Father's helpers."

"Where is he from?" Konstantine asked.

"He works at a university in Kalamazoo. He's been there for twenty years."

Kalamazoo.

"That's where Kaia's family lived," he said. "Before they were murdered."

Konstantine picked up his laptop again and did a quick search. He had to ask Louie how to spell the man's strange name, but he did find him. The first hit was his biography on the university's website, giving the names of his courses, meeting times, as well as research interests.

"Impressive," Lou said, reading over his shoulder. "I wonder where he finds the time to murder families and kidnap children while enjoying tenure."

Konstantine thought there was something familiar about the man. Either his name or his face. Had he read something today that mentioned him? He couldn't be sure. All the articles he'd gone through were a single blurry mass in his tired mind. He'd have to circle back after he rested.

"Between you and Dani we'll find everything there is to know about him, including whether he wears boxers or briefs. I'm going to guess briefs."

He liked seeing her in a good mood. He wasn't sure if it was their date—of course that's what he hoped—or if it was the successful hunt that had pleased her. Or simply to be making progress on this case after weeks of stagnation.

"And the babies?" he asked, double-checking he had the doctor's name written down before closing the laptop for a second time. "How are they?"

She shivered. He pulled her closer.

"Monstrous, I'm sure. I bet they look like little dragons now," he said.

"They're growing. Quickly."

"Aren't you afraid they'll eat you?" he asked.

She snorted. "I hope they'll get used to me long before they're big enough to eat me."

"Have you been back to see the children since this morning?"

"They're still undecided about Italy."

"You should make them. What will they do? Kick your shins?"

Lou laughed, placing her head on his chest.

It was the happiest Konstantine had been in weeks. Could he really have been worried for nothing? Had Lou only been worried about the children? Her work? Had he taken her distance personally when it had not been about him at all?

"I'll ask them again," Lou said. "But it'll be easier to gain their trust if we don't force them to do something against their will. I have a feeling they've been forced to do things all their lives."

"Is this the place?" Piper was looking out the passenger-side window of King's car at the duplex beside them.

King leaned across her, taking in the view of the chain-link fence and the chipped and decaying exterior. The sign on the fence read *Beware of Dog*.

"Maybe we'll have better luck with this dog than the last one," King said, turning the engine off.

He stepped in front of her on the sidewalk, insisting that he be the one who opened the gate. If there was a dangerous dog waiting to attack, he'd rather Piper not be the one it went after. Her face was lower to the ground.

He tried the gate's handle and found it was unlocked.

The gate creaked open. King waited, one hand still on the handle in case he needed to throw it shut quickly.

But no dog came.

"The dog's been dead for years. The sign's just there to keep people like you out," an old woman said.

Piper jumped at the sound of the voice, giving King's arm a fierce squeeze. "Geez-us."

On the right side of the duplex, a woman sat in a chair by

the door. She'd been hidden by the shadows beneath the porch's awning, but now that King knew where to look, he could make out the shape of her.

He approached. "I'm very sorry to bother you, ma'am, but we're looking for Tommy. Is he home?"

King couldn't be sure if these two shared the same residence or simply lived side by side.

"Tommy next door? He's been gone all week. He keeps them odd hours. Always comin' and goin', that one. But a young man needs money, so I can't fault him that. Unlike me. I don't spend much of anything anymore."

She lifted her glass of sweet tea. How she could bring herself to sit on the porch and drink it in this cold weather, he didn't know.

"Yes, siree. I've got all I need right 'ere. Of course, I think what's really keepin' him busy is his lady friend."

"You've seen a girl?" Piper asked. "Was she about this tall? Blond?"

The old woman nodded. "Yeah, she was. Pretty little thing. Even if I never seen her smile once."

"Can I show you a picture?" Piper asked. She was already fishing her phone out of her pocket. King let her handle it while he gave the duplex a once-over. It was a squat, low-slung row house. The outside was decent, but the yard mostly dead.

And the neighborhood wasn't much to look at either.

There was nothing but houses out here. If something were to happen, surely someone would hear something.

"Hold on, honey, I need my glasses," the old woman said. Her hands felt the top of her head for a moment, frowning. "I think I left 'em inside. Just a minute."

She went into the duplex, leaving Piper on the porch and King on the sidewalk.

"What are you thinking, boss?" Piper asked.

"I'm thinking that this is a terrible place to commit a kidnapping. Nothing but eyes and ears out here."

The old woman reappeared, her tortoiseshell glasses now balanced on the end of her nose. She took Piper's phone and squinted down at it.

"Yeah, that'd be her," the woman said. "She was here four nights ago. I saw her come in with him but didn't see her leave."

"You don't think she's still in there, do you?" Piper asked.

The old woman shrugged. "I can't tell you. But seein' as how I'm the landlady of this here property, if you give me a good enough reason, I might let you in."

"That would be illegal," King said.

"Only if you or I or this young lady here says a word about it," the woman said. "Besides, there's a smell and I don't like it. I've been lookin' for a reason to go in for two days now."

King's heart dropped. "A smell?"

"Do you always make little old ladies repeat themselves? That's what I said. *A smell.* It's why I'm out here on my porch. One, to get away from that smell, and two, because I'm hoping to catch that boy when he comes home. But I ain't seen him."

Piper must've known what she was thinking. She was watching his face closely.

"My name is Robert King. This is Piper Genereux."

"Genereux," the woman said. "A lovely name. Go on."

"I'm from the Crescent City Detective Agency, and Piper here is my co-investigator. We're trying to find the girl in the photo. Jenny Bright. She's Tommy's cousin, and it's her mother who hired us, thinking she might be in some serious trouble. I can't say for sure that Tommy is the source of that trouble. I don't want to lie to you just to get into his place, but like you said, a smell could mean a lot of things. I probably don't need to tell you which one I'm hoping it isn't."

"No, sir." The woman pursed her lips.

"But we wanted to talk to Tommy either way. As his land-lady, I assume you collect his rent?"

"Yes, sir, I do."

"And you probably know where he works," King ventured.

"I know where he *told* me he worked, and I called down there for a reference when he started renting from me two years ago. But if he still works there, I can't tell you."

She stretched, her back slowly straightening from its bent shape.

"Let me get you that key."

She disappeared, leaving Piper and King on the porch.

"Are you sure about this?" Piper asked once they were alone. "You're always harping on me that we can't use something in court if it was obtained unlawfully."

"I'm not here for evidence," King told her. "I came to talk to Tommy. I'm staying to make sure Jenny's body isn't in there."

Piper rubbed her fist across her forehead. "That would suck."

The landlady reappeared with some keys jingling in her hand. "All right, let's see what we've got."

Piper held the screen door open for her while she tried two different keys. It was the third that opened it.

"Here we go. My lord." The old woman pulled her head back. "That smell."

King was struck by it. It had the distinct stench of rotten meat. Piper was looking at him with a concerned expression.

"Maybe you should wait here with—" King broke off and looked to the woman.

"Geraldine LaPont," she said.

"With Geraldine. Just in case I find—" He couldn't finish. Opening his mouth just let more of the stench in.

Already he was imagining Ms. Bright's struck face if King had to deliver devastating news.

"I'd like to know what that smell is, but I'm happy to let you do the searching for me," Geraldine said. "That stinks to high heaven. Makes me feel sick just catching it here on the porch. I can't imagine how bad it will be inside."

"I'll stay here with Geraldine," Piper agreed. "Keep a lookout for Tommy."

"He ain't been home in days," Geraldine said. "I doubt he'd come home now, but yes, you can sit over here with me, honey."

That left King to cross the threshold into the left duplex alone. He wasn't too proud to admit that he was also nauseated by the stench. He reached into his pocket and pulled out a handkerchief, and used it to cover his nose and mouth.

He turned on the lights as he went, grateful that he wasn't doing any searching in the dark.

The place itself was tidy, which felt at odds with the horrible smell.

But there was no trash, no ashtray full of cigarette butts, no shoes thrown everywhere. There were even vacuum lines in the carpet.

At the end of the living room was the kitchen, but King looked to the three rooms further down the adjacent hallway. The first room was a bathroom.

It could have used a good scrub, but there was nothing offensive there. In the medicine cabinet, King saw an expired prescription for dextroamphetamine. The bottle had two pills on the bottom, with Tommy's name printed on the white label. There was a badly smashed tube of toothpaste, but no toothbrush, King noted. A few cleaning supplies and half a package of toilet paper were under the sink. A bottle of three-in-one bodywash, shampoo, and conditioner in the shower.

But that was it.

The other two rooms were just as easy to search.

One had a few boxes in it, as if Tommy had never unpacked them. Kitchenware. Some sheets. Some photo albums and yearbooks.

The other room turned out to be the bedroom. There was a mattress on the floor with a crumpled comforter on top. There were condoms, tissues, and a couple of issues of *Playboy* in the nightstand, but that was it. Half a glass of flat soda was on its surface beside a small lamp.

No phone charger.

No phone charger, no toothbrush, he hadn't been back in days. Clearly Tommy had vacated the premises, but for what reason, King couldn't be sure. It didn't look like he'd left in the same hurried manner as Jenny had.

King checked the closets and dresser and found some clothes. No photos of family. No suggestion of his interests.

That left the kitchen.

As soon as King stepped into it, he knew this must be the source of the smell. It was strongest in here.

"You okay?" Piper called from the doorway.

"Just fine," he called back.

He opened the trash can first, and while it definitely needed to be taken out, that wasn't the source of the smell. He looked in the fridge next.

A swarm of flies hit him full in the face.

He yelped, and before he cleared his face, Piper was there, squeezing his arm.

"What is it? What is it!" she demanded.

"Flies," he said. "What the hell were they doing in the fridge?"

Piper looked into the fridge, but before she could answer, she turned and threw up in the sink.

Apart from the usual assortment of condiments, butter,

ketchup, mayo, there was a plate centered on the top rack. On it was a heart, half eaten with maggots.

That's what the flies had been on.

And no wonder. The fridge was warm.

Of course meat would go bad in a warm fridge.

"Is that a human heart?" Piper asked between retching.

"I don't know," King said, fighting his own wave of nausea.

Twenty minutes later, Detective Dick White rolled up outside the duplex. Geraldine had wanted to throw the heart out, open the windows and see if they couldn't get rid of the rotten smell. But King was able to persuade her to wait for the detective to arrive.

Dick greeted King with a hearty handshake, but all his good humor faded once he saw the look on King's face.

"That bad, huh?"

"It looks like a human heart, the guy is a rumored satanist, and the girl I'm looking for is missing."

"That bad," Piper added.

"I can take the heart down to forensics and see if it's really human. It could be a pig's."

King wrinkled his nose. "Why the hell would he have a pig's heart in the fridge?"

"That's good eating," White said. "Pork heart with butter and onions."

He smacked his lips.

King shook his head. "Can you put a BOLO out on him? Tommy Wexler."

White typed the name into his phone. "And the girl?"

"Jenny Bright. She's his cousin."

Dick White's thumb hovered above the keys. "Why does this name sound familiar? Wait a minute. Is her mother named Carrie?"

King placed his hands on his hips. "Yes. Why?"

Dick exhaled through puffed cheeks. "She was arrested

this afternoon. She assaulted a coworker and the police were called."

"She hit someone. Why?"

"I don't know. She kept going on about her daughter. Made me write her name down, which is why I remembered it. You should go down and talk to her. Now that I know it's your case, I'll call them and let them know you're on your way."

"Does she have a bail?"

"Five hundred, but she said she can't pay it."

"She can't," King said. "But I can."

"You're too soft."

"That might be her daughter's heart in the fridge. She doesn't need to be in jail right now."

He held up his hands. "You're right. I'm sorry. I'll call Janet and tell them you're coming. And I'll get someone out here to bag the heart. Is there anything else?"

"I just need to speak to Geraldine one more time. Then I'll get out of your way."

"If Tommy did kill her, you know the DA's gonna ask you to hand over the case for a formal murder investigation."

King touched his chest. "And she'll get no trouble from me."

Not just because the DA was his girlfriend and he'd no sooner argue with her about how to do her job than anything, but also because King's objective wasn't to hang on to the case by all means. It was to find Jenny. Preferably alive.

"Ms. Geraldine?" King asked.

The old woman was back in her chair on the porch.

"Yes, sir?"

"Can I get that contact information for Tommy's work from you? Whatever he gave you, old or new, is fine."

"Sure thing." She went into the house and returned five minutes later with a number and name printed neatly on a clean sheet of paper. "I'd like your number, too, if you'll give it to me."

"Of course." He pulled a business card out of his wallet. "I'm sorry about all this."

"I'm just glad that we know what that awful smell is. Now we can clear it out."

"You aren't worried about Tommy?" King couldn't help but ask.

"Oh sure. Not in the way you is implying—*I'm* worried he might be in trouble. I have a good sense about people. I know he's a good boy, just a bit misunderstood. It's why I rented to him. I just hope you find him and he's okay."

Good boys wouldn't keep human hearts in their fridge, King thought, and slipped the piece of paper into his pocket.

13

———

Konstantine's hair was still damp from the brisk walk through the rain. Glittering droplets shone on his black sleeves as he bent to build up the fire. Given that this office was made only of stone, a single-room dwelling tucked into the corner of the courtyard, it was hard to keep it warm. The portable heater he'd bought struggled until he had the fire going to supplement the loss of heat.

Once the fire was sufficiently started, crackling pleasantly behind his chair, he sank behind his desk and began his work.

He wasn't sure how much time had passed before Lou appeared.

She came around to his side of the desk and rested her weight against it.

He took the opportunity to share what he'd learned that morning before he'd stepped out with Stefano to grab a coffee. "The boy and the girl have no public records of any kind. No school photos. Nothing on social media. They have never been to a school or a doctor, anywhere that would have such records. But apart from that, there's also the matter of their faces."

Lou's brow furrowed. "What's wrong with their faces?"

"They do not exist. I cannot find public footage of them anywhere. It is as if they have never been inside a store or a building. Anywhere with a camera."

"How's that possible? Surveillance is everywhere now," Lou said.

"Exactly. It makes me wonder if they were kept in a facility or perhaps in an underground compound. Somewhere out of sight. It is unlikely, but we must look at the unlikely now."

Lou seemed to consider this. Her eyes rested on the burning fire. He wanted to reach out and hold her.

To his surprise, she let him, slipping an arm around his neck, pushing her fingers through his hair. It was an absent-minded gesture, but it still warmed him.

"I saw a house on the night I rescued them. But it had been remote. Was it a cover?"

Konstantine shrugged. He didn't know what to tell her.

Then she said, "Do you have the names of the other children that were taken? You said there were other babies."

"I have the names they were born with," he said. "I don't know what the children are called now. Kaia, for example, was born Michelle Davidson."

He handed her a sheet of paper with the list of children that he thought were connected to Kaia and Elijah.

"It shouldn't matter," Lou said. "Just something for me to focus on."

He didn't want her to stop stroking his hair.

"What will you do?"

"I want to see if my compass will take me to the other children. I wonder if it will be possible to extract them from wherever they are without being noticed."

"That's dangerous. You don't know what you're walking into, *amore mio*."

"True," she said, her fingertips soft on his earlobes. "But sometimes I can get a feel for what's on the other end. And if someone is holding these children captive, it would be better to get them out of there as soon as possible. I can deal with the organization or whatever it is later. It will be easier."

Konstantine laughed. "Easier how?"

"If the children are safe, then I won't have to be careful," she said. Now she was smiling down at him. "And I can bring the big guns."

"You must always be careful, *amore mio*," he said. "Things are different now."

Her face stiffened. Before he could ask what was wrong, the door to Konstantine's office flew open and the laughter of children spilled into the room. Matteo and Gabriella were running full speed toward his desk until they caught sight of Lou. Then they stopped, abruptly, Gabriella bumping into Matteo's back.

She swore and slapped him on the back of the head.

Konstantine chided her, but she began to blame Matteo in rapid-fire Italian.

"Hello," Matteo was saying in English. He had improved in the last few months, but he still spoke shyly to Lou. "Hello, signora *Strega*. I missed you."

Konstantine clucked his tongue and called him a flirt.

Gabriella said nothing. She only looked at Lou with her usual wide-eyed wonder.

"Well?" Konstantine asked them. "Why did you come running into my office?"

"We found this," Matteo said, opening his hand.

Konstantine beckoned him closer. The boy was too far away to see his palm in the low light of the office.

Lou moved out of the way so the children could come closer.

Then Matteo was putting his treasure into his hand.

"Ah, *sì. Una coccinella,*" Konstantine said. He looked up to Lou. "What do you call this in English?"

"A ladybug," she said.

"*Sì,* a ladybug," he repeated. "Where did you find her?"

"She was in the kitchen on one of the big windows."

They could not tell him their story fast enough. The daring adventure as to how Matteo had spotted it first and how the cook had been afraid it was a cockroach and was going to kill it, but she couldn't reach it. And so they'd lied and said they could kill it but really they just wanted to save it. Matteo was sure to tell Konstantine that it had been Gabriella who'd climbed up onto the counters.

"Maria said that we should ask if we can keep it," Matteo finished.

"No," Konstantine said. "She should be free, just like you."

The children moaned their disapproval.

Konstantine looked to Lou for her support, knowing that if she told the children to let it go, they would not argue with her like they did with him.

"Don't you agree, *amore mio*?" he asked. "She deserves to be free, no?"

She was looking at him strangely. Her face held a mixture of tenderness and—what? Horror?

"I have to go," she said. And then, without another word, she was through the shadows.

Konstantine was left holding the small creature crawling across his palm while two wide-eyed children stared at him.

"*L'abbiamo fatta arrabbiare?*" Matteo asked.

"No, she's not mad," he assured them. "She's only busy today. Now do what I said. Put *la coccinella* on the tree outside so she can fly."

. . .

Lou stood on the edge of the observation deck for a long time, breathing the sky-high air and trying to quell the crushing confusion in her chest. She stood like that for nearly ten minutes, her face turning icy in the assault of the unforgiving wind, before she understood why she was there.

It had been seeing Konstantine with the children. Especially the girl.

With her dark hair and big eyes, her hand on his knee. The way he spoke tenderly to them.

When she'd stood behind them, seeing only the back of the girl's dark head, it had been easy to imagine that Lou was looking into her future. That she was looking at the back of her daughter's head, at the little hands placed on her father's knee.

It had brought a fury of emotion up in her until the bittersweet ache in her chest had forced her to run. Her mind kept turning to her own father. The way she had come into his office sometimes, had asked him questions, had leaned over inquisitively to peer at some small treasure she'd brought him.

It wasn't sentimentality.

She'd seen Konstantine covered in the blood of his enemies. She knew he could be as vicious and as cruel as she was.

And yet.

Her chest compressed again.

"What am I doing?" she asked the gray Parisian sky, but got no answer. Somewhere in the city below, church bells began to ring.

"What the hell am I doing?" she asked the sky again.

Only then did she become aware of the piece of paper she

was clutching. She'd fisted it at some point, crumpling one side of it mercilessly.

Now she tried to smooth it out and make it readable again.

There were twenty names on the list. She spotted Michelle Davidson almost immediately and knew Elijah's birth name must also be on that list, even though she hadn't thought to ask what it was.

Who can I take? Lou asked her compass.

Who can I take without them noticing right away?

She was hoping at least one of the children could be extracted without alerting the captives to her movements.

Even better if the child was more vocal than Kaia and Elijah. Then maybe Lou would finally get some answers from someone who knew what was going on inside.

Bonus if she could gain a sense of where the children were being held.

One by one she let her eyes slide down the list of names, pausing long enough for her compass to get a lock on the location.

And yes. It did seem that the positions it locked for each child were pretty close to each other. She noted only small incremental adjustments in her targeting as she moved from one name to the next.

However, twice, she was met with dead air.

Twice, it was only the empty cold of a howling wind that echoed on the other end.

That meant two of the children were dead.

Lou's chest clenched.

Which one can I take without their notice?

Lou's watch buzzed, notifying her of an incoming page. She recognized Dani's number. Perhaps she'd found something on the professor.

Not two minutes afterward her watch buzzed again, this time from King.

Neither page had the *911* emergency tag on it.

So she would do this first. Take one of the children, whoever was easiest to get to, and then go see what her friends needed.

But she didn't move. She stared at the gray Parisian sky, at the loud city below, and felt frozen in place.

Just admit it, a voice said. Lou wasn't sure if it was Lucy this time. She half believed it was only herself, arguing back from some deep recess of her mind. *Admit you want to keep her.*

"I can't," Lou whispered. The cold wind pulled tears from her eyes.

She knew the truth of it. Even though Lou didn't deserve it. Even though her life was not fit for a child. Even though she had no proof—*none*—that she would be a good mother. In the past she hadn't even considered the possibility, but now that it was suddenly thrust upon her, she couldn't help but wonder.

She couldn't help but dream.

You think it's wrong. You think it's too dangerous. That it's selfish. But you do *want her. Admit it.*

Lou couldn't.

She took one last look at the gray horizon and was gone.

14

Carrie Bright had been booked into the Orleans Parish Prison, the city jail for New Orleans. King had been there many times before and knew where to park and how to go about posting bail for Ms. Bright. It had taken almost an hour from the time he had learned of her arrest to the time she was released into the lobby.

That hadn't been long enough for him to prepare himself to face her.

Her face crumpled as soon as she saw him. "Oh god, it's you."

That made King wonder who she had been expecting.

"Did you find her?" she said. "Tell me you found her!"

It was obvious that something had happened in the time since King had last seen her. Then he'd managed to reassure her that her daughter was alive. Carrie seemed to hold no such beliefs now.

What had changed?

"Let's get in the car first," he said, holding the door to the street open for her.

She was crying in earnest by the time she climbed into the

passenger seat of his Buick. He was suddenly glad he'd dropped Piper off at the office before coming. He suspected that the rest of the day might very well be eaten up by this case. Better that one of them be manning the station in the meantime.

"Is she dead?" Carrie screamed.

"I—"

"Is she!"

"I don't know," King said. "We haven't found her or Tommy."

Carrie covered her face with her hands and began to cry.

King rubbed the back of his neck. "You'll have to tell me what happened."

"I got a call at work. It was from Jenny. She was crying and talkin' nonsense. She told me to come get her. I kept asking her where she was but she wouldn't tell me. Then the line went dead. And when I called her back it went to her voice mail."

Her hysteria mounted as she spoke.

"When was this?" King asked. "When did you talk to Jenny?"

"This morning. I'd only been at work for fifteen, twenty minutes tops."

King seriously doubted that the rotting heart he'd found in Tommy's fridge was Jenny's then. But that didn't mean that whoever it belonged to hadn't been a victim. Maybe Jenny would be the next victim.

"Please tell me she's okay. Please," her mother begged. Her palms were smeared black with her mascara. "*Please.*"

King didn't want to lie to her. Nor did he think he should tell her about what they had found at Tommy's before they had a more complete picture on how fast this was moving.

"I found her once—we'll find her again," King said. And because he didn't want to make promises he couldn't keep, he added, "You'll have your answers soon, Carrie. I promise."

King just prayed they were the answers they both wanted.

He took out his phone and paged Lou. Lou would be fastest. Lou would know where the girl was.

"How about we get a cup of coffee and you can tell me why you hit someone at work?"

She agreed but then spent the whole ride crying. King chose speed over quality, ordering their coffees through the nearest fast food restaurant's drive-thru. Then he pulled up in the parking lot, letting her get a few sips in before pressing her for more information.

"Why did you get arrested?" he asked gently. He offered her a paper napkin so she could wipe her face.

"When I got the call, I wanted to leave, but they wouldn't let me. Tanesha, my manager, actually tried to stop me, and I hit her. I don't know what I was thinking. I just wanted her to get out of my way so I could go to Jenny. I didn't even know where to go. I was just so scared by the way her voice sounded that I knew I had to leave. Going anywhere was better than standing behind that register wondering what the hell happened to her."

"You hit your manager when she tried to stop you from leaving work. And you were leaving work because you'd gotten a distressing call from your missing daughter."

"They're not going to care about that. They're going to look at my record and give me a harsh sentence anyway."

This was the first time King was hearing about a record. "What were you arrested for before?"

"I got two DUIs and lost my license. I'm sorry I didn't tell you before. But that's the real reason why I take the bus in and leave my RV parked."

"I didn't realize you had a drinking problem," King said. He was genuinely surprised. He was usually pretty good at spotting drunks. There was something about the skin that usually tipped him off. Drinking was horrible for a person's complexion.

"I've been sober for three years now. I go to AA twice a week." Fresh tears welled up in her eyes. "I wasn't always there for her when she was a kid. My Jenny. I have to be here for her now, do you understand?"

She turned those wet eyes on King.

"I can't let her down. I can't let her down now when it matters."

King ran his hands through his hair. "We're doing everything we can, Carrie. I promise."

"Do you think I'll end up in jail for this?"

"I'm friends with the DA," he said. "I think if I explain the situation to her, we can probably get her to drop the case or at least weaken your sentence to probation. I have a feeling there's probably no saving your job."

"I was tired of that place anyway," she said. "I want to go to beauty school. I know it's late and I'm old, but I've always wanted to do hair and nails. I'd been thinking about it for a long time. I thought if I could get through school and get a good job doing hair, maybe Jenny would come by and see me. I have this image of her and I talking, cutting up while I wash her hair. Now it feels like that will never happen. Do you think it's stupid, dreaming like this after I've wasted so much of my life?"

"Not at all," King said. And he meant it. "I didn't open my agency until last year. And I'm sixty-three."

Her shoulders sagged and she covered her face with her hands again. King tried to give her a reassuring squeeze on the shoulders, but it felt wholly inadequate. Nothing would make this better for the woman except finding her daughter alive.

"I'm so sorry. I shouldn't be carrying on like this."

"Don't worry about it," King said. "Drink your coffee while it's hot and then I'll drive you home."

While Carrie took pitiful sips of her coffee, crying quietly in his passenger seat, King thought over all he'd learned in the last few hours. He searched the facts front to back, side to side, trying to figure out what his next move should be.

He was about to give up when an idea struck him. He recalled the name on the bounced check.

"Carrie, do you know who Ashley Wexler is?"

She sniffed. "Of course. That's my ex-husband. Jenny's daddy."

King hadn't recognized it since they had a different name.

"Do you know if Jenny ever went to stay with her father? If she was receiving financial support from him?"

She wiped at her red nose with the paper napkin. "She and I never talk about her daddy. He took me to court and got full custody of her. That's when my drinking started. Part of me blamed him for that, even though I know it's no one's fault but mine. Still, it was like a silent agreement between us. I never asked about her daddy and what they did in their time together, and she never rubbed it in my face about how nice his big house was, how many beautiful girlfriends he had, how great his job was. It's hard as hell watching the man who cheated on me and abandoned me having so much good fortune, while I'm just stuck down here in the dirt. You know what I mean?"

"I can imagine."

King knew his next stop would be the father's house. Maybe Jenny called her father when her mother hadn't come to pick her up. Maybe King would get lucky and she'd be there, safe and sound.

King's phone went off. It was Detective White.

"Yeah," King said by way of hello.

"I *told* you. It's a pig," Detective White said. "It looked mighty human, but it's a pig heart."

King's shoulders relaxed. That meant they still had time. But it also meant they had no reason to hunt for Tommy. "You still have people looking for him or did you have to drop the BOLO?"

"They dropped it," White said, sounding truly apologetic. "Sorry, Robbie."

"No worries. I'll follow up on it myself."

If he was being honest, King preferred it that way. He had Tommy's workplace info and the father's home address. That would have to be enough to get him started until Lou could pull through and help him out.

King only hoped that time would remain on their side.

15

Lou wanted to stop by the villa before she commenced her mission to extract one of the children. She would ask her compass to choose an easy target, but that didn't mean she wouldn't find guns waiting for her on the other end of her slip.

When she stepped from the closet in the bedroom she shared with Konstantine, the first thing she saw was Octavia. The British Blue was stretched long on the foot of their bed, her golden eyes regarding Lou with indifference. Her tail flicked back and forth as she rested in the patch of sunshine.

"Where have you been?" Lou asked.

The cat meowed, blinking her eyes lazily. She didn't get up. That was fine by Lou. She held no illusions about their relationship. The cat's loyalty certainly belonged to Konstantine.

The most affection Lou got was a meow or the occasional brush of her head into Lou's palm, if she was the only one available to feed her.

But it was Konstantine she purred for. Konstantine whom

she followed around the villa, whom she allowed to pick her up and hold her.

If Lou tried to pick her up, she'd only get an arm full of scratches for her trouble.

Still, Lou touched one of her soft, velvety ears as she passed the bed, earning herself a swat.

In the living room, Lou removed her Picasso painting and pressed the button hidden behind it. A mere indention on the wall. She stepped back so that it could open.

In her vault waited all she could ever need.

Her bulletproof vest, which she strapped across her chest. Thigh holsters that would let her place guns anywhere but at her ribs. The idea of brushing her own sensitive breasts, even accidentally, filled her with low-grade fury.

She loaded twin Glocks before slipping one into each holster. She pulled Kevlar sleeves over her forearms. Lastly, after adding a boot knife and a four-inch blade to her ensemble, she felt ready.

It certainly wasn't the most armored she'd ever been, but it was enough for this short extraction.

That was assuming she ran into trouble at all.

After resealing her vault, Lou returned to the bedroom closet. She stood in the dim shadows for several minutes, waiting. The flow of darkness moved over her. It pulled at her. She could feel its desire to consume her.

But she held off as long as she could.

Give me the one easiest to take, she told it. *A child alone. Unguarded. Perhaps I might learn something of what I'm up against here.*

The dark current shifted, changing course slightly. And yet Lou still did not give herself over to it. Instead, she listened. It was a gift she had not used in a long time, and the muscles certainly felt out of practice.

When she had been hunting the Martinelli family, well-guarded men who always had an entourage and considerable firepower close at hand, it had been to her advantage to delay her slips like this. To listen to the dark for any hint or sign as to what she might be walking into.

Given the silence that met her now, Lou began to wonder if this part of her ability had atrophied from lack of use.

She heard nothing. Felt no sensation of heat or cold.

Then she caught the briefest rustle of a blanket. The compression of a mattress. The idea of a small body turning over in sleep.

Lou surrendered to the darkness then, letting herself be pulled from one side of the world to the other.

The boy was alone in the room. That was the first thing she noticed, her senses alive with anticipation. She expected guns or violence but was met only with a small boy asleep on a mattress on the floor. He looked to be about Kaia's age, nine or perhaps ten. His back was to her. His chest rose and fell gently.

There were no toys in this room. No posters or pictures of a family.

There was the mattress on the floor, and a second cushion in the far corner. Lou saw nothing else. What comfort could a single cushion be to a child?

She was about to take the boy when she spotted the camera. It was the sound of the device pivoting toward her that caught her attention. Then she saw the blinking red light.

There was no point in running. If they'd seen her, they'd seen her. Lou only hoped that perhaps Konstantine could use this to his advantage. If his program was able to find her face on any camera, then perhaps he could track its signal to this location and learn something about its owner.

In case he couldn't, she dropped a pin on her location using her GPS watch.

Before taking the boy, she gave the camera the finger. Satisfied, she bent down and lifted the child out of the bed, taking him, blanket, and all.

Given the lack of light in the room, Lou took only a single step with the child in her arms, moving him from the solemn room where he'd been sleeping into the bathroom of the cabin far, far away.

As soon as her boots hit the wooden floor of the cabin's main room, a head popped up. Kaia regarded her over the back of the sofa with a wary gaze.

"It's just me," Lou said. "And this one."

Lou came around the sofa, realizing the children had fallen asleep in front of the fire. Elijah was waking now, more slowly. Lou noted, not for the first time, that Kaia's hypervigilance—for better or worse—was truly impressive.

Elijah hadn't noted her footfall as Kaia had. But he'd reacted to the sound of her voice.

Lou placed the sleeping boy on the loveseat, releasing the weight of him gently to the cushions.

Kaia was on her feet now, staring down at the boy. "Where did you get him?"

Lou rotated her wrist and her GPS watch woke, glowing green. She searched for her last dropped pin.

"Michigan," she said. "About twenty-five miles northwest of Kalamazoo."

Lou looked at her.

But Kaia wasn't listening. The girl's gaze was fixated on the boy still wrapped in the blanket.

"Is that Jake?" Elijah asked, his voice trembling.

The boy's eyes opened at the sound of his name. He sat up, the blanket falling away. His gaze was unfocused, looking first at the fire, then at Lou. His brow scrunched in confusion.

Lou was about to welcome him, fill his ears with the same assurances she'd given Kaia and Elijah when she'd brought them to the cabin, but something was wrong. Lou felt the warning electricity across her skin even before the boy's gaze fell on Kaia, who was closest to him.

Kaia took a step back.

But the real trouble began the moment Jake saw Elijah.

A slow contortion overtook the boy's features. All remnants of sleep were replaced by unexplainable rage.

Without fully understanding what was happening, Lou instinctively reached for her gun, but then several things happened at once.

Jake's first move was to snatch the blade from Lou's forearm sheath.

Lou hadn't even realized he'd seen it, given that his entire focus thus far had been on the other children.

Then he was off the sofa, launching himself in one fluid pounce before connecting with Elijah.

Elijah cried out as his back hit the ground hard, but his arms were up, blocking the blade now being thrust down at him.

Kaia kicked Jake hard in the side, sending him sprawling. That was as surprising to Lou as Elijah vaulting himself over the back of the sofa.

"Run!" Kaia commanded.

Without looking back, Elijah bolted for the bedroom.

Jake rolled to his feet, running for the bedroom door in what was obvious pursuit of Elijah. The feral scream that came from the boy's lips made the hair on the back of Lou's neck rise.

Kaia grabbed him from behind and pulled, tossing the boy

across the room. He tumbled, sprawling to a stop in the kitchen nook.

"Leave him alone, Jake!" Kaia commanded.

Jake didn't seem to hear her. He had the blade in his hand again and focused his gaze on Kaia.

Lou stepped between them. "Put it down."

No response.

"Put it down or I will make you."

There. She sounded reasonable, at least to herself.

But she was trying to comprehend this bizarre scene. The feralness of these children.

What the hell is wrong with them?

It had happened so fast. Lou had expected to have a pleasant fireside chat and now she was in the middle of some sort of attempted murder that she didn't understand.

Her view of children as vulnerable, small, and in need of protection was rapidly disappearing.

Was she really about to be stabbed by this little hellion?

She had to assume so. After all, it was Kaia who had shot her the night they met.

Lou couldn't make the same mistake here. Especially since the look in Jake's eyes was far colder than Kaia's had ever been.

Kaia's compassion had always been present, even in her stubbornness.

What Lou saw in Jake's eyes was very different.

They were not the eyes of a child. They were empty of all emotion except for that unexplainable rage.

"He won't stop, Louie," Kaia told her. "He's been trained not to. Not until he gets what he wants."

"What does he want?" Lou's stomach tightened at the use of her name. She couldn't recall if the girl had ever said it before.

"To kill Elijah."

"I won't let that happen," Lou said. She had to adjust her position as Jake moved. He'd begun pacing like an animal, trying to look for a way around her.

"Then you'd better kill him first." Kaia said it bluntly, as if she weren't advocating murder but a simple task that required execution.

Louie wasn't sure she could do that.

"Louie?" Kaia's voice was high.

The little girl—and yes, Lou had to keep reminding herself that Kaia was a little girl—her façade was crumbling. Lou heard the first real notes of fear in her voice. "Louie, please."

Jake heard it too. He chose that moment to lunge.

He was faster than he looked, and the firelight spilling into the room put Lou at a disadvantage. That and the fact that she wasn't used to fighting opponents who were so...short.

Her aim was to strike him in the forehead, hopefully knocking him off his feet. Even better if he dropped the blade on impact. But he moved his head at the last moment, folding the blade, sharp side up, against his forearm in a counter block. The blade sliced across Lou's upper arm, spilling a hot stream of blood across the ground. Reflexively, she pivoted on her back foot and threw a kick.

It struck him hard, sending his small body tumbling across the room. His head made an audible crack as it hit the floor.

She swore. She hadn't adjusted her power to account for his smaller size.

Kaia was already across the room and picking up his dropped blade before Lou reached him.

At his side, Lou bent down to check if he was still breathing.

He was. Lou had only knocked him out.

Blood ran down her arm. It was a deep cut. It would probably need stitches. The Kevlar sleeve had protected much of
her forearm, but she should have worn her leather jacket.

Lou was still inspecting the wound when movement in
the corner of her eye caught her attention.

Kaia brought the blade over her head and thrust it down
at the boy's heart.

Lou caught her small arms at the last minute. They were
far enough from the fire now that Lou could slip through. She
did, dragging the girl into the bedroom by her will alone.

Lou dropped her on the floor unceremoniously. "What
the hell was that?"

She couldn't hide her anger or her surprise.

"He won't stop until he kills Elijah."

"I'll take him away," Lou scolded. "It doesn't mean you
have to kill him. He's—"

She was about to shout, *He's still a child.* But then again, so
was the little girl standing in front of her, her front now
smeared with Lou's blood. Given that and the way she still
held Lou's blade, she hardly looked innocent.

What's wrong with these kids? she thought again. *They're
crazy.*

She refrained from saying so. She didn't want to hurt
anyone's feelings.

Lou plucked the blade out of Kaia's hand. "I'll take him
away."

"But—" Kaia began.

"You won't need it. But I might." Lou said this knowing
full well she wouldn't have the heart to actually stab the kid.

"Please take him far away," Elijah said.

"When I come back, one of you is going to tell me what
the hell is going on. Or I'm going to bring the rest of the kids
here, one by one, until someone gives me answers."

This was a bluff, of course. In no way was Lou going to

chance these children trying to kill each other again. But at the same time, she needed answers.

Her mission tonight had been a disaster because she hadn't considered that the real danger was the child itself. She'd expected guns, and mayhem and perhaps psychopathic henchmen—but not murderous children.

She wouldn't make the same mistake twice.

"Promise me." Lou pointed a bloody finger first at Kaia, then at Elijah. "*Answers.*"

"Promise," Elijah said.

Kaia only glared at her.

When she went out into the living room again, the front door to the cabin was open and the boy was gone. Cold winter air blew inside, making the fireplace sputter and spurt.

Lou groaned inwardly. She should have known he would run. It hardly mattered. She could use her compass to find the boy easily. He couldn't get far in snow that would be up to his waist.

"I'll go get him," she told the children. "When I'm gone, close that door and lock it."

"It's a trick," Kaia said simply. She was staying quite close to Lou. "He'll want you to leave, thinking he's out there. Then he'll attack us when you're gone."

No sooner did Lou turn her attention to her inner compass, trying to get a lock on the boy, than she knew Kaia was right. Her focus was drawn to the kitchen, to the cabinet beneath the sink.

Lou motioned for the children to stand back. Kaia pushed Elijah into the bedroom and closed the door. She watched as Lou went to the sink and tapped the cabinet door with her boot.

Nothing. Silence.

"How do you know he's in there?" Kaia asked. "Is it your—"

"Shhh." Lou leaned over, opening the door slowly, being sure to keep it between her and whatever might be inside.

She'd only gotten it halfway opened when Jake burst out, screaming.

Lou had just enough time to grab him by the back of the neck and pull him through the dark.

The Alaskan night rose up to greet her, firming under her boots as she released the writhing child. He whirled on her, his face a snarl.

"What did they do to you?" she asked him. "What the hell did they do to you?"

She couldn't believe a child would simply grow up like this. He had been made into whatever he was now. Jake, Kaia, Elijah. They were all made.

Lou was one hundred percent certain of that.

Kaia and Elijah might have better control over themselves than this one, but Lou needed to remember this moment now.

This was what she was *really* dealing with. Every single one of the children would be this dangerous, and it would be best she didn't forget that.

Jake's breath came out in heavy pants. His eyes searched her body from head to toe.

"I don't have another weapon for you to steal," she said.

This was a lie. She had two guns and more knives.

The boy seemed to reach the same conclusion. He lunged.

Lou pulled one of the Glocks and pointed it at him. She had no intention of shooting a child, no matter how monstrous he might be.

That was a line she wasn't willing to cross. Not now, not ever.

Fortunately, he didn't force her to cross it. He saw the gun and spun on his heels. Without looking back, he bolted in the opposite direction.

"Looks like you *also* know what a gun is," Lou said to herself.

Kaia too had known what a gun was and how to use it.

That meant this wasn't the first time they'd seen one. And it begged the question of who the hell had shown guns to the children before.

The boy was still running. Lou watched him disappear into the night, her mind throbbing with its confusion.

It was too cold for him to be out here in February. But it was also the safest place she could think of. He was at least one hundred miles from civilization. There was no one he could hurt.

There were wolves and moose who could certainly trample a person. But Lou wasn't convinced the wolves would be able to take down a child like this.

Still, she would have to work quickly.

After releasing a frustrated sigh, Lou holstered the Glock.

She took one last look at Jake before side-stepping through the dark to find Konstantine.

He was in his office, bent over his desk, a gentle fire roaring at his back. She could hear rain hitting the courtyard's cobblestones outside his door.

"Do you have somewhere I can store a child?" Lou asked.

Konstantine didn't even look up. "I've already told you that you can bring the children here. It's—"

"No," Lou said. And there must have been something in her voice because he looked up, his eyes widening at the sight of her bloody arm.

"I have a situation," she told him.

He put his pen down. "What's happened?"

"I rescued a child. I *thought* I was rescuing a child. But then he tried to kill Kaia and Elijah. I have a feeling they might all be like that. I can't take my chances bringing them here, but I also don't want to leave them with those people, if this is what they did to them. I need a place where I can put them where they'll be safe, but they also won't be able to hurt themselves or anyone else."

"You're bleeding badly, *amore mio*."

"*Konstantine*."

"We can ask Isadora to put them into medical comas?" he offered.

"We can't sedate the children forever," she said.

"I don't know what else to tell you."

"What about that place you built to contain me. Before we were—"

"No," he said apologetically. "I never made anything like that again. I'm sorry, but I don't have such a place."

He pressed his lips together.

Of course, she knew what he was talking about. Years ago, before they were allies and she was only the murderer of his father, his brothers. When she was still hunting down everyone related to Martinelli, Konstantine had feared that one day Lou would find him. That when the day came, and if she couldn't be reasoned with, he'd wanted to be prepared. So he'd built a padded room that could hold her. One so full of light that even her gift couldn't save her. Except it hadn't been Konstantine who'd used the room against her.

It had been his usurper, Nico.

"Is Isadora's clinic big enough for all of the children? There's got to be at least sixteen in all."

"*Sì*," he said.

"This is a *short-term* solution," she insisted.

Because she couldn't imagine putting children into comas for the rest of their lives. That seemed nearly as cruel as killing them.

"Yes," he said. "I will call her and tell her you're coming. When will you bring the child to her?"

"Immediately."

"All of them?" he asked.

"No, just the one." Now that she knew the children had fangs and claws of their own, she would have to make the extractions more carefully. And this said nothing of their captors. They had to truly be monsters if this was what they could do to an innocent child's mind.

"I'll bring Jake now. And after I talk to Kaia and Elijah, I'll figure out what to do about the others. Once I know what the hell I'm dealing with."

"Where is this Jake now?" Konstantine asked. His eyes kept sliding to her bleeding arm. But Lou couldn't think of that. She could tell by the way it was going numb that it would definitely need stitches, but first, Jake needed to be secured.

"Running around the Alaskan woods somewhere," she said.

Konstantine lifted his cell phone from the desk and began dialing a number. "I'll tell Isadora you're coming. Do you want her to give you a sedative first? It might help you subdue him."

"No," Lou said, almost laughing. "He'll probably just plunge it into my leg or something. In fact—"

She removed her guns one by one and put them on his desk. Then her blades.

"I'm leaving these here. I'm tired of getting hurt by my own weapons."

Konstantine's eyes widened. "He cut you with your own knife? Hello? Yes, Isadora."

He fell into a string of rapid-fire Italian that Lou struggled to follow.

"Tell her I'll be there in a second," she said.

Lou stepped through the dark, leaving Florence behind her. When she put her feet down again, the world had frozen over. Snow crunched beneath the weight of her boots. Her breath fogged white in front of her face.

Movement on her right and the sounds of soft panting caught her attention. She turned and saw the boy was still running, barefoot, through the trees. He hadn't stopped this whole time?

Lou took off after him, making no effort to hide her pursuit. Though she did cheat.

With darkness on her side, one step behind him became one step in front of him. She braced herself before he ran full tilt into her arms, turning at the last moment to redirect most of his frenetic energy.

It hardly helped. He was still screaming and thrashing as Lou took two steps back and delivered them both to Isadora's clinic.

"Santa Madonna!" Isadora darted aside to escape the kicking legs now trying to strike her. She issued orders in Italian to the women crowding the room. "*Questo bambino è un diavolo!*"

It took all five of them, Lou, Isadora, and the three assistants, to force the boy onto a bed and straighten out his limbs enough that Isadora could inject him with a sedative.

It took several minutes before his thrashing weakened, his limbs went soft, his face evened out.

Isadora wiped her brow. "Is he possessed?"

"No," Lou said. She didn't believe in such things. There were too many evil people on Earth to blame anything other than humans themselves. "Someone made him this way."

"Santa Madonna." Isadora crossed herself.

Once the boy's breath evened out, Isadora accepted a second syringe from one of the assistants and injected the boy again.

"Just to be sure," she explained. "Konstantine said you needed him to remain unconscious."

"Not forever," Lou said. "Just until I can figure this out."

"Whatever this is, *Strega*, you don't have to explain it to me." She waved the situation away. That was until she saw Lou's bleeding arm. Then she was swearing in Italian again.

"Right. Can I get some stitches while I'm here?" Lou asked.

16

King found the ghost tour company that Tommy worked for without much difficulty. He realized as he looked at its old stone façade facing the opposite church that he must have walked past this place a hundred times in the years since he'd started wandering the Quarter. He simply hadn't had any reason to notice it until now.

When he crossed the threshold, he found a bald man behind the counter. The man wore head-to-toe black, his t-shirt serving as an advertisement for the place. The counter, too, supported an enormous banner which read *Award-winning ghost tour! You'll have a hell of a time, or your money back! See the bloody heart of a pirate ghost! Scares guaranteed!*

"Looking to book a tour?" the man asked, his cheerful baritone filling the small space.

"Actually, I'm looking for Tommy," King said, resting one arm on the counter. "Is he in?"

The man's gaze narrowed. "No, he's not. Is there something I can help you with?"

King wasn't sure why he was being met with suspicion. And because it wasn't the reaction he'd been expecting, he had to consider his next words carefully. If he turned the boss off completely to his cause, then this might prove to be a dead end.

"His cousin Jenny is missing." King produced a photo of Jenny, the one Carrie had given him when he dropped her off at the RV after posting her bail. It was one of those senior-year portraits. The girl's hair and makeup had been done. She posed beneath a large live oak tree, moss grazing her shoulder. Her smile was bright.

"Jenny's mom thought she might be with Tommy."

Better to start there than accuse the boy of satanism outright.

"Did you check his place?" the boss asked.

"I did, and met his landlady, Geraldine. She's not seen him. That's why she sent me your way."

The boss's expression softened. "Well, shit. Now you've got me worried. I hope he's okay."

"You haven't heard from him?"

"No," the man said. "I haven't seen him all week."

"Do you have any reason to believe he's in trouble?" King asked. "Any history of drugs or drinking? Have you seen him hanging out with a rough crowd? Anything like that?"

"What an employee does on their personal time is none of my business," the boss said, his voice growing hard again.

"And you haven't seen Jenny?" King asked.

He shook his head. "Nope."

King had the distinct impression that he was lying about that.

He reached out and lifted the brochure for the tour company and gave it a once-over. "Can I keep this?"

"Sure."

"Thank you for your time." King folded the brochure and

put it in his pocket. Then he turned to go, trying to understand why his skills kept failing him during this case. Usually people opened up to him. *Usually* all he had to do was ask the right questions and he could at least get enough information to illuminate his next step. But this time, it felt like every step he took was met with resistance.

King turned back at the last minute. "Can I ask you one more question?"

The guy shrugged as if to say, *We both know you're gonna ask it anyway, buddy.*

"What's your opinion of Tommy? As a person. Does he seem like a good guy? Always on time? Trustworthy?"

"He seems like a scared kid to me," the boss said, and again King saw that hint of softness seeping back into his demeanor. He'd seen the same tenderness in Geraldine.

This kid really must be quite the charmer, he thought.

"Why do you say that?" King said.

"He's skittish. He struggles to make eye contact."

"Sounds like terrible traits for a tour guide." King laughed. The boss did not.

"He's great on the tours. Animated. Funny. It's like he becomes a different person. I think it's the only time I've ever seen him happy, which is why I was worried when he didn't turn up for his last few shifts."

"Did you file a missing person's report?" King asked.

"I don't like cops. They're just as likely to kill you as save you," he said. The words felt a little pointed. King began to understand why he wasn't covering much ground with this guy. Hadn't someone just told him he looked like a cop?

"I'm not a cop. I'm just trying to help a mom find her daughter." King took another stab. "Do you know if he ever got involved in anything weird?"

The man snorted. He gestured around the shop as if

pointing to all of it. "I don't know what you're talking about, man. We're all into weird shit here."

ONCE ISADORA FINISHED PUTTING eight fresh stitches in Lou's arm, Lou returned to the cabin. The first thing she saw when she stepped out of the bathroom was her blood drying all over the floor.

She would have to clean that up.

The bedroom door opened.

"You're back," Elijah said. He ran to Lou, but stopped short of embracing her. She wasn't sure the kid had ever hugged an adult in his life. He looked as unsure as to what to do next as she was.

She placed a hand on his head.

"Watch out," she said, and gestured at the floor. "You'll get your socks bloody."

"I couldn't find the cleaning products," Kaia said. She was on the couch, looking into the flames.

"I'll take care of it," Lou said.

"What happened to Jake?" she asked. "You didn't kill him, did you?"

She heard the disappointment in the girl's voice. An eight-year-old girl. *Disappointed.* In *Lou.* For not committing murder.

It took Lou several moments before she could say, "He's somewhere he can't hurt anyone."

She didn't want to put the idea of a coma into their heads. What if they started to worry that she would do the same to them? They might try to fight her or, hell, kill her and escape.

"We're going to talk," she said. She gestured at the sofa. "Sit down."

Elijah went to the sofa and took a seat beside Kaia, so close their thighs were touching.

Lou took a seat on the loveseat to their left. Their eyes kept sliding to her stitches.

"It's not as bad as it looks," she said. "Certainly not as bad as when you *shot* me."

At least Kaia had the decency to lower her eyes at that.

"It's *very* apparent to me that what I don't know about your situation puts you in danger. You have to start filling in these gaps for me. *Now.* No more excuses, or I'm going to make another mistake. Do you want me to bring any of the other kids here?"

"No!" Kaia said without hesitation.

Elijah wasn't as quick to respond. "What about Paula? Or Nathaniel? They might be okay."

"No," Kaia said again. "You don't know that."

"And why is that?" Lou asked. "Are they like Jake?"

Lou stopped herself from saying, *Are they also murderous little monsters?*

At first Lou thought they were going to refuse to tell her. But then Kaia's face softened in the firelight. She looked tired. Way too tired for a kid. After a long look into the flames, she said, "It's not their fault."

"Was it Father who made them this way?"

"He made us do things," Kaia said.

"Or sometimes he let people do things to us," Elijah said.

A cold rage rose up in Lou. She caught herself clenching her fists and forced herself to relax them.

"That doesn't explain why Jake wanted to kill you," Lou pressed.

"He kept Jake apart the most. I don't know what happened to him when he was gone," she said.

"It must have been bad," Elijah said.

"He was only brought out for the games," Kaia said.

"Games?"

"That's what Father calls them. Sometimes they're okay. But most of the games are bad."

"The puzzles," Elijah interjected. "Kaia always solved the puzzles first."

"Because if you made a mistake, someone got hurt," Kaia said. "I don't want anyone to get hurt."

Lou had to remind herself to take a steadying breath. To remain where she was, even though everything in her itched to grab this so-called Father and play a game of her own.

"Has Jake killed someone before?" she asked.

Elijah was looking at Kaia as if he needed permission to speak. Lou wondered if she should try another angle, but the girl surprised her again.

"The game is called One," she said. "He puts two kids together and says there can only be one."

"They weren't always kids," Elijah interjected.

"No," she admitted. "It wasn't always us."

Us.

"When I saw Jake, I knew he was playing One," Kaia said.

"Why was he targeting Elijah instead of you?" Lou wasn't sure that it mattered, but she was trying to understand what was going on in these children's minds, and exactly what the hell had been done to them.

"Because of the rules of the game," Kaia said. "He would have killed Elijah first. Then he would try to kill me."

Lou didn't miss the *try*.

Leaning forward, she searched Kaia's face. Finally, the girl met her gaze. Her eyes were full of so much sadness. It hurt Lou's heart.

"Are there really no other children I can save?" she asked. "None that I can bring here without them attacking you or Elijah?"

Kaia's eyes began to fill with tears. "No."

. . .

LOU'S first instinct after leaving the children was to go to Dani and Piper's apartment. She wanted more information on this bastard called Father. She only hoped that Dani's search had proved fruitful.

When she stepped through the dark of the cabin's bathroom into their living room, they were at the kitchen counter eating dinner.

"Lou-blue!" Piper called, trying to slurp the last of the spaghetti she'd been eating into her mouth. "Where've you been?"

"I paged you hours ago," Dani said.

Right. Lou had forgotten about that. King too. But neither had been marked as emergencies, so she'd assumed they could wait.

"Sorry. Something happened," she said, shrugging out of her leather coat and throwing it over the arm of the sofa.

Piper spotted the stitches immediately and whistled. "Who the hell stabbed you?"

"No one."

"Liar. Wait. Didn't an eight-year-old just shoot you? Was it another kid?" Piper frowned. "Where are you finding these children?"

Dani's eyes widened. "Oh! I have to show you what I found!"

Her fork clattered to her plate. She rushed to the armchair in the corner of the room and started rifling through her work bag.

"Here, here!"

She pulled out a large manila folder and took it to the coffee table. She opened the folder and pulled out page after page.

"I've spent all afternoon reading this guy's research, and it's fascinating. It's all about the connection between trauma and psychopathy."

Dani shoved the pages toward her.

"Summarize it for me." Lou knelt down by the table.

"He argues that it's not only childhood trauma that causes children to grow up to be psychopathic. He says certain genetic predispositions such as a parent, especially a mother, with mental illness increase a child's likelihood to develop psychopathic tendencies, as well as a toxic or dangerous environment. Chronic abuse."

Lou thought of her own mother's pill-popping. Had the combination of her cold nature and addictive tendencies contributed to who Lou was now? Until this moment, Lou had always blamed the Martinelli family and their execution of her family. That her father's death was responsible for the rage and despair that had driven her desire for revenge. It hadn't occurred to her that perhaps her mother's own personality might have played its part.

Dani must have realized the connection as soon as she did. "I'm not saying that's why you—"

"Lou's not a psychopath!" Piper cut in, wiping spaghetti sauce off her face. "We've been over this."

"Agreed," Dani quickly added. "I'm just saying that this guy's focus is on how these contributing factors increase the likelihood of certain psychoses. Anti-social personality disorder, sociopathy and psychopathy. He's obsessed with this stuff. It's all he writes about. He's got hundreds of articles on it. Seriously, he's published a remarkable amount of research in the last fifteen years."

"Try not to sound too impressed with the bad guy, babe," Piper said, frowning.

"Right, sorry." Dani laced her fingers and put them on the table.

"He's using the children for his research," Lou said. Her anger hardened to a cold pit in her stomach. "I think he's trying to make killers."

Piper lowered the article she'd been holding. "What?"

Lou told them what Kaia and Elijah had shared with her about their captivity. And also what Konstantine had uncovered about the murdered families. Then she told them about Jake.

Now that Lou had time to consider all of these details together, a clear picture of the situation was forming in her mind.

This so-called *Father* must have targeted their families specifically because they had infants. He went about collecting the babies for his research the way laboratories collected animals for their experiments.

And how long would it go on if Lou didn't put a stop to it? Would the next wave of his research be generational? Would he start breeding the children as if they were rats?

"Are you freaking kidding me?" Piper said, dropping the papers onto the coffee table. "You're telling me this sicko murdered a bunch of families and then kidnapped the babies in the name of research?"

"He couldn't have killed all the families himself," Lou clarified, remembering what Konstantine had said about overlapping times for some of the incidents. Distances that couldn't have been traversed by normal means. Not unless this so-called professor was like her—and Lou wasn't ready to believe in such a horrifying possibility.

"You're telling *me*"—Piper's voice was still rising—"that all these kids have ever known is this sick fuck? How did he even find them?"

Something sparked in Dani's eyes. She snapped her fingers. "Wait! I think I know that one."

She began frantically shuffling the pages again, spreading them across the coffee table. "He had a practice. He doesn't anymore, but about twenty years ago he was a practicing psychiatrist. He focused mostly on women. Married and single. In many of his papers, he *claims* his research came from those women. What if these babies came from those women? I wonder if we could go through his client list and see if any of their names are the same.

"Client lists should be confidential," Piper said. "Right?"

Dani gave her a pointed look. "Nothing is confidential if you throw enough money around."

Piper clucked her tongue. "Way to flex on me, babe. Why can't you pretend to be poor like Lou. At least for the sake of my ego?"

Piper was gesturing at Lou's half-destroyed leather jacket lying over the arm of the couch.

Lou made a mental note not to mention that Konstantine had closed an entire store just for Valentine's Day.

Dani's fingers were flying over her keyboard. "Do you remember the names of any of the children? Their birth names?"

"Konstantine said there was only one from Kalamazoo, where his practice was from. The others came from all over the country. One was even from Canada."

Dani's fingers paused in their incessant tapping, hovering over the keys. "They couldn't all be his patients then."

"No, he had help," Lou said.

"You don't think that all the killers were psychiatrists like him, do you?" Piper was touching her throat as if the idea were unthinkable. "Man, doctors freak me out enough already. I'm still not over that murdering nurse you found six months ago."

"Research like this is often shared among colleagues," Dani said. "It's very possible that most of the patients weren't his, but simply cases he knew about. He was very active on the conference circuit back then. It's possible colleagues were sharing information, unaware of the danger they were putting their patients in."

Lou remembered the killer she took from the art museum. "Does his research ever talk about psychopathy in adults or only in kids?"

"Oh, no," Dani said, unable to hide her fascination. "He talks a great deal about the psychopathic compulsions in adults. He never mentions anyone in particular, but it's very clear he's studied them just as much as the kids. It's also evident that his passion lies in what makes a psychopath rather than how they express that psychopathy as an adult. I think you're right about what he's been doing to the kids."

"What if he found these psychopaths and recruited them?" Lou asked. "What if he directed them to kill these families, to hurt the children, to do all of it for the sake of his research?"

"He let them hurt the kids?" Dani asked, tears gathering in the corner of her eyes.

Lou said nothing.

"Jesus." Piper ran her hand through her hair.

None of them spoke for a long time.

Finally, Piper said, "He's got to be a really sick guy."

"And a dangerous one," Dani said, her brow knit together. "Think about it. Who is more anti-authority than a psychopath? And here he is willingly interacting with them? Telling them what to do? What keeps these killers from turning on him? From murdering him or torturing him, especially to protect their own identity? He has to have *serious cojones* to mess with these people. Or maybe he has some leverage on them."

"Whatever leverage he has on them, it's got to be working," Lou said. "It makes me not want to have this baby."

Their heads snapped up. Piper grabbed her hand across the table. "What?"

"They're so small. They're not safe. How could I possibly make a kid feel safe?" Lou was whispering to herself, but their reactions were so strong she might as well have shouted it.

"Are you kidding me!" Piper exclaimed.

"Don't say that," Dani added.

"You make kids feel so safe."

"I—" Lou began, but they wouldn't let her get a word in.

"No, seriously. Remember that sex-trafficking thing that we got sucked into by that crazy woman, Diana?" Dani pointed her pen at Lou, then Piper.

Lou could tell that Piper was glad Dani was the one who had brought this up. Lou had not forgotten either how Diana Dennard had wreaked havoc on Dani's PTSD.

"I remember," Lou said.

"That little boy held on to your neck *so* tight. What was his name?"

"Shai Wilson."

"Shai!"

Lou hadn't forgotten him. Sometimes he still prayed to her, and she still answered his call, slipping into his bedroom on the nights when bad dreams woke him and his fear was brightest in his mind. He was only a little younger than Kaia.

"If I trusted anyone to keep a kid safe, it would be you," Dani said.

Piper threw up her hands. "That's what I told her! But she was like 'I don't want to be like my dad.'"

Dani frowned. "Like your dad how?"

Lou wasn't sure what to say exactly. It was hard to articulate an emotion that was little more than a fearful clench at the base of her throat.

"People make mistakes," she said finally.

Dani's brows lifted. "You do realize that you're a lot stronger than your father, don't you?"

Lou said nothing. She fought against the urge to protest, and they must have seen it.

"I'm serious," Dani said. "Not only could you outgun him, but what about your incredible gift?"

"He saved my life, but not his own," Lou said.

"He didn't save you." Piper threw up her hands. "Your gift saved you. It was never your father. He threw you in the pool so you could *save yourself.*"

There. They'd said it. Something that had long lingered in the back of Lou's mind. A dark realization that she'd moved away from every time the truth had come close to consciousness.

"You did what he couldn't," Piper said. "Props to your dad for being a righteous do-gooder or whatever, but he doesn't compare to you. You hear me? He couldn't hold a candle to you, and I'm going to be so bold as to say I don't think he'd mind me telling you that either. I think he'd agree with me."

The knot at the base of Lou's throat only tightened.

"You've known every time we were in danger," Dani said. "I can't think of a single time I needed you that you didn't come. What makes you think you wouldn't be there if your kid needed you?"

"I can't come if I'm dead," Lou said.

"Oh geez," Piper said. "We're all going to die sooner or later. Hell, the way I've been drinking coffee while taking these freaking exams is going to finish me off."

Dani scowled at her. "It's not the coffee, babe. It's all that sugar you eat."

Piper rolled her eyes.

"But Piper's right. If you die—" Dani began.

"It'll never happen," Piper interjected.

"—*if* you die, even if you and Konstantine *both* died, the kid will still have us," Dani finished. "Me and Piper and Mel and King."

"I'll be honest. I'm not mom material, but I can be the cool gay aunt. I'm *excited* to be the cool gay aunt," Piper said. "And we'll love the hell out of your kid. You know we will. But be forewarned, I'm going to buy those annoying-as-hell games that make all the noise. You're gonna love that."

17

It took King almost forty minutes to navigate the rush-hour traffic across downtown New Orleans before taking the Lake Pontchartrain Causeway to Mandeville. When he pulled into Ashley Wexler's driveway, for a moment all he could do was sit there and stare at the house.

It wasn't a mansion, but it was certainly large. There were no pillars or butlers or servants rushing about a grand estate. Wexler wasn't displaying the same kind of wealth that Piper had described Dani's family having, but there was something gaudy about the place nonetheless. The way the whole house looked a bit like a fairy tale with its spires and glossy windows, the decorative touches that made King think of a gingerbread house.

It was inviting in an ominous sort of way.

King also wondered just how much money this guy had to make in order to keep up the care on such a place. The seasonal storms weren't kind to real estate around here, and the size and age of the house alone would require consistent attention to sustain this level of maintenance.

Someone inside the house peeled back a curtain and looked out at his car.

He should have known that a Buick like his would stick out like a sore thumb in this land of Porsches, BMWs, and Mercedes-Benzes.

King stepped out of the car.

The front door opened even before he reached the top step.

A tall man with thick black hair and bright eyes stepped forward. He'd been blessed with good looks and an athletic body.

"Can I help you?" the man said. His face was natural, friendly.

But the eyes were cold. And for King, it was always about the eyes.

"I'm looking for Ashley Wexler. Is he home?" King asked.

"That's me," the guy said, his smile fading. "What's going on?"

"I've been hired by your ex-wife to find your daughter. Were you aware that she's been missing for over a week?"

King decided to go from the date that the roommate last saw her rather than when Lou did. If he was really the one who went by the apartment and wrote the bum check—King was open to the possibility that he'd sent an assistant or some lackey to do the job—then he'd already know that she was missing.

"I wasn't," he said. "Have you gone by her apartment?"

"I did," he said. "I got your address from the roommate, actually. Seems like you wrote her a check that didn't cash."

There. A flash of anger.

"I never wrote her a check," he said. "I haven't been to that apartment in ages."

"Then you might want to check your checkbook, Mr. Wexler."

"Look here. My daughter knows where I am. If she needs me, she knows she's always welcome here. I have far more to offer her than her mother does. That's for sure."

Wexler's ears were growing red.

"It would seem so." King gestured to the house. "She would come to you if she were in trouble."

"Of course," he said defiantly.

"But she hasn't?" King pressed.

"No."

"Do you know of any friends that she could be staying with? Did she mention any trips, maybe? Or a new boyfriend she might be spending a lot of time with?"

"No," he said. "But she did mention Tommy, her cousin."

King shifted his weight to the other foot. "Tommy is your nephew, correct?"

"Yes, he's my sister's son. Though he's been like a son to me ever since my sister died."

"And how long ago was that?"

"Almost twenty years," he said, removing his glasses. He cleaned them with the edge of his polo shirt before sliding them back onto his nose.

As he bent to look down, King saw a scratch on the side of his neck. It could have been a cut from shaving. Or from a fingernail.

"And when you say she mentioned her cousin, what did she say?"

"I don't want to say anything bad about my own nephew —" he began.

But you will anyway, King thought.

"—but he hasn't been the same since my sister died."

"How old was Tommy when she died?"

"He was six. He started experimenting with drugs, hanging out with the wrong crowd—"

"At *six*?" King asked, being intentionally obtuse.

Anger flashed in Wexler's eyes again. "No. As a teenager. He was always getting into trouble at school, started listening to that rock music that makes your ears bleed. Awful stuff."

King noticed that the man seemed to enjoy the sound of his own voice. He was falling into the rhythm of speaking in a way that showed it. King was fine with that. Let the man talk and maybe King would learn something.

"His trouble peaked in high school when he got arrested for killing that animal. I tried to get him out of it——"

Not *tried to stop him*, King noted. "What kind of animal?"

"A cat. But there wasn't much I could do for him. My neighbors are assholes."

Wexler pointed up the street at the house across from his own lot.

"Why he had to go and pick their cat, I'll never know."

"He was here?" King asked.

"Yeah, he lived with me until he was sixteen. After that, I told him he could get a job and a place of his own if he hated it here so badly. Last I heard he was slumming it in that shithole. I assume that's where Carrie found you? She hasn't risen above her circumstances, I'm sure."

King was now doing his best to check his own anger. "That shithole?"

"New Orleans. It's a godawful place. I only go there when I absolutely have to. Which isn't often. Thankfully."

"Let's circle back to your daughter. What did she say about Tommy exactly?"

"Only that he was trying to find her. She sounded a bit scared. That's why I went by her place to see if she was all right."

And here we have our first lie, King thought. *You said you haven't been there in ages.*

"But she wasn't there?" he asked, waiting to see if he would catch himself in his own lie and backtrack.

"No."

"And you haven't heard or seen from her since? You said she didn't come here, but there were no other phone calls? No pleas for money? No text messages or emails?"

"No, nothing," he said, shifting his weight from one leg to the other. "She must be with Tommy. I'd check his place."

"Your daughter called you scared, so you go to her apartment to see if she's okay. But when you don't find her, you also don't call the police or put in a missing persons report?"

"My daughter is a grown woman. What she does with her time is her business. I resent that you're implying I don't care about my own daughter."

"You're right," King said, not bothering to correct him. Something about this guy was rubbing him the wrong way. He wasn't sure if it was how he spoke about his ex-wife or just his general pompousness. "My apologies."

King reached into his wallet and pulled out one of his cards. He handed it over to the man.

"Here's my number. If you do hear from Tommy or your daughter, I would appreciate it if you would give me a call."

King had zero confidence the guy would do any such thing.

Wexler looked down at King's card and arched a brow. "You are in the shithole. Right in the middle of it."

"That I am," King said. "Some of us like that shithole."

And with that, he turned and descended the steps of the porch, returning to the Buick without a backward glance.

Once he was inside the car, he ignited the engine. He waited for the heater to sputter to life before throwing the car in reverse.

He was about to back out of the driveway when he saw her.

In the upstairs window, plain as day, Jenny was holding back the drapes, looking down at him.

His heart lifted with relief.

Not dead. She's not dead.

He was about to lift his hand and give her a little wave, but she turned, looking at something—or someone—over her shoulder. At the last minute she pulled away and the curtain swished back into place, blocking the room from view.

King began backing out of the driveway. He wasn't sure why, but he hoped that if Wexler did come to the window, he would assume that King hadn't seen her.

As he navigated his way out of the ritzy subdivision back toward the causeway, King kept replaying the way the curtain had swished into place.

Had Jenny stepped away from the window? Or had she been pulled away from it?

In either case, why had Wexler lied to him? Why hadn't he wanted King to know that Jenny was there, safe and sound? Was it just an innocent lie to hide his embarrassment about the bounced check?

Or did he really hate his ex-wife so much that he wanted to let the poor woman suffer? He must have understood how distraught she was, if she was willing to go to a detective for help in finding her daughter, even if she had no money to speak of.

He did strike King as the kind of douche who would enjoy torturing someone like that. Especially an ex.

"What a prick," he muttered.

But there was something else too. That part about Tommy. Why would he almost insinuate that Tommy might be to blame for Jenny's disappearance if he knew that Jenny was safe and sound in his own house?

King dialed Piper's cell phone.

She answered on the second ring. "What's up, boss?"

"I want us to find out everything we can on Ashley Wexler, the ex-husband." He spelled the name for her. "Financial records. Anything about a dead sister or their family. Whatever you can get your hands on. Ask Dani too. I don't care if the info is obtained legally or not."

"New suspect?" Piper asked.

"Maybe. Let me know what you find."

"Sure thing. Stay safe out there," Piper said, and hung up.

King tapped his phone against his chin.

Tommy.

"Where are you?" King wondered aloud. "I really need to speak with you, kid."

18

Konstantine stood over the unconscious boy, his arms crossed. When asleep, the boy didn't look like the animal Lou had described to him. He looked only like a sleeping child.

"Will this hurt him?" he asked, turning to the doctor at his side.

"The coma?" Isadora asked. "I would not recommend using this method forever. Children aren't meant to spend their lives in sedation. But for a couple of weeks, perhaps as long as a month, it is possible to keep him comfortable. But you need a long-term solution. *E hai detto che ce n'erano altri?*"

"*Sì*, there are others."

"*Quanti?*"

"I'm not sure. As many as fifteen." He wouldn't count the two that he'd already met. Though they hadn't been very friendly, especially the girl, they seemed in possession of a certain level of self-control. He didn't think they'd have to sedate them.

"*Mio dio*," she said. "Do you have a plan? Where they can be kept?"

"I'm working on it." The truth was, the plan he'd managed to cobble together in the short time since this problem had arrived was threadbare. He'd been honest with Lou when he said he'd never tried to construct anything like the original containment cell he'd meant to use against her. But certainly such places existed. He could find somewhere the children could be kept and possibly rehabilitated for society. He'd reached out to many of his contacts in the last few hours, before walking to Isadora's clinic.

It was only a matter of time before someone got back to him.

That was the good thing about having Padre's immense wealth at his disposal. Someone would make him a decent offer as long as Konstantine was willing to pay the price.

Konstantine felt the pressure change between his ears before she stepped into his periphery.

"*Amore mio*," he said, turning to her.

Isadora stepped away from the bed. She gestured for Lou's arms. "*Fammi dare un'occhiata.*"

Lou showed her the stitches.

Isadora adjusted her glasses on her nose, bending closer to inspect them. "They're getting infected. Have you washed them in those magic waters of yours?"

Konstantine snorted.

Because the doctor had never seen the nightmare landscape for herself, she clearly thought of La Loon as some lovely, mystical place rather than Hell itself.

"No," Lou said. "I'll go tonight."

That meant she intended to hunt soon. Would it be too much to ask her to take him along?

"Who are you looking for?" he asked.

"One of the professor's henchmen. If I can interrogate one of the killers who help him, maybe I can get some answers. I want to know how many kids are still alive, what sort of shape they're in." She nodded toward the child sleeping in the bed. "No more surprises."

"They might not know," Konstantine warned her. "If this man is as versed in psychological warfare as you've said, it's possible he has lied to his assistants, not just to the children. Can I go with you?"

"It's easier when it's just me," she said.

Konstantine caught sight of the doctor in the corner of his vision. He turned, noting her concerned face. "*Sì, dottoressa?*"

She was looking at Lou. "Be careful, *Strega*."

Lou arched a brow.

The doctor nodded toward Lou's arm, which was resting at her side, her forearm pressed into the side of her belly. "Your stitches."

Lou only regarded her for a moment. Konstantine wondered if she would chastise the woman for her concern. An infected patch on Lou's arm was hardly a worry at a time like this. And hadn't she seen worse from *La Strega*?

Hoping to prevent any conflict between them, Konstantine said, "She'll wash her arm soon. She'll be fine."

The doctor was unmoved by his assurances. In fact, if he wasn't mistaken, her expression was stern.

Lou surprised him by the tenderness with which she finally spoke to Isadora. "I'm being careful."

The doctor's shoulders relaxed then. "Good. Very good."

LOU RETURNED Konstantine to the church, then she went home.

As she stood in their bedroom, a piercing thought struck her.

Where would we put a bassinet?

The novelty of the idea was shocking. Also the quickness

with which her mind—with little effort—worked out the details.

There was another bedroom in the villa, but Lou didn't think she could sleep so far away from her child. At least not at first. Not until she was sure that she was safe, that she would remain safe.

And so it was decided almost instantly. There, on her side of the bed, in that generous space between the bed and the closet she used for her departures, that would be the best place for a baby to sleep.

Because if anything did happen, it would be only a matter of steps before she could take the infant in her arms and be through the darkness, somewhere safe on the other side of the world.

Have you decided then? the little voice in her head asked. *Have you decided this is your path—despite all odds? Are you going to make this child a promise that even your father couldn't keep?*

Her insides twisted.

She pushed these thoughts away. She forced her mind to focus on the task at hand.

Lou went to her secret treasury and began exchanging her weapons. She needed bullets small enough to wound but not blow someone apart with a single shot.

She took her time with the blades. Since they would be doing most of the work, she wanted to choose something that would feel good in her hands. Something smooth.

In the end, she decided on six knives of varying sizes.

Her hand hovered above her father's bulletproof vest, remade several times over. It was far out of date, but Konstantine had kept it functional because he understood its sentimental value. She ran her hand over the vest, feeling the fabric pull at her fingertips.

She decided to put it on at the last minute. She was more than a little aware of the fact that it felt good, snug across her abdomen. She touched the place where the vest and the possibility of life growing inside her overlapped. It was the closest her father would ever get to her child.

Now you're just being sentimental, she chided herself. She supposed it might be the hormones. She'd heard that pregnancy could make a woman emotional. Lou's target had better hope that her mood swings ran on the softer side then —lest her neatly contained rage decide to surface.

Someone close to him, Lou thought. *Not the professor himself, but someone close. Someone who knows the situation. Someone who can tell me what's going on.*

Her compass spun, whirled. But it didn't lock on anyone.

It occurred to her that no one might know the situation. If the professor was smart, he'd keep his schemes to himself. She needed to simplify her targeting.

After consideration, she thought, *Someone who can tell me his weakness.*

Her compass snapped into place.

Lou closed her armory, putting the painting back in place, and went to the closet. Before she'd fully closed the door behind her, she was through.

Her foot found solid ground again in a hallway. It was dim, a row of doors opposing each other on each side. It was empty of people, and Lou had a moment to consider if her compass had betrayed her. But no. She could hear the faint tapping of someone working away at a computer. Light spilled from a room across the dark hallway.

She'd not been able to get any closer because the person was bathed in bright light. That was why she was in the hallway outside their door.

Fine. She would drag them into the corridor if she had to.

When Lou took a step toward the office just ahead, the lights overhead began to activate.

Without thinking, she sprang forward, dashing into

the office and its insufferable source of light. The man at the computer half turned, pushing his glasses up on his nose.

His eyes widened at the sight of her, and whatever question he'd been about to ask died on his lips. He sucked in a deep breath as if he meant to scream. But Lou slammed her hand over his mouth, yanking him backward by the hair and hitting the light switch.

The room went blessedly dark. Lou stepped through the shadows, holding the writhing man in her arms as she moved from one side of the world to another.

"Oh god, oh god, oh god oh—"

"I want to ask you a few questions," Lou said, pressing a blade to his throat.

"Please—please. I don't know. I swear. He doesn't tell me anything. He doesn't tell anyone anything."

"Has he ever asked you to hurt the children?" Lou's breath fogged white in front of her face.

He hesitated.

Lou plunged the blade into the top of his thigh, and he howled.

"I'm sorry," the man screamed. "I'm so fucking sorry!"

"You know the children. You know what he does to them. So answer me."

"I type up his research. I keep notes. I swear. I swear. I barely even speak to the kids."

"But you knew what he was doing and you didn't stop him." Lou drew the blade across the man's bare chest. "Did you?"

When he hesitated again, Lou's real work began. She carved his chest, the tops of his thighs. She slipped the blade between his ribs more than once.

She wasn't sure how long this went on, only that enough time had passed for her fingers to freeze, making it hard to hold the blade. The blood all over her hands and the knife wasn't helping either.

"You can't tell me anything about him? His weaknesses?" she purred in his ear.

The man's eyes fluttered. He was going to pass out from shock if she wasn't careful. Then her game would be over.

Lou slapped his face.

"His weaknesses?" the man repeated. He looked down at his clothes, as if seeing them for the first time.

"Yes," Lou said encouragingly. "What does he care most about?"

"The truth," the man said. "He only wants the truth. That's his weakness."

"The truth of what happens when you hurt children?" Lou asked.

"The truth of psychopathy. He's desperate to understand it. To master it. It's all he cares about."

All he cares about.

Lou grabbed the man by his hair and pulled his neck back, looking down into his eyes. "He'd like to meet me then."

"Yes, he would. He knows about you," the man said, his throat bobbing against her blade. "He wants you to come."

Lou buried the blade to the hilt in the man's neck. Blood flowed down the front of his torso, over Lou's arms and waist.

Lou stepped back, taking the knife with her. The blood flowed all the harder without it in the way.

She wiped the blade on her shirt, but since her shirt was also soaked with his blood, it hardly mattered.

The battered man had stopped breathing.

"Useless," she said. She ran a hand down the front of her bulletproof vest and sheathed the blade.

As Lou stood beside the lapping water, with the snow-covered woods around her, she had this feeling of not being quite herself. It was still the familiar irritation that she'd had for weeks, and yet its edges had softened to something like sadness.

"Is it hormones?" she whispered.

She dropped the man on the embankment and rotated her shoulder, ridding it of the tension she'd accumulated from holding him up.

"Fucking pregnancy hormones?"

The corpse didn't answer. No wonder, she thought, as she considered the mutilated remains. Had she lost a little bit of control of herself in those final moments with a blade in her hand?

He knows about you. He wants you to come.

"Of course he does," she murmured. If this *Father*, this professor, was as obsessed with psychopathy as his work suggested, Lou would be a temptation he couldn't resist.

Could she use that to her advantage?

She grabbed the useless lackey's leg and dragged him to the water's edge. She entered first, tugging the corpse behind her like a child's beloved toy.

His initial buoyancy faded as Lou went out deeper into the lake. The water filled his clothes and pulled him under. Lou walked on. The ice-cold water as black as the night above rose to her waist, then to her chest, before she took a breath and sank beneath its surface.

Holding the corpse close, she watched as the water shifted. From dark gray to red. From cold to warm.

Her boots scraped the roof of Angelo Martinelli's car, and this was her signal to push for the surface. She didn't always encounter the car when she crossed to La Loon. She'd come across it only a few times since she first carried it from Baltimore four years ago.

Four years.

Four years ago, she'd been hunting Konstantine. *And now look at us.*

She broke through the surface of Blood Lake, the scent of sulfur hitting her in the face even as she cleared her eyes of red water.

The two moons greeted her as well as the haze of the distant mountains. But she had only a moment to enjoy the haunting landscape before a tremor in the water drew her attention. She spun toward it, expecting to see the dorsal fins she'd grown used to. Sometimes these waters were infested with such creatures who had no problem yanking a corpse from her hand.

But there was no dorsal fin.

Only turbulent water.

Then she saw the enormous black body, serpentine in its glory, rising up from beneath her.

She dropped the corpse and reached for her gun.

She was too slow. She was already being lifted out of the water.

To Lou's crushing relief, it was Jabbers. She was on the beast's back.

Lou swore, placing both hands, including the one now holding the gun, on the creature's scales.

"I dropped your dinner," she said.

On the shore, Lou slid off Jabbers's back, her boots hitting the soggy embankment.

"Were you hunting?" Lou asked, running a hand over her black body. "That's good. I was afraid you weren't eating."

Lou had read about blue whales, spiders, and other animal mothers who didn't eat until their children were weaned.

The beast snapped her jaws in answer.

"If you're still hungry you can go get that guy." Lou pointed over her shoulder at the lake.

But Jabbers seemed more interested in Lou. She kept pressing her snout into Lou's stomach and sniffing.

After a full minute of this rough inspection, she chuffed.

Lou sank to the water's edge and submerged her arm. It wasn't until she'd washed off the blood that she realized she was bleeding.

One of her stitches had popped. Isadora was going to give her a hard time about that unless these waters did swift work on her wound.

Jabbers entered the lake once more. Two powerful contractions of her sleek body were all it took to propel her from the shore. Then she dove out of sight, leaving only an expanding ring of ripples in her wake.

Once her tail broke the surface in a furious thrash.

Lou remained in the shallows, soaking her arm, in no hurry to return. She was feeling a touch tired, another new experience for her.

Mood swings. Exhaustion.

"When does it stop?" she asked the beast climbing out of the lake.

Jabbers was chewing on something. If Lou had to guess, that particular chunk of meat must have been a leg at some point in its previous life. But before she could be sure, Jabbers swallowed and it was gone.

Then the two of them were simply sitting on the shore together, looking out at the nightmarish horizon in silence.

Jabbers had cleaned one taloned paw and then another before Lou asked, "Is it hard to be a mother?"

The beast let out a low whine.

Lou wasn't sure how to interpret that, so she went on gazing at the eternal twilight.

19

King's phone rang, and because he didn't recognize the number, and because he was in the middle of composing his argument for Beth—a strong argument, he thought, as to why the DA shouldn't pursue a case against Carrie Bright; she was only a distraught mother, after all—he didn't answer.

Then it rang again.

No one ever called him repeatedly unless it was urgent.

"Hello?"

"Yes, Mr—uh. Oh hell, I've forgotten your name, honey."

King wasn't sure if this was a scam or trick, so he only said, "Can I help you?"

"It's Geraldine," she said. "Tommy's landlady."

His brow evened out. "Geraldine, yes. I'm so sorry I didn't recognize your voice. What can I do for you?"

"He's here. He's here and it looks like someone hit the poor boy upside his head. It wasn't you, was it?"

"No, ma'am," King said, wondering why she would call him if she thought he was the culprit.

"Good. Can you get over here? I really do think he be in trouble, and I don't want nothing to happen to him."

"He's home now?" King asked, looking at his watch. "Just got there?"

"Sure did. Said he was going to lay down for a bit before he went to work, but I don't believe it. Hurry if you can."

Piper had been behind her desk typing up a report that was due to the DA's office first thing tomorrow. A summary of a robbery case they'd been asked to assist on. It would have to wait.

He was waving at her and then at the door.

"We're leaving?" she whispered. "Right now? Oh, okay."

She stood, shutting down her computer and pulling on her coat. She was shoving everything into her backpack as King double-checked his pockets for his keys. His wallet.

"We'll be there in a few minutes, Geraldine. Just sit tight. Call me if he tries to leave. Stop him if you can."

"Sure, sure."

They were halfway down Royal Street before he pocketed his phone.

"What's happening?" Piper asked. "Because I don't have a taser or pepper spray or anything."

"Hopefully we won't need it," he told her. "Tommy's home."

"Oh. That was the neighbor lady? She was nice. I liked her."

They hooked a left onto Peter Street and passed Melandra's Fortunes and Fixes. King looked through the window instinctively, and there was Mel behind the counter, talking to one of her shopgirls. Mia, was it? King could never remember their names.

Piper was waving at them. King, too, threw up his hand as an afterthought.

Melandra returned it, her face scrunched in question. No

doubt she was wondering why they were in such a hurry, especially as they walked right past the shop door, headed for the Buick parked in the alleyway.

He'd have to tell her what happened later.

King unlocked the car and Piper swung herself into the passenger seat. She placed her backpack between her feet and buckled up. "So what's the plan? Are we going to rough him up? Make him talk? Get him to tell us where the hell Jenny is?"

Right. King had forgotten to tell her about what had transpired at Ashley Wexler's house. He filled her in on the way to Tommy's. It didn't help that they were sharing the road with the lunchtime traffic.

"At least she's not dead," Piper said, exhaling with visible relief. "But I don't like that he lied to you. Why would he do that?"

"I think he wants Carrie to worry about her."

"But she's not. You told her where her daughter was, right?" Piper's voice was stern. Almost scolding.

"Of course I did."

"What did she say?" Piper was opening her phone and composing a text to someone.

"She's still concerned. As I am. But we both assume that she must have called her father when Carrie wasn't able to come to pick her up."

"He's lying about having her in his house to make his ex sweat. That's cold, man. What a douche."

King put the Buick in park outside the chain-link fence that said *Beware of Dog*. Geraldine was on the porch in a coat this time. She stood when she saw them, waving them forward.

"He's still in there. I heard him yelling at somebody on the phone."

"Did you hear what they were yelling about?" King asked,

adjusting his duster across his shoulders to protect himself from the blast of icy wind assailing the back of his neck.

"No. The walls are not that thin. But he sounded upset. Poor boy."

"Is there a back door?" King asked.

"No, but there's a window. Are you saying he might throw himself out of it if he hears you knock?" Geraldine was giving him a scrupulous look.

"Anything is possible."

"I'll go around back," Piper said. "I'll yell if he jumps."

King waited until she was out of sight before he raised his fist and began rapping on the door.

"I don't understand why you don't like him. He's a sweet boy," Geraldine said, her arms folded.

"I never said I didn't like him."

"Don't trust him, then. Why don't you trust him?"

Because Carrie and Ashley are telling me he's a satanist who tortures animals to death.

"Tommy, are you home?" he called out. He knocked again.

Geraldine remained at his arm.

"Tommy?"

She clicked her tongue. "Give the boy a minute to put his pants on. Lord."

"King! King!" Piper called from the back.

King was off the porch and around the corner before she could shout his name for a third time. He regretted moving that quickly. His ankles were burning from his jump off the porch.

What the hell are you thinking? he chastised himself. *You're too old to be chasing anybody.*

But it had seemed that not that long ago, he had had it in him to chase suspects for miles on foot, even while wearing a vest and all those DEA-issued weapons.

Fortunately, Tommy wasn't a runner.

He was hanging out the back window, his feet dangling.

"Tommy, honey, what are you doing?" Geraldine asked. She appeared on the opposite side, blocking Tommy's alternative exit.

"Ms. Geraldine," he said, and released the window. He collapsed to the ground.

"Honey, you've got more sense than that. Why you jumpin' out of my windows for?"

"I'm sorry." Tommy looked as confused by the scene as she was. His eyes darted from King to Piper and back to King again. "I'm sorry. I thought you were somebody else."

"Who, baby? Who are you running from?"

Movement caught King's eye and he turned. The neighbor was peering out from behind her curtain, curlers in her hair. Her brow was raised, lips pursed in judgment.

"Maybe we should take this inside," King offered. He didn't want to have this conversation out in the open.

"Let's use my side. I've got the space heaters going and I made tea," Geraldine offered, already hobbling away. She was leaning her weight to the left as if her right knee and hip bothered her.

Five minutes later, the four of them were sitting in Geraldine's tidy living room. Piper and Tommy were on the couch together, both holding a glass of Geraldine's sweet tea.

King was in a kitchen chair that had been brought over. Geraldine had laid claim to her recliner, spinning it on its swivel away from the television until she could face the three of them.

"Now, honey, tell us what's going on?"

King didn't insist that he be the one to ask the questions. It didn't seem right since he was in her living room, drinking her sweet tea, sitting on her kitchen chair.

"I'm sorry I ran," Tommy said. "I thought you were someone else."

"Who did you think I was?" King asked.

"My uncle. I've been trying to stay off his radar."

"Are you talking about Ashley Wexler?" King set down the tea and pulled out his notepad and a pen.

"Yes."

"Do you have problems with your uncle?" he asked.

Tommy barked a strangled laugh, empty of any real humor. "That's an understatement."

"Did you know that Jenny is missing?" King asked.

"I hope so. I told her to run," Tommy said. He sat his glass down on a coaster.

King frowned. "Why"

"Because she's not safe. Not until the gate closes."

Piper tilted her head, her scribbling pen hesitating. "What kind of gate we talkin' about here?"

"There's a gate that only aligns with the ley lines once every twenty years."

Geraldine waved her hand at him as if shooing a fly away. "Baby, what are you talking about?"

He didn't answer her.

King scratched his temple with his pen. "I'm going to need you to back up for me, Tommy. Start by telling me the last time you saw Jenny."

"I saw her a week ago. I went to her place to warn her."

"About the ley lines?" Piper asked. King could tell she was struggling to keep her voice professional.

"Yeah. I told her that if Uncle Ash reached out to her, if he promised her anything or made up some bullshit about a vacation, a get-together, father–daughter time—whatever the hell he said, it didn't matter. I told her to stay away from him until the gate closed."

"You think that he could hurt his own daughter?"

"Only when the gate is open. That's the only opportunity to get whatever he wants from the other side. But it has a blood price. You can't use the ley lines without paying the blood price. He's not going to waste her. Or me."

King felt that he had firmly traveled to the other side of looney land, but he wanted to keep Tommy talking. Maybe if the young man said enough, King could figure out what was going on in that head of his. But he was struggling to form his next question.

Piper beat him to it. "How do you know all of this about the ley lines?"

"I started learning about them after my mom died. I wanted to understand what happened to her. Why he killed her."

"You think your uncle killed her?"

"I *know* he did."

Piper already had her phone out. "It says here she was in a car accident. Her car ended up in the Mississippi River."

"It's a lie," Tommy ground out, real fury coating his words. "That bastard killed her. I fucking know he did."

"Easy now. Watch that language in my house. This is the Lord's house," Geraldine said. "Who killed your mama?"

"My uncle Ash. Her brother. He thinks I was too young to know what I saw, but I wasn't."

"What did you see, baby?" Geraldine asked.

For a long time, Tommy didn't speak. His eyes were wide, lost somewhere deep in his memories. Then he said, "I woke up in his arms. He was carrying me. I asked him where we were going and he told me to just go back to sleep. And I think I did. But I woke up again because my mom was crying. No, she was *screaming*. I opened my eyes to see what was going on, and she was bent over me. I thought it was her tears hitting my face, but it was blood."

"Oh my god," Piper said.

"And I'll never forget what he said. He said, 'You dumb bitch. You could've had another.'"

"Lord Jesus in Heaven." Geraldine pinched her eyes closed. "Sounds like your uncle is a sick, sick man."

"Are you sure he killed her?" King asked. This earned him a hateful look from both Geraldine and Piper, but he pressed on. "I mean, did you see him actually hurt her?"

"When he pulled her off of me, I saw the knife in her back. That's when I realized he was going to stab me with it, but I guess she got between us. So he had to use her."

King's hand hesitated in its scribbling. "Use her?"

"For the blood price. It was supposed to be my body—he can use anyone as long as they're of his blood. It was supposed to be me but she got in the way. Then he—he—"

Tommy began to cry.

Geraldine wrapped her arm around his shoulders.

King's mind raced with the possibilities. He replayed his conversation with Ashley, the way the man had tried to cast doubt and uncertainty on Tommy's character. He'd wanted King to believe that Tommy was the sick one. Was it possible that he'd also filled his ex-wife's head with these thoughts, long ago, back when they were married? Anything to draw suspicion away from himself?

What was more likely? That this kid was in the throes of a schizophrenic breakdown or that Ashley Wexler murdered his sister?

Tommy didn't feel like a killer. He was talking crazy, without question. King hadn't understood half the nonsense out of his mouth. But his pain was clear enough. King didn't find it hard to believe that he'd seen something terrible as a kid and was suffering from it.

"What was your mother's name, Tommy?" he asked.

"Lily Wexler." Piper and Tommy had spoken at the same time.

He wrote it down. "And she died twenty years ago?"

Tommy wiped his face with the tissues Geraldine gave him.

"There was never a trial? Never any suspicion that your uncle was the one responsible for your mother's death?"

"No. They said her injuries were from the windshield glass going through her torso. But that's a lie. It wasn't the windshield that went through her like that."

King rubbed his forehead. "I'm a little lost. What does your mother's death have to do with Jenny's disappearance?"

"He'll do it again, if he can," Tommy said. He blew his nose. "It's gotta be me or Jenny. We're the only blood kin he's got left."

"What does he think he gets out of killing you?" King knew that murderers often made up elaborate fantasies to justify their actions. Sometimes they even claimed God told them to do it. But King couldn't help but wonder what particular delusion was in play here.

"When the gate is open, he can make a deal with the devil. But he's got to pay the blood price or his wish won't come true."

"What if I told you that when I spoke to your uncle, he told me that you were the one into devil worship," King said, searching his face for a reaction.

Tommy laughed bitterly, swiping at his red nose. "I wouldn't be surprised. He's been trying to get at me ever since I went to the police and said that he killed my mom. They didn't believe me because I was only six. He tried to make them think I'm sick in the head. That I'm the one who hurt those animals. He did that."

"Do you have any proof?" King asked.

"Proof!" Tommy cried, standing. "I have boxes and boxes of proof. I've been following him for years. Tracking his movements. Trying to prove what he did to my mom. I brought that proof to the police station and they referred me to a psych ward. You cops don't want *proof*."

Geraldine pulled him back into his seat with a gentle tug.

King held up his hand. "I only ask because if you think Jenny is in trouble, then it would be best if we had a reason to arrest him before he got that chance to hurt her."

"Hopefully he won't find her. When she came here, I gave her all the money I had. It wasn't much, but I hoped it was enough to get her away until the gate closes."

"And what if I told you that she's at his house? Right now."

There. King saw real terror in the kid's eyes. He wasn't lying. He really believed all of this, as incomprehensible as King found it.

"Then she's dead," Tommy said. "He's gonna kill her."

"My Lord," Geraldine said, and crossed herself.

Piper shook Tommy. "Don't say that. We can still stop him. Can't we?"

Tommy ran his fingers through his hair. This low light made the dark circles under his eyes more prominent. "There's a meeting tonight. It's supposed to be a rehearsal for the main event. I can show you where they are, but I can't go in."

"Maybe if you stayed in the back or—"

"*No*," Tommy insisted. "I can't go anywhere near him."

Fresh tears fell from his eyes.

"I'm not going to risk getting killed. She can't have died for nothing. No matter how much I might deserve it."

Piper squeezed his shoulder. "Don't say that."

"When does this gate close, baby?" Geraldine asked. "When will you be safe? For another twenty years at least."

"Saturday," he said. "Saturday night is the last night. If we can make it to dawn on Sunday, we're safe for another twenty years."

King wasn't sure what to believe. Was Tommy really worried about Jenny? Did he really believe his uncle capable of murder? Or were these lies to misdirect them?

His doubt must have shown on his face.

"What do you think, boss?" Piper asked.

"He doesn't believe me," Tommy cut in. "No one ever does, but I know what I saw. I know what really happened to her."

"I think we'd better sneak into this meeting," King said. "I don't know if we'll be able to get any evidence that will actually hold up in a court of law, but we can try."

"You'll see," Tommy said, his eyes dark. "Then you'll know who's the real monster."

20

Lou's hair was still wet from a shower when she went to check on Kaia and Elijah. As she stepped from the dark bathroom into the cabin, she found them at the kitchen table. They had a puzzle between them, half completed. From what Lou could see, it was the Taj Mahal, or at least most of it, with a welcoming blue sky at its back.

"That bored, huh?" she asked.

"We're almost out of wood," Kaia said without looking up. "We didn't know when you'd be back."

Lou didn't take this personally. It made sense that they should doubt her. After what they'd been through, why not expect the adults in their lives to let them down?

"I wouldn't have forgotten," Lou told her.

They said nothing. Elijah was watching her from the corner of his eyes, stealing glances at her.

"What is it?" she asked him.

"You have blood on your jacket."

She looked down.

So she did. "I took another one of Father's helpers. Glasses. Tall. Red-blond hair."

They met each other's eyes but said nothing.

"He never hurt you, did he?" Lou guessed.

"No," Kaia said. "But he didn't help us either."

Elijah pressed one of the pieces into place. "He took a lot of notes."

"He certainly won't be doing any more of that." She took a seat at the table. "Is there nothing else you can tell me about him?"

"Father?"

"Yes," Lou pressed.

"He likes to play games," Kaia said simply.

"You mentioned that. What kind of games?"

"There's the 'finding game," she said, pressing three pieces into place, one right after the other.

"There's the 'who first' game," Elijah said.

"There's the 'quiet game,'" Kaia said, and Elijah's hand stilled above the puzzle.

"That was the worst game," he said.

"Did you have to hide?" Lou ventured, crossing her arms.

"No. It was who could be quiet the longest," Elijah said, trying one piece and finding it didn't fit.

"You had to be quiet even when someone hurt you," Kaia said.

"I'd like to play that game with him," Lou told her, her blood boiling.

"Kaia's the only one he played nice games with," Elijah said matter-of-factly, sifting through the pieces on the table.

Before Lou could ask what he meant by that, Kaia rose, pushing away from the table. She went to the fire and threw on another log.

"Don't build that up," Lou said from her seat. "We won't be here long."

Kaia turned, still holding a piece of wood in her small hands. "What?"

"I'm taking you to Italy. You'll be safer there."

"Safer? Why?" Kaia put the wood back on the pile and turned on her. "You're going after him, aren't you?"

"You *are* a clever girl," Lou said.

"Don't call me that."

"Father called her that," Elijah whispered.

Lou pretended not to hear.

"He'll hurt you," Kaia said.

"He'll try," Lou said.

Kaia searched her face, and as she did so, Lou struggled to understand what emotion she was seeing. Fear?

"Even if something happens to me, you'll be safe with Konstantine," she told them.

"No," Kaia said. "You can't."

"I—"

Lou couldn't get a word in.

"No!" Kaia clenched her little fists at her sides. "You can't kill him."

"He's not your real father," she said gently. "He killed your family and took you."

"I know."

If Kaia didn't want to spare the monster because of some sentimental reason, then what was going on?

"*I* want to kill him. It's got to be *me*."

Lou was going to dismiss this ridiculous claim, except the girl's whole body was shaking.

"You're a kid," Lou said gently. "You shouldn't have to kill anyone."

"It has to be me. If you don't promise me that you won't kill him then I'll have to stop you. I'll have to—to—"

"Kaia—" Elijah looked afraid, his eyes large and round.

"I need this! I *really, really* need this or—or—I'll just—"

Lou didn't laugh. She didn't shake her head or tell Kaia to stop kidding herself. Instead she looked at her. *Really* looked at her, casting her mind back to when she had been twelve years old herself. In the days, weeks, months, and years after Angelo Martinelli had taken everything from her.

Back to when Lou's only reason to stay alive was revenge. When her only armor against soul-crushing madness was her determination to destroy the Martinelli crime family.

How would she have felt if someone had taken that from her? If someone had looked at her and laughed? Had called her a child?

"You're eight years old," Lou said. Lou hadn't brought herself to kill anyone until she was seventeen.

"I—" Kaia opened and closed her fists again and again. "I can't kill him *now*, but I will. One day I'll do it. I swear I'll do it."

Lou puffed up her cheeks. "You're calling dibs? *Really?* So not only do I have to fight him without knowing enough about him, I'm not supposed to kill him either? Can I maim him at least? Break some bones? Bleed him out a little bit?"

Kaia gave this far too much consideration, her face pinched with seriousness. "He won't die?"

"If I stick a blade in the right place, he won't die," Lou said. "You can even shoot someone a few times if the caliber is small enough. And your aim is good."

Kaia's face evened out. "You're teasing me."

"No, I'm not." Lou leaned toward her. "But be honest with me. Do you *have* to do this? Because if you force me to make this promise, it's going to put me in more danger. Don't ask this of me unless you really have to have it."

After another long pause in which those green eyes searched Lou's face, she said, "I have to have it."

Such conviction. Was this what Lou had looked like when she'd vowed to destroy Fernando Martinelli?

"But I have your permission to hurt him as long as I don't kill him?"

Again, those adult eyes.

You're too young to look at me like that, Lou thought.

"You can hurt him," Kaia said. "But I get to be the one who kills him."

"If I make this promise, can I trust you to behave in Italy? Will you listen to Konstantine and be nice to the other kids? They're tough, but they're not like you. They're not going to play those kinds of games. You have to promise *me* you won't hurt them."

"I promise," they said.

You two are going to be the death of me.

"Fine. It's a deal." Lou sat back in her seat and regarded them both. "Now go get your things."

KONSTANTINE SPENT the afternoon preparing for the arrival of the children. He spoke to Matteo and the others, warning that they would have visitors. That there would be a language barrier, if nothing else. He also told them to be nice—but not stupid. If it felt like these newcomers were going to cause trouble or do something dangerous, they were to tell him immediately. And to protect themselves.

With that business aside, there was only the matter of making sure they could fit two cots into the spare room.

Lou had said she'd already brought them clothes weeks ago when she'd rescued them, but that they'd need new coats. The Canadian climate was much harsher. Their coats too heavy.

They would be free to roam here, with a bit of pocket money and a chaperone. Matteo would have to do. He had the best English out of the children. And he was a good, responsible boy. He would tell Konstantine if anything happened. And Gabriella had the will to match the other one. Perhaps they would even become friends.

He gave the room one last appraisal and nodded approvingly. Then his ears popped. He turned to find Lou and the children stepping forward from the corner.

"Hello," Konstantine said, putting his hands on his hips. "How was the fastest trip to Italy? Better than flying half a day by plane, no?"

"I've never seen a plane before," said the boy.

The girl wasn't smiling either. *Dio mio.* He would have to work on that. He didn't like children to be so serious. There was plenty of time for misery in adulthood.

"This is your room," Konstantine said, pointing at the two beds with their new sheets and pillows. "And here is a wardrobe for your clothes. You can use that chest for your toys."

"We don't have any toys."

"I'll go back for your games," Lou said.

"Where are we?" Kaia asked, stepping past him into the room.

"Florence, Italy. Do you know where that is on a map?"

"I've never seen a map," Elijah said.

"Yes," Kaia said. "It's in the northern part of Italy. In the middle."

"Yes," he said. "That is correct."

He reached into his pocket and produced a handful of euros. He gave thirty to each child. Enough for food or something that interested them, but not enough to get them into trouble.

"What is this?" the girl asked.

"Money," Lou said, leaning against the doorway. "Have you seen it before?"

"No. I've heard about money."

Konstantine arched a brow. "What did you hear?"

"It makes people do bad things."

He saw the fury behind Lou's eyes before she looked away.

She must be thinking what he was thinking—that these children knew nothing of the world. That they must have lived all their lives in the grip of their captors. It made him feel more than a little murderous himself.

"I'll find them a tutor, *amore mio*," he promised her. "They'll catch up."

But Lou was already pulling her shades down over her eyes. Though whether she wished to hide her feelings from him or the children, he couldn't say.

Konstantine checked his watch. "I'll take you down to dinner now. Introduce you to the others."

The boy looked elated. For him, this was clearly an adventure. The girl looked pained.

"Aren't you hungry?" Konstantine asked.

"She's always hungry," Elijah laughed.

She elbowed him in the gut. "Shut up."

"Now, don't fight. Come to the kitchen with me."

The introductions were anti-climactic. Matteo, Gabriella, and the others were already well into their meal when Konstantine walked in with the children.

He introduced them, said they would be staying with them here at the church for a while. He was wondering why they were only staring at him until he realized they weren't.

Their large, surprised eyes were fixed on Lou. *La Strega*.

Lou seemed to realize she was the focus of attention at the same time he did.

She took advantage of it, coming closer to the table.

"Behave," she said, though it was unclear whom she directed these instructions to. "All of you."

A chorus of reassurances erupted from the children.

Her watch buzzed. "King needs me. Are you okay here?"

"*Sì, sì.*"

She left him at the kitchen table with the children, unsure

of what to say next. He searched each face in turn before smiling.

"After dinner, why don't we go to the piazza for gelato," he said. "But they need coats. Someone share with them until I can take them shopping. *Chi ha un cappotto in più?*"

"I will take them shopping," Matteo volunteered, coming out of his seat as if he intended to leave this very instant.

"*Anche io!*" Gabriella cried, also rising.

"*Anche io!*" the children echoed. "*Anche io!*"

"Okay. Okay. *Calmatevi.* We can all go." Konstantine held up his hands. "But first, *eat.*"

"Shit, man. A lot of this is checking out," Piper said.

King looked up from his computer. "What do you mean?"

She shook a handful of manila folders at him. "I mean I've been going through these notes that Tommy made about Wexler and a lot of it really happened. Places Wexler really went. Things he really bought. Shady meetings he really had."

"What about the sister?" King asked.

Piper's fingers flew over the keyboard of her laptop as she tried to sort through what felt like hundreds of articles that she'd read. She'd been at it all day, her eyes burning from looking at the screen.

She yawned and said, "Okay. Listen to this. A young mother, Lily Wexler, was pulled from the Mississippi River today after the New Orleans Police department received an anonymous tip from a local homeless man."

She hesitated, scanning the screen.

"Go on."

"The anonymous caller told officers that they had seen the car careen off the road, slide between the gap in the safety barrier, and plunge headfirst into the river. The car had already sunk below the surface by the time the authorities arrived. Divers were called to the scene and the body was retrieved. It appears that she died from her injuries. The young woman was not drunk nor were any narcotics found in her system at the time of her death. But there was a wound in her chest that was most certainly the cause of her death. 'People fall asleep at the wheel all the time. If you feel tired, pull over,' Police Chief Reginald Dreyfus told reporters at the scene of the accident.

"Lily Wexler was only twenty-six years old. She is survived by her young son, Thomas, her parents, Donald and Dolores Wexler, and an older brother, Ashley."

King's brows lifted. "What do we think happened?"

Piper looked away from the screen. "I think he killed her and drove her car into the river."

"I'd like to know more about her injuries."

Piper straightened her back. "Who can we ask?"

"The medical examiner. He's a nice guy. Finneas. Call down there and see if he'll see us. This case is before his time, so hopefully he won't feel insulted. No one likes having their work checked."

She dug in her backpack for her phone. "What should I tell him?"

"Just that you're working a case that is connected to her death. Don't get too excited. This could be a dead end."

Piper frowned at her phone.

"What?" he asked.

"I just got an email from Dani. It's the financials we asked for," she said, dragging her thumb over the screen. "Ashley Wexler isn't doing so great."

Piper rose, crossed the office, and went to the other side of his desk. She showed him the report on her phone.

He squinted at the screen. "Reading that hurts my eyes. Email it to me."

Five minutes later he had the financial reports pulled up

on his own computer, with Piper standing behind him, reading over his shoulder.

He pointed at the screen. "This here is when he was still married to Carrie. They owned a trailer out in Gretna, but only her name was on it. And no wonder, his credit was awful."

King moved the documents around on the computer's desktop.

"Now look here."

"Everything goes from red to black," Piper said. "How? Did he get a new job?"

"He opened a consultancy firm, but his client list is empty."

"Are we talking about a shell company to hide dark money?" Piper asked.

"I don't know. But this is two months after his sister died. Look. He bought a house. A BMW."

Piper stepped back and held up her hands. "Okay, but are we really saying that Satan—the devil dude downstairs—gave this asshat money because he sacrificed his sister? Are we really saying that?"

King rubbed his brow. "It's more likely that he used the insurance money that Tommy inherited from his mother's early death."

"How would he even get that?"

"Because he became Tommy's guardian. He took custody of the boy right after his sister died."

"Geez," Piper said. "And no one thought that was suspicious?"

King was still squinting at the screen. "Sacrifice or not, his luck didn't last. He's back in the red. Look at all this debt. He spends like crazy."

"Can we find out if he's got a life insurance policy out on his daughter? And maybe Tommy too?" Piper asked.

"Companies don't usually disclose that kind of information," King said. He closed his laptop and stood. "You know who we should ask?"

"A life insurance person? What are they called? Advisers?"

"Melandra," King said.

Piper snorted. "Mel? What does she know about life insurance?"

"No, about the ley lines. Magic. All that nonsense about gates. Let's ask her."

"She's a fortune teller. Not a satanic priest. What's she going to know about ley lines and deals with the devil?"

"She might surprise us."

King waited for Piper by the agency's door while she packed up her things.

The last of the day's light was shining gold along the top of the buildings as they walked down Royal toward St. Peter.

Fortunes and Fixes was empty when they entered.

King held the door open and Piper crossed the threshold first. It was always a little sad when she came into the shop now. She missed it. The scent of incense hanging in the air, the flicker of the chandelier's lights, and the ghostly sound effects.

Fortunately, the shopgirls weren't in today. They were sweet. Piper just struggled with jealousy whenever she saw them doing the job that she'd loved for so long.

Lady pressed her cold nose into Piper's hand.

"Hello, beautiful girl," she said, kneeling and rubbing her face on the dog's neck. "Who's pretty? Who's the prettiest of the prettiest girls? *Who?* Tell me who?"

"Do you have a minute?" King asked.

Piper looked up to see he was talking to Mel. She was behind the counter, scribbling something on her notepad.

An inventory list.

Piper's heart clenched. *I used to make the inventory lists.*

"What's going on?"

Piper waited as King caught Mel up on their conversation with Tommy. About his belief that Wexler killed his mother.

"I don't know about ley lines," Melandra said when he finished. "I've heard of them, but I'm not sure what they have to do with devil worship or selling your soul."

"But you *do* think someone can sell their soul?" King asked, leaning on the counter.

Mel pushed him off, rubbing at the glass until she'd removed the smudges he'd made.

"She doesn't like it when you touch the glass, man," Piper said.

King took a step back.

Mel went on, "Of course. I think people sell their souls all the time. Satan ain't got nothing to do with that. Anytime you go against your heart and do what you know you shouldn't, you hurt your soul."

"That's upsetting," Piper said. She accepted a kiss on her cheek from the dog. "Sometimes people have to make tough choices."

"All you've got in this life is your integrity," Mel said. "Remember that."

King was rubbing his chin. "I'm trying to figure out if it even matters. What does it matter if Ashley Wexler is a satanist or just a murderer? Plenty of killers believe crazy things to justify killing their victims. Him believing that he's fulfilling some pact with the devil in exchange for wealth sounds like a run-of-the-mill delusion to me. Regardless of his motivation for killing, if he really killed his sister, it's more than possible he will kill his daughter or nephew."

Piper stood, much to Lady's dismay. "Killers are more likely to repeat a crime if they didn't get caught the first time. You told me that."

"Yes, but not all killers are serial killers," King told her.

"Then forget about the ley lines. This guy just might be hoping to cash in on another life insurance policy," Melandra said. "Do you think it's important to know whether or not he's really communing with the devil? It won't be the devil writing the check either way."

He saw her point. Whether Tommy was a liar, delusional, or traumatized didn't matter. It only mattered that they made sure Jenny didn't get hurt.

King shifted his weight. "I want you to come with me. Tonight."

"Wait, wait," Piper said. "You're actually going to sneak into the devil meeting? What if they catch you?"

"I'll ask Lou to take us."

"You're assuming it'll be dark enough. What if they're at an Olive Garden or something? Last time you said they were playing Taylor Swift!"

Mel laughed.

"I don't think this will be the same group," King said.

"Who are you messaging?" Piper asked as she watched King's fingers fly across the screen of his phone.

"Louie. If Tommy's right, then the meeting starts in two hours. Surely two hours is enough notice for her to turn up."

"I have to say, I'm not sure what you think I can do at this meeting for you," Mel said, running her fingers over her braids. "I'm not sure I was so helpful at the last one."

"Hard evidence would be ideal. But I'd be satisfied just to see Wexler with my own eyes." King turned to Piper. "Show me how to use night mode on this camera. You did it before."

That was true. Weeks ago, a vandalism case had them walking the cemeteries at night. He'd wanted to document some of the damage but there hadn't been much light. That's when Piper told him about night mode. He had marveled at how, if the camera was held still enough for long enough, he could take night pictures that were nearly as bright as those taken during the day.

He'd been half in love with the feature since.

"Sure thing, boss." Piper opened King's camera on his phone and played with the settings.

"Mr. King, you have to walk me through this," Mel said. "You want us to sneak into this meeting with Louie's help. You want to take pictures of your suspect, and get evidence that he means to do someone bodily harm, and then—what? What exactly is my role in this? I already told you that I don't know anything about devil worship."

"You're my moral support," King said, looking up at her through his lashes.

"Then what the heck am I?" Piper asked.

"You're *technical* support. Photos. Audio recordings. Video. You'll help me set up everything."

Piper opened her mouth to speak but was struck by a strange thought. Clear as day. It was the way King was looking at Mel.

Oh my god. He likes her, she thought. *King likes Mel.*

Like, *likes* her likes her.

His posture, the way he leaned toward her. The way he was quick to smile, quick to laugh.

But above all, it was that heavy eye contact.

"Oh. My. God." The words were out of her mouth before she could stop herself.

They both turned their gazes on her.

Mel arched a brow. "What? What's wrong?"

Before Piper could speak, the storage closet door opened and Lou stepped into the shop. She wore her mirrored shades and a clean leather jacket.

She gave the three of them a once-over before saying, "What did I miss?"

21

They chose Jim's Jambalaya for their late lunch. Piper wondered if food this spicy would upset Lou's stomach. Weren't pregnant people supposed to be nauseated all the time? Yet she watched Lou eat a whole skillet of cornbread covered in honey butter, an entire fourteen-ounce strip steak, and a mound of garlic potatoes before she finally came up for air.

King and Melandra were staring at her.

"Don't you eat in Italy?" King asked.

Mel slapped his shoulder gently. "Don't ever comment on how much a woman eats."

"I didn't mean anything by it," King said. "She just seems hungry."

Lou looked at her demolished plate and then at Piper.

Piper shook her head. "Don't look at me, man. Eat whatever you want."

She was going for nonchalance, but the truth was she was still reeling from the knowledge that King liked Mel.

King.

Liked Mel.

This was a disaster. What if he was stupid enough to pursue her and then they broke up and then she had to choose between them?

Slow down, she told herself. *You're getting too far ahead of yourself.*

The idea of the match gave her tremendous anxiety. Even more anxiety than the idea that Lou was going to have a kid.

Melandra was watching her. "What's wrong with you? Your gumbo too spicy?"

There are too many secrets at this table. Too many things changing at once. That's what's wrong with me.

Instead, she said, "As if."

She lifted the hot sauce from the table and tapped out several red drops onto her food. This was for show, of course.

Feather-light lips brushed the back of Piper's neck. "Hey, love."

Dani stepped into view, pulling out the empty seat beside her.

"Y'all look cozy," Dani said after everyone said their hellos. "When was the last time we got to eat together like this? Was it Louie's birthday? Are we celebrating something?"

Piper froze, trying to remain as still as possible.

Lou said nothing. It was King who said, "We're going undercover tonight to see if Ashley Wexler is the real satanist."

Dani's brows lifted. "Oh really."

"As far as Tommy explained it, there's some sort of blood ritual beneath one of the old crypts across town. We're going to sneak in and see if there's any truth to that."

"And if there's not?" Dani reached across the table and took a menu.

"Then it's likely that his uncle killed his mother for the insurance money, and the boy is just confused about what he saw. Or he's schizophrenic. That would also explain all the paranoid delusions."

"Sounds like this Wexler is a sick bastard either way," Dani said, turning the page. "Oh, the crawfish bucket looks good."

Dani waved to the waiter.

Once the business of ordering was done, she asked, "How's it going with the professor?"

Mel arched a brow. "The professor?"

"I admit, I haven't been able to stop thinking about him," Dani said. "He's horrifying. Absolutely horrifying. I hate being reminded that there are people like him in the world."

It was Piper who answered Mel. "There's a guy who teaches courses about psychopathy, but turns out he's the psychopath. He murdered like twenty families and kidnapped their babies so he could experiment on them and turn them into little monsters."

"Games," Lou said. "Kaia says he plays a lot of games."

The waiter returned with Dani's glass of wine.

"Can I get another cornbread skillet?" Lou asked.

"Sure thing, ma'am."

King pressed his lips together and Piper thought about kicking him under the table. But at least he didn't say anything to Lou.

"What do you mean, *games?*" Mel asked, adjusting the bangles on her wrists.

"That's what the children called them," Lou said. "It sounds like he had a lot of them. Ways to get the children to do what he wanted."

"He was probably testing their reactions," King said.

"So, when will you be killing the bastard?" Piper asked. Her face felt hot.

"I promised I wouldn't."

"*What?*" Mel, Dani, and Piper all said at the same time.

King was frowning.

Dani asked, "What do you mean, you promised?"

"Kaia wants to kill him."

Piper leaned forward and hissed across the table, "The *eight*-year-old?"

"Yes," Lou said plainly.

"The *eight-year-old kid*," she repeated. "The one who shot you?"

"She wants revenge for what he did to her and her family. I understand that."

No one spoke. What could they say? They knew where Lou stood on this.

"Did she ask for your help in killing him?" Dani shrugged out of her coat, laying it across the back of her chair. "Like are you supposed to take them somewhere or—"

"No," Lou said. "She wants to do it herself. When she's older."

"You're going to need to build a case against him then," Dani said. "We'll need hard evidence to send him to prison. At least that way she'll know where to find him when the time comes."

A hush fell over the group as the waiter put the cornbread skillet on the table.

"Thanks," Lou said, taking the dish of whipped honey butter and slathering it on the bread.

"Oh, I should've ordered cornbread," Dani said, waving at the waiter again. "Can I get one too, please?"

"Sure thing, honey." The waiter dismissed himself.

Dani turned her attention to Lou again. "Do you have any evidence that he's the one who took the kids or killed the families?"

"Konstantine said that someone scrubbed all the articles. How could he fund that level of media suppression?"

"If I'm remembering correctly, his mother left him a lot of

money when she died," Dani offered. "I suppose he could have hired someone to scrub all the stories. But that would be a massive effort."

"If this guy is backed by a patron of some sort, it's possible he won't stay in jail even if you arrest him," King said. "Depends on how powerful his friends are."

Piper held up her hands. "Wait a minute. Is there even a possibility that this could be backed by a shady organization?"

King shrugged. "I heard stories when I was working in the DEA. I don't think it's entirely out of the question. I can see the interest certain agencies may have in trained killers. The military for one."

"They're kids. Not soldiers," Dani said, her disgust evident.

"I didn't say it was right," King said. "I just said I wouldn't be surprised."

Piper did remember King's old partner Chaz trying to shoot him in his apartment. Apparently, he'd been corrupt for years.

"Greedy people. Man, they're the worst," Piper said before forking her gumbo.

"If he tries to disappear, I'll kill him." Lou's mouth was full of cornbread. "Kaia will just have to forgive me."

"Maybe it won't come to that." Dani placed her hand on Piper's thigh under the table. It made Piper's whole body melt. "If we break this story open wide enough, even his backers might drop him in an attempt to distance themselves."

Piper placed her hand on top of Dani's and squeezed. Piper enjoyed seeing the color spread across Dani's cheeks.

"Then we break it open wide," Piper said. "Make the bastard such a pariah that even this so-called patron is afraid to bail him out."

King leaned back in his chair, casually laying an arm across the back of Mel's chair.

Mel didn't even seem to notice.

"Ow!" Dani cried. That's when Piper realized she'd been squeezing her hand too hard.

"Sorry," she muttered, and released her.

"You'll have to expose not only him but also the cover-up," King said. "Cast light on these possible accomplices, too."

Dani exhaled, running her bruised hand through her hair. "I don't know if I can do all of that by myself."

"Konstantine will help you," Lou said. "He's got connections."

"We should talk and coordinate then," Dani said. "We'll need something concrete."

"I have Kaia and Elijah," Lou said. "He had an assistant that was recording something."

"Data? Notes? Details of these so-called 'games'?" Dani asked.

"I don't know," Lou said. "But it's got to be something worth recording. We just need to get that record."

Lou's watch buzzed. She looked at the time before slipping the last bite of her cornbread into her mouth. "We need to leave soon if you want to sneak into that place."

"Where should our jumping-off point be?" Melandra asked.

The waiter returned with Dani's meal, placing the crawfish bucket on the table in front of her.

"Your cornbread will be out any minute. You need anything else, hon?"

"No, thank you." When they were alone again, she asked, "Wait, who's *we*? Do you have to go?"

She was staring at Piper.

"I don't."

"Then don't," Dani said. "You have an exam to study for anyway. And I don't love the idea of you down in some devil crypt. Come home with me instead."

"It *will* be safer if Lou has fewer people to keep track of," King added. "If it's just the two instead of three."

"There's already three," Piper said. The words were out of her mouth before she thought of what she was saying.

Dani's hand tightened on her leg, and that more than anything told Piper she'd screwed up.

"But now there will be only two," Dani said. "Because you're coming home with me."

Piper tried to catch Lou's eyes, hoping to see that she wasn't mad at her for almost slipping up.

But if Lou was pissed, Piper couldn't tell. Her face was unreadable.

"It can be only one if you want," Melandra said. "I'm still not entirely sure what I'm adding to this excursion."

"Come on. You went to that other meeting with me." King was batting his eyes at her again. "We're in this together."

"Will you be okay if—if I don't go?" Piper asked Lou.

"Don't worry." Lou sucked honey off her fingers, but she still didn't look up. "I'll keep everyone safe."

KING HADN'T BEEN sure before, but now he was certain. Something was up between Piper and Lou. Piper had slipped up twice now. Both times she'd been on the verge of saying something, only to pull herself back at the last second.

King knew better than to press the issue. If the girls wanted him to know something, he'd know. Until that moment, he'd consider it none of his business.

Whatever it is, we'll handle it, he thought. It was reassurance for his own peace of mind, as much as an affirmation of the promise he made to his dead wife, Lou's aunt, years ago. *Everything will be okay.*

"Do you have everything you need?" Lou asked.

The three of them were standing in King's apartment, Melandra, King, and Lou forming a triangle beside his massive coffee table.

"I'll focus on getting pictures with my phone. Maybe a video. Can I give you a recorder?" he asked.

He turned to Mel.

"Where am I going to put the recorder?" she asked.

"Tommy told us to dress all in black and to hide our faces. You don't have a black jacket? You can put the recorder in your pocket and just let it run."

Mel swore under her breath. To Lou she said, "Just tell me you're gonna stay close. If this goes a hundred kinds of wrong, I would like to be promptly returned to my apartment. Please and thank you."

Lou cracked a smile. "I'll stay close. But I could also just take the guy."

"It will help our case more if we can prove he holds these delusional beliefs. Better still if we can catch him trying to sacrifice someone."

Mel clucked her tongue. "I thought you wanted to keep Jenny alive."

"I said *trying*, not succeeding," he said. "We need something concrete if we want to put this guy in jail. Besides, tonight is only supposed to be some sort of rehearsal or preliminary meeting."

Mel didn't look impressed. "What is your plan *exactly*?"

"You keep asking me that. I swear, it'll be fine. Tommy said there will be enough people that we can blend in."

"How does he know that?" Mel held up a hand. "And this is the same guy who had the pig's heart in his fridge? Ten minutes ago, you said he could be schizophrenic. Why are we following his advice?"

"That's why we're going. To verify if he's crazy or not. Apparently, he's been trying to prove that his uncle is a murderer for a while now. He claims he refuses to be gaslit into believing his mother died in a car accident."

Mel put her hands on her hips. "And what if he's not crazy? What if we find the real satanists and they ask, why the hell you here in our demon party? The devil don't know you."

"That's when Lou will pull us right out of there. Before anything happens. Right?"

Lou gave a sharp nod.

"And if Jenny is there?" Melandra asked.

"If Jenny's there and she happens to be in danger, Lou can take her first."

"I have done this before," Lou said.

King looked from Lou to Mel. "This is only slightly more dangerous than our night at Mabel's."

King went into his bedroom and got the recorder. He checked the tape, making sure that he could hear his own voice after a brief playback. Satisfied that it worked, he also rummaged through his closet and found a black bomber jacket that Mel could wear.

In the living room, he held it out to her. "Here. It'll be big on you, but it's black."

She slipped it on.

For a moment all he could do was look at her in his coat. "Cute."

She shrugged an oversized shoulder. "It's warm."

There was a beat of silence. King broke it by saying, "If you're ready, I'll turn on the recorder and slip it into your pocket now."

She held her arms up so he could access the pockets.

When he finished, he noticed Lou was staring at him.

"What?" he asked.

Her lips quirked. "Nothing. You ready?"

"Yes."

Mel's arm hooked into his and his body warmed.

Before King could speak, the world shifted. His dim apartment fell away, cold stone walls erected in its place.

As happened every time he slipped with Lou, his stomach felt as if it had been drop-kicked. His head spun. He reached out to steady himself, but the only thing to grab on to was Mel. Lou had already stepped away from him.

"Whoa," Mel said, holding up his weight. "Where are your sea legs, Mr. King?"

"Sorry," he said. "I've never gotten the hang of that."

"Shhh," Lou hushed them.

King opened his eyes and was glad to see the room wasn't spinning. However, they were in a crypt. A stone sarcophagus rested in the center of the space, the door to the cemetery at their back. But straight ahead was light tracing the outline of a door.

Lou went to it and pushed until it opened wider on a candlelit stairway.

"Are you ready to go down?" she whispered.

King hesitated. If Lou hadn't been able to take them closer, was it because there was too much light down there?

Lou seemed to understand. She said, "Candles can be extinguished."

He released Mel. "Then let's do it."

"I have my pepper spray," Mel assured him. "And my claws."

He snorted.

"I have two Berettas," Lou said.

"I feel better knowing that," Mel said. "Lead the way."

King felt he should go first, but Lou was already

descending the steps. Her boots were silent on the stone as the stairway curved out of sight.

Mel moved to go next but King grabbed her.

"Mel, you should walk behind me," he said. "In case there's trouble."

She arched a brow at him. "Do I look like I want to be at the back? I'd feel safer up her ass, thank you very much."

King suppressed a laugh. "Go on then."

She turned away from him, and he caught the scent of the jasmine oil she rubbed behind her ears.

Then it was only him left in the crypt.

He cast one last look behind him at the moonlight pouring through the crypt door, then stepped into the stairwell.

Every five feet, a candle burned, creating a halo of light along the stone steps.

At the bottom of the steps was another room. Four stone walls and no candles.

Lou and Mel stood at the base of the stairs, looking at the cobwebs and dust.

"That way." Lou pointed toward a hallway to the left. An identical one led to the right.

"You're sure?" he asked.

She didn't humor him with a reply. She only started down the hallway.

They were halfway down it when King heard voices.

Soft whispers that seemed more ethereal than human. The sound of it made the hair on the back of his neck rise. But still he walked on.

At the end of the hallway, two steps led down to a large cavern.

It was full of people. Everyone was in black. Most had their faces covered so that only their liquid black eyes shone in the dim candlelight.

A hand tightened on his.

It was Mel. "I think you owe Tommy an apology. This don't look like no delusion to me."

"Remain calm," he said, speaking directly into her ear. "Continue with the plan."

Mel gave a nod, moving around the edge of the room.

They kept to the shadows.

Most of the people were chanting something. That was the reason for the haunting voices he'd first heard in the hall outside. And they all seemed to be facing the same structure.

On the far wall, centered, was a large stone slab. It had been decorated with candles, skulls that looked very human, and lush red flowers. Carnations? Garden roses? King couldn't tell from this distance.

A man in a black robe stood behind it, his face covered by shadows.

King itched to move nearer but was afraid of getting too close to the candle flames, considering that they would surely illuminate his face.

A cold hand closed around his wrist and he almost screamed.

It was Lou, pressing a wad of black cloth into his hand.

Face coverings. She'd left them to get face coverings.

Mel was already pulling hers on. The fabric covered her hair and the lower half of her face. Only her eyes could be seen. The rest of her body was hidden under his massive jacket.

King put his mask on too, adjusting it so that only his eyes were exposed to the cold underground air.

His breath was hot against the fabric, moistening the cloth. But he couldn't worry about that now.

Lou, he noted, hadn't bothered to cover her face. She wore her usual mirrored sunglasses and battered leather jacket.

That was all the protection she seemed to think she needed.

But he also noticed the way people moved away from her instinctively. As she cut a path up the side of the room, approaching the altar as if for a better look, they scuttled away like she was the devil herself.

As if touching her might set their own clothes on fire.

"I want to move closer too," Mel whispered into his ear. "Maybe I can pick up what he's saying."

King wanted to stop her, pull her back. Keep her close.

But she was already following in Lou's wake. That left him with no choice.

It was brighter by the altar. Probably because there were more candles.

Now he could finally see what had been placed on the altar itself.

A ginger cat. Its eyes closed. Its body still.

Was it dead?

He didn't believe a cat would lie like that if it were still alive.

His heart sank.

That's when he saw the blade.

He stepped forward. He had moved without full awareness of what he was doing, only that he wanted to stop the blade from striking the cat.

A tight hand seized his arm.

He whirled to find Lou holding him firmly in place.

Melandra's eyes were wide with fear.

Then the blade struck the stone.

The cat didn't move. Its body didn't even jerk.

Already dead.

It had already been dead or close to it. Either way, the poor creature had felt nothing at all.

You sick fucks, he thought.

"The altar has been consecrated," the man called out, raising his bloodied blade to the light as if in offering. "The gate is now open."

"Praise be unto Him," the crowd chorused.

"Pictures," a voice whispered.

It was Mel, nudging his elbow.

Pictures. Right. He'd been so struck by the sacrifice of the cat that he'd forgotten what they'd come for. He pulled out his phone, glad again that Piper had shown him how to darken the screen so that it wouldn't cast light.

To be sure, he checked his settings one more time under the cover of his coat before opening the camera application itself.

He snapped a photo inside his jacket of absolutely nothing, further confirming that he wasn't about to give them away.

He was relieved that the phone made no sound and cast no light.

He took a few photos of the altar with the cat's still form.

"Anyone?" the man called again.

"I have an offering," someone called.

No, King thought. *Shit.*

Because it was a voice he recognized. Ashley Wexler was as haughty and arrogant down here beneath the earth as he had been on his porch.

A figure cloaked in black separated itself from the crowd. A second figure stumbled at his side.

"I feel sick," a young, feminine voice said.

"Lie down here," Wexler commanded.

He eased the girl onto the slab, pulled her legs until they stretched long.

The man, still holding the blade, reached forward and touched the girl's forehead. It took King several beats before he understood he was painting symbols on her face—her forehead, her cheeks—with the cat's blood.

Now they were undressing her.

But before King could look away, he saw her face.

Jenny.

"Oh my—" It was Mel, her voice fearful. Her fingers bit into his arm. "Oh, no. Are they—"

A horrifying realization dawned on King then. This was no dress rehearsal.

Wexler really meant to sacrifice his daughter.

Tonight.

22

K onstantine returned to the villa late. After dinner, he'd walked around the piazza with the children, pointing out the stores and museums. He did his best to explain the monuments and art, all of which was but the barest sliver of Florence's rich history. The boy, Elijah, had been enthusiastic from the start, but even Kaia's eyes had filled with wonder by the end of the night.

Now Konstantine was tired, his feet sore. He was glad to be home.

Meow.

Octavia trotted to him as he entered the kitchen. He spoke softly to her in Italian as he refilled her bowls with food and water.

He let her eat while he poured himself a glass of wine and readied himself for bed.

He'd only just settled beneath the covers, with the British Blue on his chest, a paperback in hand, and the glass of wine on the nightstand, when his phone rang.

It wasn't Lou, he knew. She would simply find him if she had something to say.

"Hello?" he asked.

"It's me," a woman said.

"Ah, Elizabeth," he said. She was the director of the facility near Chicago.

"I wanted you to know that we're ready when you are. Everything is prepared. We've hired extra staff and settled the rooms. I've also ordered additional safety measures to be put in place, but I won't be able to give you a firm estimate on expenditures until after the children have been evaluated and we fully understand what will be needed to ensure their care."

"But you are ready to take them?" he asked.

"Yes, whenever you would like to move forward."

He was glad to hear it. She was the slightly more expensive of his two options, but she had more experience with violent children. She would know what to do.

"When can we expect them to arrive?" Elizabeth asked.

Konstantine didn't have an answer for that. He knew that Lou was frustrated with her inability to gain more information on the man who had kidnapped and tortured them. He also understood that the fortress in which they were kept was difficult to penetrate.

"I'm sorry, I can't tell you," he admitted. "It's proving difficult to extract the children from their situation. But I will keep you posted."

"What can you tell me of their situation?" she asked. "You only mentioned before that they were dangerous."

"It isn't their fault," Konstantine said. "You must be sure to treat them with kindness."

There was a pause. "Of course. We won't use force unless necessary."

He thanked her and ended the call. Octavia purred on his chest.

Konstantine's eyes fell on the closet door, but it didn't open.

"Where is she?" he asked the cat. He opened the book and tried to find where he'd left off. The night before, he'd fallen asleep somewhere just before the hero confessed his feelings to his star-crossed lover.

But his mind kept wandering. There was something about this operation he didn't like.

It was the numbers.

How many children could she possibly extract before this professor noticed? Assuming he hadn't noticed her already. If he didn't see her aid Kaia and Elijah, certainly he saw her walk into his lair and retrieve that monstrous child that now slept in Isadora's clinic.

To have so many children to save meant surprise wouldn't be on her side. Surprise was one of Louie's strengths. Now she didn't have it.

He would have to talk to her before she went again.

He would go over her plan with her until he felt at ease. She would do that much for him, he thought.

He was failing to read the same paragraph for the fifth time when the closet door was kicked in. Lou burst into the room. She was covered in blood and holding a dead cat.

Octavia hissed, coming up onto her paws, her back arched.

Konstantine tried to soothe her, but she was already sprinting from the bedroom, howling in her wake.

"What happened?" he asked, sitting up and tossing the book away.

She looked down at her clothes. At the dead cat.

"I'm not sure where to begin."

KING COULDN'T LOOK AWAY. It wasn't only that Jenny was naked on the altar, her face painted in cat's blood. It was also the horror of the moment, and the strange energy that had entered the room. The bodies around him began to sway, to shift, almost in ecstasy. Someone bumped into him, knocking him into Mel.

"Pictures," she hissed in his ear.

He pulled out his camera and snapped several shots of the altar. Of the whirling bodies. His shaking finger actually shifted the camera into video mode, and he took a fifteen-second video before realizing he'd done it.

This can't be happening, he thought as Wexler ran a hand over his daughter's naked body.

The hair on the back of his neck stood on end.

He didn't want to believe that this man would kill his own daughter just for some sick delusion that he would gain something from her sacrifice.

Only he had to believe his eyes.

Because here was Jenny, drugged and whimpering. Here was Wexler, accepting the blade offered to him by the hooded priest.

"No," King said, jolting forward.

Several things happened at once.

Somehow the sound of his voice cut through the frenzy building in the darkness, and the undulating bodies jerked to a halt. All eyes shifted in his direction.

Then Wexler was screaming.

"Who was that? Who *the fuck* was that?"

He was holding the blade and staring at the empty slab.

Jenny was gone. King had caught the barest glint of candlelight reflected in her mirrored shades before Lou disappeared, taking Jenny with her.

Good, he thought. *Get the girl to safety first.*

Except now everyone was looking at him, their eyes shifting from Wexler cursing at the altar to King. Mel moved closer, pressing her body against his side.

A well of protectiveness rose up in him. Except there was

little he could do. The door was at the back of the room. There was no avenue of escape open to them. They were cornered between the wall at their back and the altar in front of them. A sea of bodies stood between them and the only way out.

"Who are you?" Wexler was pointing the bloody blade at King.

King put his phone in his pocket but didn't speak. There was too much of a risk that Wexler would recognize his voice.

Instead, he considered his next move.

He could use his body to shield Mel until Lou returned or—

Wexler lunged. The blade cut through the air and connected with Lou's forearm.

King hadn't even seen her appear in front of him.

She was simply there. Then with the slightest shift, she threw Wexler across the room. He spun out of sight, taking out several of the bodies closest to them.

The satanic priest—which was how King kept thinking of the hooded cat killer—was over the altar a second later.

He threw something at Lou. A bucket of water?

It hit her back, sloshing down the side of her body.

Lou froze.

As if sensing the fury rising in the room, everyone nearest her took a step back. Then another.

Lou pulled a gun and shot the priest through the head. His brains sprayed across the altar and the far wall.

The gun report was so loud that King's ears rang, his head splitting. Mel jumped at his side and he wrapped his arms around her instinctively.

Lou fired a second shot and the panic began. Bodies started pushing and shoving for the back door, forcing themselves into the hallway that would lead them up and out of the crypt.

As they trampled each other, Lou calmly holstered her gun and walked to the altar.

King pulled down his face covering. "What are you doing?"

"We're taking the cat."

She gathered the poor, lifeless beast in her arms and turned to them. "Are you ready?"

"You can certainly get *me* the hell out of here," Mel said, abandoning King's side. "I've seen more than enough."

She reached out for Lou. "Oh, heaven. Where can I touch you without—"

Before King could get his bearings, the dark was swallowing him whole again.

The crypt fell away and his apartment reformed around them.

The shocking sight of a naked girl painted with cat's blood greeted him. She was sprawled on his couch, looking like she'd been dropped there.

She probably had been. Lou hadn't had time to cover her or make her decent given that they were two seconds away from being stabbed with the sacrificial blade themselves.

"Lord tell me that's not all your blood."

King thought Mel was talking to Jenny. But the girl was unconscious.

Then he saw Lou. Half of her body was soaked in blood from head to toe.

"I think it was a bucket of pig's blood he threw on me," she said simply. "Are we good here?"

"Wash your hair twice. We'll clean up here," Mel said, her nose wrinkled. "And what are you going to do with that cat?"

"Bury it. Properly." Lou left them without another word.

King stood there looking from the unconscious girl to the blood puddle Lou had left on his floor.

"What's wrong? You saved the girl," Mel said. "You should be happy."

"I'm trying to figure out what the hell just happened."

"It doesn't matter. Call the ambulance," Mel said. "We'll get someone to watch her until this so-called gate closes. Maybe Detective White can get an officer to stand outside her door too, if she ends up in the hospital."

King called the ambulance, then Detective White, doing his best to explain the bizarre situation.

When he hung up, Mel said, "I thought she shot that guy for throwing a bucket of blood on her. Lord knows I'd be angry as hell too. But it was about the cat, wasn't it? She killed him because he hurt that cat."

King was glad she'd put a blanket over Jenny, covering her.

"I'm sure it was," he said.

In the distance, he heard the sirens approaching.

"THAT'S WHAT HAPPENED?" Konstantine said. Lou had stripped down at the doorway, which normally would have been a welcome sight.

However, holding the dead cat and covered in blood, she was far more horrifying than arousing.

"I'm getting blood on the tile," she said.

"We'll clean it," he assured her. "Go shower."

Instead of heading to the bathroom, she went into their closet.

"*Amore mio?*"

Lou reappeared with the dead cat in an old shoe box. She placed the box by the closet door.

"I'll take care of it after I shower," she told him, as if he'd expressed concern for how long the cat's corpse might be in the house.

He waited until after she'd showered and changed before he told her about the phone call from Chicago.

"If they don't need me tomorrow, I'll go then," Lou said.

He assumed *they* were her friends in New Orleans.

"You could wait," he said.

"No," she said. "I don't want to leave them there any longer than we have to. He's done enough damage."

"What are you doing?" he asked.

She didn't look up from her watch. "I'm sending King the coordinates to the crypt. In case he needs to take the police there to collect evidence. I dropped a pin when we arrived."

He almost laughed. Louie. His dear luddite. She'd not even had so much as an email address when he'd met her. She'd had a more primitive version of the GPS watch she wore now. And he'd been surprised that she'd accepted his gift of a considerable upgrade. Now, to see her sending messages and using its features as if she'd always done so amused him. It had only taken him years to convert her.

"Stop smiling," she said. "I know what you're thinking."

"I'm thinking that I should help you with the cat," he lied.

"Not now," she said. "Now I need sleep."

23

King stood outside the hospital room with Detective White. Through the glass window they could see Carrie Bright at Jenny's bedside. She was crying softly into the mattress while her daughter slept.

The doctor had said she'd been given a dangerously large dose of heroin, but she would pull through. She might need rehab or support to make sure she didn't develop an addiction.

King was about to speak, but Detective White's phone rang. King had no choice but to wait.

"They found the crypt," White said. "There are fingerprints, a lot of blood, and a few strands of blond hair."

"Hopefully Jenny's," King said. "Any sign of Wexler?"

"The judge just signed the warrant to search his place, so they're about to head over there now. But the uniform parked outside said his car isn't there and the house is dark. I don't think he went home after last night's—"

White didn't seem to know how to finish.

"We did identify the priest. Abbot Wilmoth. He worked

at the credit union in Freret. No priors. Unmarried. No kids. He looks boring as hell on paper."

"Banker moonlighting as a satanic priest," King laughed. "I'll have to make sure I stay friendly with Dana when I make my deposits."

White pursed his lips, putting his hands on his hips. "Why is it you get all the freaky shit, man? Have you considered sticking to missing dogs and purse snatchers?"

King snorted. "I don't mind weird."

"Obviously." White laughed. "I'll stay here until O'Malley arrives."

"Thank you," King said, and shook his hand.

"The media is going to have a field day with this, once it gets out. Satanic cult in an old New Orleans cemetery? The tourism department will love it though." White was watching the mother and daughter through the glass window.

"What about Tommy?" King asked.

Detective White shook his head. "We went by the kid's place but he wasn't there. His boss hasn't seen him either."

"Are you going to look into his mother's death?" King asked. "He was convinced that Wexler killed her the way he was going to kill Jenny. After what I saw, I have to say, I believe him."

"I'll see what I can do. Here's O'Malley," White said, motioning up the hospital corridor. "I want to go to the house and see what they dig up."

King arched a brow. "Who's looking for weird shit now?"

White waved a goodbye before pushing open the door to the stairwell and disappearing out of sight.

"O'Malley," King said. "I'm going to step in and have a word with the mother, then I'll get out of your way."

"Yes, sir," he said.

King clapped him on the shoulder and went into the hospital room, closing the door behind him.

As soon as Carrie saw him, her face broke with relief. "Mr. King."

King accepted her hands, letting the woman squeeze so hard it hurt. Still, he didn't complain.

"Thank you. Thank you. Thank you," she said, wiping at her nose with her sleeve. "I can't thank you enough. And I got a call yesterday saying the charges will be dropped. I don't have to go to court or anything."

"That's good," he said, patting her hand. "But your ex is still out there."

"I can't believe it. I can't believe it was Ashley all along."

"Do you remember when his sister died?"

"Oh god, did he kill Lily too?"

"Tommy thinks so."

Her face pinched. "I need to apologize to that boy. I feel terrible for those things I said about him. I should've never believed Ashley. Just shows you what a terrible judge of character I am."

A self-deprecating laugh escaped her.

"You chose to work with me and everything turned out all right," he said.

"Until she wakes up. Until she sees my face and knows that I'm here, I can't—"

Her voice broke. King gave her a reassuring pat on the shoulder.

"I've got a friend who puts a lot of stock in dreams," King told her. "She would tell you that the fact you even had that dream about your daughter, that you were willing to do what you could to protect her—that's proof enough that you're a good mom who cares. Jenny will see that."

"Thank you," she said again, fresh tears falling. "Thank you so much for giving us a second chance."

King's heart clenched. He'd been given a lot of second chances in his life. A second chance to love Lucy. A second chance at a career he loved, that he could be proud of. A second chance at building a life worth living. To fill his life with people he cared about.

He squeezed her hands. "It's been my honor."

AFTER THEY BURIED THE CAT, Lou spent the afternoon with the children. They didn't have school that day, which meant they spent most of their daylight hours on the steps of Konstantine's church, playing soccer.

Lou was pleased to discover that the language barrier wasn't a problem when it came to playing. Children were marvelous at finding workarounds. And when they struggled with the technicalities of one rule or another, Matteo had just enough English to get them by.

Lou watched as Kaia abandoned the game and came to sit by her on the steps. Her eyes tracked Elijah running up and down the cobblestone walkway, intercepting the ball from one of the taller boys and cheering.

Finally, she said, "Konstantine said he found a safe place for everyone."

Lou sat up, resting her elbows on her knees. "It's like a hospital. They'll have their own rooms. Doctors and people who can take care of them. No more games. No more getting hurt. Will they be happy, you think?"

"Some of them," Kaia said. "But some of them like the games now."

"Would you rather I left them there?"

"No." Kaia shook her head. "I want them to get better."

"Me too." Lou ruffled Kaia's hair despite the act earning her a furious look. Then she stood.

"Where are you going?"

"To get those kids," she said. "I think they've been there long enough, don't you?"

Kaia chewed her lips, her anxiety clear. "Don't forget about the games. It's not safe."

"Are the games always dangerous? Even the so-called nice ones?" Lou asked, slipping her hands into the pocket of her leather jacket.

"Yes," Kaia said, in full seriousness. "Always."

As LOU STOOD in her armory, surveying her options, she tried to let her experience retrieving Jake inform her decision of how to arm herself. Most of her toys were too violent to take on a simple extraction mission. More than that, it was hard to decide what she would feel comfortable using against a violent child. She didn't want to shoot them or even cut them. A taser felt too risky. She wasn't sure their small bodies would recover from a shock as easily as an adult's. There was certainly no need for the flamethrower. At least not until she emptied the facility of the children. Then she might have the chance to go in with some real firepower and lay the place to waste.

She hadn't forgotten her promise to Kaia either. The more she'd spoken to Dani and Piper, the more she was sold on the idea of letting the world know what that monster had done.

She felt Konstantine behind her before he spoke.

He came to her, slipped his arms around her waist, and rested his chin on her shoulder. His hand touched her belly and a strange fluttering shimmered through her.

Tell him, she thought.

Tell him.

But if she told him, he might ask her not to go tonight. She wasn't ready to be told what she could and couldn't do. She wasn't ready to confront his possible anger. She already saw how he fought to quell it when she narrowly escaped dangerous situations. What would he say if he knew that she was risking them both?

After, she decided. *I'll tell him when this is over.*

"All ready, *amore mio*?"

She said nothing.

"What is it?" he asked.

He spun her so he could look into her eyes.

"Is it really only the children?"

Lou's heart skipped a beat. "What do you mean?"

"Something is bothering you," he told her. "I didn't want to say. I don't want to force you to talk about it if you're not ready, *but* I feel it. I'm not wrong, am I?"

She considered lying. She considered telling him it was nothing, if only not to worry him. But Lou had only to look at their lives to know that Konstantine wasn't the sort of man who needed to be protected from unpleasantries.

"You're not wrong," she told him. "There's something."

He placed a hand on each side of her neck. "Tell me, *per favore*. Whatever it is, *amore mio*, we will fix it. Whatever you need, whatever you want—I can—"

"Stop." She pinched her eyes shut. She couldn't handle the soulful pleading. In his voice, his eyes. "I can't do this right now."

"Because you need to go?"

"Because I need to go," she echoed.

"But I'm not imagining it. There is something wrong?"

Wrong? It would change their lives forever. But that wasn't the sort of thing she could say to someone and then disappear for several hours.

She grabbed the back of his neck, coming up on her toes to kiss him on the lips. He let her. With her mouth just over his, she said, "I'll tell you when I get back."

She stepped out of his arms. She needed to remain

focused on tonight. She couldn't let her mind be divided. That could lead to her getting hurt, or the children.

Or our child.

Our child.

Ours.

"You *will* tell me when you get back," he said. "Promise me."

She kissed him once more. "I promise."

Only then did his shoulders ease.

"Then I can wait." He released her. "I told Elizabeth to expect you tonight."

Lou snorted. "I can only imagine what you said."

"She's been with us for a long time. She's heard the rumors. I'm sure she's more than a little curious to see you with her own eyes."

"No time like the present."

She turned to leave but he caught her wrist. He held her there on the threshold between her armory and their living room.

"Be careful, *amore mio.*"

She removed the hand holding her, brushed a kiss across his knuckles and then released him. "More than ever."

Lou didn't wait to hear his reply. She couldn't stand the way he was looking at her with his imploring eyes, so deeply green as to make her heart ache. She went to their bedroom closet and stepped through the darkness.

24

The first child was easy to take. Lou found her sitting on a cot in a sparse room much like Jake's. A book lay open in her lap as Lou stepped into her bedroom at the edge of the light cast by the far lamp. The girl looked up, revealing brown eyes so dark they looked nearly black beneath her flaming red hair. Her mouth began to form a question, but Lou was already pulling her through the dark before the words could pass her lips.

One more step brought them into an office. A woman with glasses and a blond bob jumped, startled. The phone and mug she'd been holding slipped from her grip.

"My god. It's you." She looked from Lou to the blooming coffee stain on her clothes. "Oh, sorry."

"Here's the first one," Lou said, releasing the child.

The girl only stood there, looking from Lou to the doctor and back, still holding her book.

Well, this one is docile, Lou thought. She wondered what the trick was.

"Are you ready for the others or not?" Lou asked the doctor.

"Yes, yes. Just a moment."

The doctor reached up and grabbed the lanyard off her neck. At the end was a small device. She pressed the button and footsteps sounded in the hall immediately.

Two large orderlies appeared, pushing their way through the narrow office door. "Dr. Christfeld?"

"Yes, we're starting now. Please take this one—what's your name, sweetie?"

The girl didn't answer. She seemed to be studying the situation.

"Well, there will be plenty of time to get to know each other later. Once all your friends arrive."

This caught the girl's attention. "They're coming too?"

The orderly took the girl gently, his wary gaze reluctantly pulling away from Lou.

"They're clever," Lou warned them. "Mind your weapons and your keys."

"Oh yes, of course," the doctor said. Her eyes kept sliding to the Beretta in Lou's right hand.

"I'll get the others," Lou said.

"Right. I'll just—" The doctor glanced down at the mess on the floor. "I guess I can take care of this later. I—"

Whatever she meant to say next was swallowed by the darkness. Lou was already in another room.

This target was not so calm. He started swinging the moment her boots hit the floor. He landed a decent blow to her kidney before she managed to turn him around and trap him in a fierce bear hug.

Still his nails raked across the back of her hand as he tried to break her grip. And when that didn't work, he bit her.

It didn't stop her from pulling him through the dark to the hospital. This time the doctor was in the hallway outside the girl's room. They were asking her if she'd eaten, if she wanted water.

The questions ended abruptly when Lou's boots squeaked against the polished floor.

"He's a biter," she said, prying him off her.

The larger of the two orderlies grabbed the boy by the back of the neck, holding him at arm's length.

"I've got him," he promised.

The doctor opened a door across the hallway and turned on the light, revealing a second room much like the girl's.

"Come in here if you please, young man."

Lou was able to extract eleven children. Six girls and five boys. There were more that needed to be moved to the hospital, based on the list she'd memorized in her head.

Caleb Killian.

She let her compass spin, locking on the next child. But when she emerged from the shadows, she found a vacant room.

Confused, she spun slowly.

The bed was rumpled but empty. There was a chair in the corner but it was empty too. This room had no toys and no personal effects.

Lou knew her compass couldn't be wrong. If it said there was a child here, it was here.

Come out, come out, wherever you are.

A sharp stab in her calf made her cry out. She stumbled back, her hands catching her against the opposite wall. Then her knees folded and she hit the tile.

That's when she saw the eyes under the bed, shining in the dark.

Slowly, a boy, no more than six years old and as scrawny as a skeleton, pulled himself out.

Lou reached for him, and immediately knew something was wrong. Her arms were too heavy. Her body unresponsive to her commands. Then the shadows in the room began to shift and move around her.

The boy held up an empty syringe and smiled. It was a haunting smile that didn't reach his eyes.

Lou was about to abandon this attempt when the room suddenly filled with light, flooding every corner. It seemed to come from every direction, burning her eyes.

Lou tried to slip, tried to call the darkness to her, but nothing happened. Her back remained pressed against the cold wall, the world stubbornly solid around her.

From the doorway, a shadow said, "Good job, Killian. You've won the game. Though how did you get ahold of my medicine, you sneaky boy?"

Lou used the last of her strength to push three buttons on her GPS watch. But she couldn't even be sure she'd pressed the right ones.

Her hands were shaking.

Then someone was taking the watch. A bootheel stomped it, crushing it into the floor.

"You won't be needing this," the shadow said.

King was lying in bed next to Beth when his phone buzzed. He sat up and opened the message.

He frowned, unsure of what he was looking at.

Thirty seconds later, his phone rang. It was Piper.

She didn't even say hello. "Did you get a text from Lou?"

"I did, but I don't know what I'm looking at."

"It's a dropped pin from Michigan. Why would she drop a pin? Is she stuck? Does she need to be rescued? Oh god, Dani just got the same message. What's happening?"

The fear in Piper's voice made his own heart speed up. "Just slow down. Give me five minutes and I'll call you right back."

He threw back the covers, searching the floor for his pants, his underwear.

Beth sat up in bed, her braids falling over one shoulder. "Is everything okay?"

"I'm sorry, but I have to go," he said.

"Sure, sure," she said, waving him on. "Do what you've got to do."

He dressed quickly and grabbed his coat off the back of the chair. He was about to barrel out of her bedroom and down the stairs before he turned back at the last second.

"I'm sorry," he said again. He gave Beth a hurried kiss. "I owe you breakfast."

"Be careful. Don't go speeding and wreck."

He kissed her again and left.

On the sidewalk outside of her Prytania Street townhouse, he checked the time. It was one in the morning.

Instead of calling Piper back, he searched his contacts for the only Italian number he had. Konstantine answered on the third ring. It would be early in the morning there, but it didn't matter.

"*Sì?*" he said. "What can I do for you, Mr. King?"

"Is Lou with you?"

Silence rang on the line.

"No," he said. "Is this an emergency?"

"I think she just tried to get ahold of me, but I don't understand the message. I just wanted to make sure she's okay."

"I will call you back," Konstantine said, and hung up.

King was left standing on the sidewalk in the cold morning, looking up and down the moonlit street.

It was a terrible feeling, to be consumed with urgency and yet not know what the next move was supposed to be.

Keep her safe for me, a voice whispered through his mind. It was Lucy. Sweet Lucy. Dead now for three and half years.

I need you to keep her safe for me, Robert.

"I'm trying," he said, and began walking in the direction of his Buick.

KONSTANTINE CALLED LOU FIRST, but her phone buzzed on the nightstand beside him.

So Konstantine called the doctor in Chicago. Christfeld confirmed that Lou had appeared ten minutes ago but that she hadn't come back since. That this break was, in fact, her longest since she'd begun.

She asked him if perhaps this was all the children? Were eleven all that could be saved?

Eleven.

He told the doctor he would be in touch once he knew more and ended the call.

With his phone resting in his lap, Konstantine's stomach twisted with worry. He had not received the same text message that King and the others had. Perhaps Lou was simply sending them information on the case? She had mentioned that Daniella was building a story that would expose the man and his evil deeds, bringing his actions to light.

Perhaps nothing was wrong then.

Maybe she only had a body to dispose of. If she'd killed one of the monsters responsible for these horrors.

If that were that case, she would be delayed.

He'd half convinced himself that this was the case when his phone buzzed again.

It was a message from Lou.

His heart clenched.

He opened the text and saw the dropped pin.

. . .

AFTER KING PARKED THE BUICK, he walked past Fortunes and Fixes toward the agency. He wanted to check on the girls first—Dani and Piper—to make sure they weren't panicking over Lou's message.

He entered the agency, making sure to lock up behind him. The last thing they needed was some drunk reveler stumbling into the office. Once he was confident they were safe, he knocked on their apartment door at the back of the room.

"It's me. Are you up?" he called out.

Footsteps sounded overhead as someone ran across the living room above and then down the stairwell.

Piper opened the door, breathless. "Oh good, you came. We're freaking out."

At the top of the stairs, he found Dani sitting at the kitchen island with her laptop open. The blue light from the screen was reflected in her glasses as her fingers flew furiously over the keyboard.

She nodded in the direction of the steaming coffeepot. "Get a mug if you want."

Piper didn't sit down. She was pacing. "She's in trouble. I know she's in trouble."

Dani pushed her glasses up on her nose. "Just give me a minute. I have to find the first one."

King didn't know what *the first one* was, but he poured himself a cup of black coffee and came to the island. He couldn't bring himself to sit.

Piper continued to pace back and forth across the living room floor.

"I tried reaching her, but I got no answer," King said.

"Same here," Dani said, leaning toward the screen.

"What are we looking for?" King asked, feeling like he'd walked in on the middle of something.

"We're trying to find out if these coordinates are the same as the ones she sent before. If they are, we're fucked."

King didn't understand. He told them so.

Dani spoke while continuing to scroll. "Lou sent me a pin like this earlier. We were planning to swarm the place when the story broke. News vans, cops, whoever we could get out there so that we could document what happened in real-time. Break the story wide open so that it would make it all over the news."

Piper added, "Since he suppressed all those murders and baby-snatching before, Dani thought we needed to hit the guy hard out of the gate or he might just cover it all up again."

"Cell phone footage, social media, we were planning on using it all," Dani explained. "It'll be a major effort. I've brought just about every connection I have into this."

"I still don't understand what it means if the pins are the same." King took a sip of the coffee. It was still too hot to really enjoy.

"Because she wouldn't send the same thing twice," Piper said. "She's a beast of efficiency. She wouldn't repeat herself and she definitely wouldn't send a key smash."

King's brow pinched. "A key smash?"

"Open your message again," Dani said, without looking away from the computer. "Scroll past the image to the text below."

The text below. King hadn't even seen any text. He opened the message again, and it was the map that filled his screen, giving him the impression that was the entire message. But it wasn't. He thumbed the image away, and sure enough, there was a collection of nonsensical letters below it.

"What is that? Is it short for something?" he asked.

"No. We think she hit those keys by accident. Maybe she was in a hurry or maybe she wasn't looking at the screen.

Either way, the implications aren't good," Piper said. "God, what's taking so long."

Dani waved her away. "It's a lot of information. This folder is huge. Ah, here it is."

She bent close to the screen, looking from the phone to her laptop and back again.

Her shoulders slumped. "It's the same. She was in Gein's facility when she sent this. I think it's safe to assume this was a call for help."

"Shit, shit, shit," Piper said, grabbing her hair. "What if she's dead? What if she's fucking dead right now?"

"Take a breath," King said.

Piper did not take a breath. "What if someone got the drop on her and she's trapped in that hellhole with those little murder kids? How are we going to get to Michigan? How are we going to rescue her?"

King held up his hand. "We don't know what's happened. We can't assume she's dead or captured. She could just be busy."

"When I freak out Lou always comes. She *always* comes. I'm freaking the fuck out and *is she here right now?*"

Dani took Piper by the shoulders. "You need to calm down. We can't help her if you lose it."

"Okay. Fine, okay." Piper covered her face and went to the couch. She put her head between her legs and began to take loud, exaggerated breaths.

Dani turned to him. "The quickest way to get to Michigan would be with Konstantine's help. He has a plane. He can mobilize a team. We need him on this. Have you spoken to him?"

"Yes, but he was going back to bed."

"Back to bed!" Piper cried. "You would think he'd care more about saving his own ki—"

"Piper!" Dani screamed over her.

But it was too late. King had heard the words clearly.

Suddenly it all made sense. The hinting. The near slip-ups. The subtext in their conversations.

He ran a hand down his face. "She's pregnant."

"Konstantine doesn't know," Dani said. "And Lou needs to be the one to tell him when she's ready. Don't blab about it before she can tell him."

She was scowling at Piper.

"I'm sorry," Piper said, looking up from her hands. "I'm just scared, okay. When I'm scared she comes, but she's not here and that means she's not okay. Lou's not okay. If she was okay, she would be here."

Tears streamed down her face.

King put his coffee on the counter and took a seat on the couch beside her.

"Lou's tough," he said, placing a hand on her back. "Even if she can't get herself out of a situation, she'll hang in there until we can get to her."

Piper sniffed. "You're right. I know you're right. But I promised I'd always be there for her."

You and me both, kid.

"When should we call Konstantine?" Dani asked.

"Now!" Piper said.

"Yeah, probably." Dani rubbed her chin. "Even with a private jet, it'll take him hours to fly to get everything together and meet us in Michigan."

"Meet us?" Piper's voice was hopeful.

"There's a nonstop flight out of MSY in three hours. If we're on it, we'll be in Kalamazoo before the sun rises. I don't know what we can do when we get there. We certainly don't have the means to storm some secret facility full of murderers, but maybe we'll have a plan by the time we arrive."

"I'll start packing." Piper hopped up from the couch and ran from the room.

"I can't go," King said. "I have to stay here with Jenny until we can be sure her father is behind bars. But you two go. What will you do when you get there? I hope you're going to let Konstantine's people do the fighting."

"That would be best. I'll try to get everyone together before the story breaks. If I can coordinate with Laura and her team, we could have this out in the world within forty-eight hours. The media is very different now than it was twenty years ago. If we blast this through every channel, I'd like to see this fucker try to suppress that."

A bang and crash rang out from the bedroom as something tumbled out of an unseen closet.

"I'm fine," Piper called.

King stood and pulled his phone out of his pocket. "I'll call Konstantine now."

"King," Dani said.

He looked up.

"I meant what I said about not telling him. This sort of thing is really important for a woman. Don't let it slip that she's pregnant until she's ready to have that conversation."

"I won't," he said, a little hurt that she didn't trust him. "I promise."

And he had his own reason for not bringing it up anyway. If Lou was hurt, if she miscarried, he didn't want to set Konstantine up for the heartbreak of losing a child.

He'd gone through that loss with his first wife, Fiona, when she'd miscarried at eighteen weeks. It had been hard on both of them, and their relationship was never the same after.

Dani was still looking at him.

"I promise," he said, and dialed Florence for the second time that night.

25

Konstantine kept looking up, hoping to see Lou emerge from the darkness at any moment. But as the hours passed, as his sleepless night turned into a bleary-eyed morning, she still didn't return.

She didn't come no matter how hard he thought of her. No matter how he longed for her in his mind or his heart. She remained stubbornly absent as he commanded Stefano to assemble a team of their most trusted. As they called his people in Chicago and Detroit, giving them the rendezvous point and projected meeting time.

He gathered more than a hundred men and women who were set to descend on the place Lou had marked.

But would that be enough?

If this so-called monster had managed to somehow ensnare and trap Louie, *La Strega*, what could a hundred men do? Hadn't he seen her lay waste to more souls than that in a single frenzied night?

Or she's dead—No. He wouldn't even consider it a possibility. It might be a matter of skill. It might simply be that the monster had found a way to use the children against her.

Children had always been her weakness. Like him, something in her could not bear to leave them behind. Was it because their own childhoods had been so tragic? He didn't know. He knew only that it was time to go to the airport and Louie still had not returned.

He was certain then that she was not simply dropping a body in La Loon. She'd been gone far too long for that.

Promise me.

Those had been his last words to her.

Had he known this would be the result of her hunt, he would have uttered something more meaningful. He wouldn't have wasted his last moments begging her to assuage his own fears.

It hardly mattered now.

It was time to go.

He put his computer, phone, and tablet in his bag and stood. He traced the stone pathways through the church. Down narrow hallways, his shoes echoing loudly off the walls.

Then he was in the cathedral, the door just ahead. Stefano stood on the stone steps outside, cupping his hands over a cigarette.

"The car's ready," he called out, and nodded in the direction of the waiting vehicle as if Konstantine couldn't see it for himself.

"No!" someone cried. "No, let go of me! Konstantine! Konstantine!"

Konstantine stopped, turning toward the sound.

"I have to tell him. I have to! *Konstantine!*"

"What is going on?" he called, still unsure of where that desperate voice was coming from.

Then he saw her break into view. Kaia was running full tilt up the aisle in his direction. Matilda was on her heels, trying to catch her. He waved Matilda off.

"What's wrong?" he asked the girl. "Be quick. I have to go."

"Is it true?" she asked. "Is it true that Father has Louie?"

"What do you mean?"

"Matteo said Louie is in trouble. Is it true?"

Konstantine would have to question Matteo later to know where he got his gossip from. Gossip was a liability.

"She didn't return when she was supposed to," Konstantine admitted.

"Then he has her in the white room."

Konstantine put his bags on the ground. "What?"

"She needs the dark. She has to have the dark to escape, doesn't she?"

"Yes." He knelt in front of the girl. "What do you mean, 'the white room'?"

"Father has a white room. If he knows about the dark, he'll put her in the white room."

Ice slid down the back of Konstantine's neck.

"Are there shadows in the white room?" he asked.

"No." She shook her head. "He puts us there to punish us. Because the white room is the scariest room. If he has her in the white room, then she's too far from the door. She can't even get out like I did. She's too far!"

"Konstantine," Stefano said. "We need to go."

"Put my bags in the car," he told him, before turning back to the girl. "Kaia, why is the white room the scariest?"

"It's—it's like a nightmare," she said. "A nightmare you can't wake up from."

Konstantine felt as if he'd been kicked in the gut. He was going to be sick.

He squeezed the girl's shoulders. "I have to go."

"Take me!" Kaia said, her face pinched in fear. "You can tell Father that he can have me if he gives you Louie."

"I can't." He patted her cheek. "Louie would never allow it."

AN HOUR LATER, they were in the air above France, the jet traveling five hundred miles an hour, due west. Konstantine's eyes were fixed on the clouds outside his window.

"We will be there in seven hours. Try to sleep. You look like shit," Stefano said. He sat in the seat across from Konstantine. He opened the mini bar between them and began to pour himself a glass of wine.

Konstantine could no sooner sleep than jump from this plane. His mind kept racing, thinking again and again of what Louie must be going through. What fury and pain must be coursing through her now.

This situation reminded him of Nico, when his adversary had used a room to trap Louie three years ago in an attempt to turn her against him. It had to be a room like that, he thought. Something done with the lighting to ensure there were no shadows.

But how had he known? How had the bastard known that Louie needed the darkness? How had he known?

"You will be useless to her if you don't sleep," Stefano said, regarding Konstantine over the rim of his wine glass.

"I know." His mind was not clear. "But I can't."

Stefano leaned forward, pitching his voice low so the other men in the back of the plane could not hear him. "She is *La Strega*. Whatever has happened, she will survive it. How many times have we seen her shot? Stabbed? Half drowned. It doesn't matter if he's thrown her into the fires of Hell, she will walk out of it. *Sai che ho ragione*."

"I want to believe you."

"Then do." Stefano slapped him on the thigh before leaning back in his seat.

Konstantine turned his eyes to the window again, his gaze focusing on a horizon he couldn't really see.

Hold on, he prayed. *Please, Louie, hold on. I'm coming.*

LOU'S first few attempts at waking did not work. She rose to consciousness, only to slip under again. In those moments, she caught glimpses of faces, words exchanged. None of it made sense. There was no cohesiveness to hold on to. Nothing tangible enough to form a reality.

The only consistency was the unrelenting light.

When she rose to true consciousness at last, her head was killing her. It felt as if someone had buried a hatchet in her skull and left it there.

And the light was still unbearable. She opened her eyes only to pinch them closed again. She couldn't stand it.

"It's bright, isn't it?" a voice said. It was smooth as silk, pitched low, seductive in its measure. "I would offer to dim the lights for you, but we both know I can't do that."

The humor tinging the words was good-natured. It was the same tone he'd used with his students the day she'd crashed his lecture.

"Do you want to know how I figured it out? How your amazing gift works?" he asked.

"Because you bought a vowel," Lou said.

"It was when you took Rupert," the hypnotic voice droned on. "My assistant. A very good assistant, actually. I'm rather disappointed that you took him. I assume that he's dead, since he's gone and you're here. When you came to this facility last time, you entered into the hallway, which was dark. Not directly into his office. That, perhaps, could have been a coincidence. Or I thought, maybe you wanted to look in on him *before* you made your move, as to not enter blindly. But then the lights in the hallway came on and you ran. There was no one there but you *ran*. And when you took Rupert, you turned off the lights. That's when I realized you were running from the light. Why would you run from the light and keep to the shadows, *unless*—"

Lou tried to sit up and couldn't. There was an intense weight pressing against her back and her arms were unresponsive. No wonder. She was in a straitjacket. That was why her arms weren't working.

The white room. The straitjacket. It was giving her déjà vu. Hadn't she been here before?

Hadn't Nico done the same thing?

No. Not exactly. That room had been padded. This one was white tile and concrete walls.

And this room was so much brighter. So bright, in fact, that her eyes swam trying to conjure shapes and images on the very walls themselves.

"I killed the last man who put me in a straitjacket," she said. Strictly speaking, that wasn't true. It had been Konstantine who had shot him in the head four times. But Lou had caved in his nose first.

"Oh, I've no doubt you're dangerous. Gift or no gift. Even though I've stripped you of your weapons, I know better than to come any closer to you than I am now. I have a good sense about people, you see. You could say that it's *my* special gift. And when I look at you, I see more darkness than I've ever seen in a person before. If you don't mind me saying, it's incredibly seductive."

Given the man's position beneath the lights, she couldn't see his face. It was blurred, unfocused.

"This room," she said.

"Yes, it's a white room. This form of torture is still quite common in Iranian prisons. It's meant to deprive you of your senses. Drive you a little mad. But I have a feeling it would take more than a white room to drive you mad. Unless you're already mad?"

"No."

"I didn't think so. You seem to have a tremendous amount of self-possession. That's not always compatible with other psychopathic traits. Psychopaths can lie, beguile, pretend. But full self-control, it's rare. It's why so often they're caught, sooner or later. Do you ever use these techniques yourself when you hunt? Or does your gift allow you to bypass developing such skills?"

Lou rose to her knees, intent on crossing the room and showing the good doctor her *psychopathic traits* firsthand.

She managed only two steps before she was yanked back, her knees hitting the tile. Pain shot up to her hips, but she didn't cry out.

"My, you are strong," he said. "That chain must weigh more than two hundred pounds."

"Why?" she asked through gritted teeth.

"I've chained you to the wall to limit your movements. And I used ankle shackles because I thought it was best not to underestimate you. I've seen how fast you move."

Cold fury burned in Lou.

The doctor leaned forward. "See? There it is. You want to tear me apart with your bare hands, and yet you don't so much as scream in frustration."

"I'm patient."

He laughed. The good, hearty laugh befitting a mall Santa. When he stopped, he said, "*Patience.* I suppose I haven't taught them much patience. Kaia is perhaps the most patient of all. You're right though, whether you realize it or not. The most successful killers do have the ability to delay gratification."

Lou's mind sifted through her options. She didn't have her weapons or most of her clothes. She'd been stripped down and bound by the straitjacket. No boots, no blades. Her bare ankles were shackled to each other. She couldn't see the chain at her back, but it felt heavy.

No hands, no feet, no help.

What did that leave her with? Her voice? Her teeth?

The assistant—before she'd killed him—had told her that the professor's desire, above all, was to master psychopathy. To understand it.

"Rupert said you studied psychopaths," Lou said.

"Did he? Psychopathy is my life's work. But I'm still trying to discern if you are in fact a psychopath. How many people have you killed? Including my Rupert?"

"I don't know."

"A rough guess will do," the professor said.

"Five hundred."

The truth was Lou had lost count somewhere in the low three hundreds. But that had been years ago. Dmitri Petrov, the Russian mob boss, had accused Lou of killing more than four hundred of his men, not including his son. Lou was inclined to believe him.

"Five *hundred*," the man said. "And how old are you?"

"Twenty-eight."

"How old were you when you first killed?"

"Seventeen."

These were easy questions to answer. What could he possibly do with such facts?

"More than five hundred dead in eleven years. I must say, that is incredibly prolific. I assume it's your gift that allows you to be so proficient?"

"Yes," she said. She didn't correct him and point out that she had *gifts*.

"How did you come by such a gift, may I ask?"

"It's hereditary."

"*Hereditary.*" He rubbed his chin, looking more like a professor than ever. "Father?"

"Aunt."

"Fascinating. And where is she now?"

"Dead."

"Was her death what triggered your thirst for killing?" There was something hypnotic about his voice. And the casual way in which he asked questions made it easy to answer him.

Lou felt she could tell him anything at all.

"No," she said.

"But it was a death."

"My father's."

He snapped his fingers. "See. I knew there was a connection to your father. It was a feeling I had. I tell you, I'm good with these things."

Lou said nothing.

"Tell me about your first kill...uh, you never told me your name."

Lou had to make a decision here. She could lie to him. Or she could tell him the truth, knowing he could simply search the internet and find her story. And would that story interest him? Buy her the time she needed to come up with a plan?

"My name is Louie," she said. "Louie Thorne."

"Louie Thorne," he repeated, musically, as if committing it to memory. "Tell me about your first kill, Louie."

"His name was Gus Johnson. I stabbed him in the neck with my father's blade and he bled out."

The professor was not impressed by this. "I see. Had you killed anything before that? Animals?"

"No," she said.

"No? You went straight to humans? Ambitious."

"I like animals."

"Do you? And children too, it seems. That's an interesting

deviation. Let's return to your first kill. Why him? Did he hurt you?"

"He betrayed my father."

"Ah, I see. There's some sort of loyalty complex here," he said knowingly. "What did you do with the body?"

She hesitated. "I took it to the bottom of a lake."

This was not a lie exactly. But she knew that the professor wouldn't be able to comprehend what she really meant by this. How could she describe a place like La Loon to him?

"I see." He rubbed his chin. "Do you always take them to the same lake? With five hundred bodies, I can't imagine one such place could hold them all. Unless it's a *very* big lake."

Lou said nothing.

The professor was not discouraged. "I wonder what the water represents for you. Why you must give the bodies this ritualistic cleansing at the end of each kill. Do you know why? Did anything happen with water on the night your father died?"

Her heart twisted. "Yes."

"Will you tell me what happened the night your father died?" he asked. He pulled his chair closer by its seat, and when he settled back into it, she could see his face at long last.

He looked just as he had the day in the lecture hall, his face a mask of curiosity behind his tortoiseshell sunglasses.

Sunglasses.

"Where are my sunglasses?" she asked.

"If I promise to return them to you, will you answer me? Maybe I can give them to you after you've eaten. You must be hungry. You've been asleep most of the night."

Most of the night.

Then her friends must know something was wrong. She remembered trying to send a dropped pin before the drugs overtook her. But now her watch was gone, and she had no idea if the message even went through at all.

But Konstantine would know. When she didn't come home, he would know.

Lou just had to buy him time.

"My father was an agent for the DEA. He arrested the son of an Italian crime boss. The mafia wanted to send a message, so he sent his people to my house. They shot my mother upstairs in bed and then they came after me and my father."

"Where were you when the bad men found you, Louie?"

"We were outside in the backyard. We were talking by the pool."

"And what happened when the bad men entered the backyard? Did they shoot your father?" The professor sounded almost sympathetic. Encouraging. Lou could tell he'd spent a lot of time talking to children.

"Yes, they shot him."

"How many times?"

"Nine," she said.

"Did you see this?"

"No," she said.

"What did you see?" he asked, coaxing her.

What did she see? She saw her father lifting her. She saw the fear on his face as he threw her into the pool, the silent prayer on his lips for her life. And as she sank into the depths of the black waters pulling her down, she saw his white shirt darting away, drawing Angelo Martinelli's gunfire away from her.

"Not much," she said. "He threw me into the pool so I wouldn't be shot."

The professor arched his brow. "Into a pool? How interesting. That explains the lake."

Lou hadn't meant to tell him about the water, and yet she'd shared this secret with ease.

Guard your mind, a voice whispered. *Guard your mind against him.*

Who was speaking to her? Her father? Lucy?

"How old were you when he was shot?" he asked.

"Twelve."

"And do you think of this night often?" the professor asked. "Do you replay your parents' deaths in your mind, even now, sixteen years later?"

"Yes," she said.

"Very good," he said. "It's nice to talk about the things that hurt us, isn't it? I find it liberating."

There was that voice again. The hypnotic therapist voice. She had to be careful with that voice. It relaxed her. Soothed her.

It was dangerous.

Maybe Louie really wasn't the only one in the room with a gift.

The professor was smiling. "I must say, I'm so glad you found me, Louie. I believe I'm going to learn a great deal from you."

26

Piper felt as if she couldn't keep her skin on. From their wait in the New Orleans airport, through boarding, through the plane ride itself, while Dani got their rental car. Through the drive north along Highway 131 until they pulled off at a roadside diner. And even now, as they sat in the booth, their coffees in front of them and breakfast platters on the way. Her whole body buzzed with frantic energy.

"Can you stop bouncing your leg?" Dani begged. "It's driving me nuts."

"*I'm* going nuts," Piper groaned, putting her forehead on the table only to jerk upright again. "I keep praying she's not dead. I'm agnostic and I'm *praying*."

"I think Gein would view it as a waste to kill her." Dani didn't look up from the laptop she'd been furiously typing on. "He'll be too desperate to know how she ticks."

The waitress returned to their table, one hand in her apron. "Can I offer you two more coffee while you wait?"

"Yes, thank you." Dani forced a smile. She waited until the

woman slinked away before she said, "I'm more worried about her miscarrying and blaming herself."

"God, now that's what I'll be worrying about." Piper's stomach turned. She said nothing as she reached for the little packets of creamer and sugar at the end of the table. She added generous amounts of both until her coffee was the color of smooth caramel.

She knew she needed neither caffeine nor sugar at a time like this. Her nerves were already shot. But the act of tending to her coffee, holding and drinking the warm beverage, all of it provided some small measure of comfort and reassurance.

Dani closed her laptop. "Let's just eat, relax, hydrate. We meet Laura and her team in two hours. Then we'll go to the house together."

"We don't know that it's a house," Piper said.

"Konstantine sent me a satellite image. It's probably not *only* a house, but it looks like one."

"When is he supposed to arrive?"

"Three hours," she said. "I haven't told Laura everything, so we'll need to get clear on what the story is."

"I'm sure he'll just doctor the footage. Do you think she told him about her pregnancy before she got caught?"

"Unlikely," she said. "I'm half convinced that Lou won't tell him until she's in delivery."

Piper ran a hand through her hair. "A *baby*. Do you want babies?"

"No, I want a Pulitzer," Dani said.

Piper had been about to take a drink of her coffee, but snorted, spilling it on the table. She mopped it up with a thin paper napkin.

"I mean, we'll do it, if you want kids," Dani said.

Piper placed a hand on her chest. "Whoa. At least let me propose first."

Dani tried to hide her smile and failed. "How do you know I won't be the one proposing?"

"Don't you *dare*." Piper squeezed her leg under the table. "I want—"

The waitress put two platters full of eggs and hashbrowns on the table. Piper also had a biscuit smothered in sausage gravy on hers.

"Salt, pepper, and ketchup are all on the table. You girls need anything else?"

"No, thank you."

Dani's phone buzzed. A second later, so did Piper's. They both leapt for them.

Piper's face fell. "It's not Lou."

"No, it's Konstantine," Dani said. "He's almost here."

Lou woke to his voice. She'd been slipping in and out of consciousness. She knew part of this was dehydration. Hunger. Despite his promise of dinner, the professor hadn't returned after his initial interrogation. But he wasn't her problem now.

It was the lights. They were getting to her. She'd started to see shadows along the wall. Human-shaped and moving. Once she'd called out hello only to be met with a sinister hissing.

A second time she thought she saw one dancing just past her knees, and she strained to reach it, half believing she could simply fall into it and save herself.

But now the shadow was gone and someone was speaking.

"I asked you if you killed Jake," the voice said again, in the same measured tone. "Or any of the other children?"

"No," she said.

"Are you just saying no, or do you mean it?"

She said nothing.

"If I give you a drink of water, do you promise not to bite me?"

Again Lou said nothing. But then a cup was pressed to her lips. She wanted to spit it into his face. To headbutt the cup and enjoy the look as water dripped off his glasses, his chin.

She did neither. She drank the whole glass and did nothing.

"How cooperative," he said. "I hadn't expected that. I wonder what your motivation is. Are you plotting your escape? Trying to keep your strength up so that you can tear me limb from limb once you're free? Is that what you want?"

I want to keep her safe. My baby.

"Isn't it *I* who should be mad at *you?*" he asked her, in the plaintive tone of a parent. "You took my children away."

"They're not your children," she said. "You killed their families."

"Not all of them. Most of them were abandoned by mothers with drug addiction. Desperate women who needed the two hundred dollars I offered more than the baby they didn't want. But I didn't want my sample size to be *only* children from drug-addicted mothers. So I admit that I branched out."

Most of them, she thought. "How many do you have?"

"You've just taken eleven, so I suppose now I'm down to forty-six. We started with sixty-three, but accidents happen."

Lou swore.

"Rather more than you calculated, I'm guessing," he said, with a hint of amusement. Then the amusement was gone. "You should've never taken them. You don't know what you've done to my research. How important it is. But then again, you yourself are a tremendous find. You might very well make up for the loss. I still wish I had Kaia, though."

"Why?" Lou was speaking to the shadows on the floor again, opening and closing her eyes in hopes they would focus. The one closest to her looked like Jabbers, sliding serpentine along the floor in front of her.

"I'm allowed to have favorites. She was proving to be an exception, like you. You know, research is most exciting when something unexpected happens. Nearly all the children followed a rather formulaic path in their development. The right combination of nature and nurture seemed to amplify the potential psychopathy dormant in their personalities. Kaia is interesting because she is fiercer than the others. I dare say *fearless*. But she also possesses an empathy that isn't present in most of the subjects. I'm *desperate* to know why. Are you aware that you're leaning to the left?"

Was she? Lou felt as if she were above, looking down from a great height.

"You know," he went on, "this room doesn't usually affect me. In part because I limit my exposure, but also because I wear these special glasses, which dims the effects of the light. But as I sit here with you, I can almost swear I see the darkness moving toward you. There's so little of it, but it's as if it's stretching toward you. Are you doing that? Can you call the darkness in a room?"

Lou felt as if she was falling and jerked. She pinched her eyes closed and found the light still bright against the back of her lids.

"Is it only the room that makes me feel this way?" she asked.

"No. It's also the drugs I keep giving you," he said. "Nothing too dangerous. Unless you're pregnant."

"I am pregnant," she said.

She felt like she was in a dream and reality was warped around her. She couldn't even be sure she'd spoken at all.

"What?" A rough hand grabbed her face. "What did you say?"

"I'm pregnant."

"*How* pregnant?" The grip tightened on her chin so hard it hurt.

She opened her eyes. "Eleven weeks. Maybe twelve."

Or maybe not at all. Not anymore, a callous voice said in her mind. *Maybe what he's given you has already killed her, and who is to blame for that?*

Her chest compressed. It was so tight Lou couldn't breathe. Couldn't speak.

When she looked up the chair was empty. She was alone in the room. She hadn't even felt him release her jaw.

"I'm sorry," she whispered.

Who are you apologizing to? The voice seemed to be coming from the walls themselves. From the shifting shadows playing across the stark white surfaces.

"To her," she said. "To the baby."

Someone grabbed her face roughly again. It wasn't the shadows come to life. It was the doctor. He was back.

"Drink this," he said. "Drink this *now*."

She opened her mouth and swallowed. Whatever it was, it burned.

"I'm putting in an IV drip and I'm taking blood. If you want your baby to survive, don't fight me on this. Given the straitjacket, it'll have to be in the leg."

Lou felt a sharp pinch then a burning sting, but her body was too heavy to move. Not one of her muscles obeyed her.

Time skipped. Or maybe she'd fallen asleep. It was hard to tell given the uniformity of the walls around her. She could only say that when she woke, she felt different. Some of the weight in her limbs had abated. The terrible headache she'd had before was back, but at least she felt more alert.

Alive.

But now her father was in the room. He was sitting in the professor's chair.

"You're dead," she said to him.

"Yes," he said. "And you'd do well to remember that."

He smiled, spoke as if this were a joke.

"I miss you, Lou-blue."

She pinched her eyes shut and opened them again. He was still there.

"I'm crazy."

"No," he said.

"Dreaming?"

"Not quite."

"Then how are you here?" she asked. The words came out tight, strangled.

"I've never left you, Lou-blue," he said. "Never will."

"Who are you talking to?" someone asked.

Lou turned toward the sound of the voice and found the professor standing there. He was holding a tray. Lou could smell the food from where she was, straining at the end of her chains.

"Look at that salivation response. No need to ask if you're starving. You clearly are. Let's fix that."

Lou looked to the chair again and found it empty. Her father was gone.

"I'm sure that the last thing you want is to be fed like a little bird, but you need to eat. Think of the *baby*."

Lou's skin crawled. She didn't like the way he'd said it.

"If you're pregnant, then you must be sexually active. Do you kill your mates after intercourse?"

Lou almost laughed. Her face must have betrayed some measure of her humor.

"So you *do* kill them?"

"Almost. Once."

She'd spared Konstantine because he'd been rather persuasive—and rather beautiful. Far more beautiful than his brothers and father. She wondered if his good looks came from his mother. It was painfully obvious to her now that she'd never asked about his mother because she'd been afraid it would hurt him.

But she could have asked about the good things. What her voice had sounded like. What he remembered best about her. What he loved most about her. There was a photo of her in their living room. She'd been very beautiful, with his same green eyes. She'd been standing in front of a large row of sunflowers, one hand holding a white hat to her head, her other arm thrown around Konstantine's shoulder. He must have been twelve or thirteen at the time, his smile as bright as hers.

"Do you know who the father is?" Gein asked.

Lou laughed. Why did everyone keep asking her that?

"Yes."

"Is the father psychopathic like you?" the professor asked.

"Not like me."

"But he *is* a killer."

Why did he sound so interested? So excited?

"When the situation calls for it," Lou said. "He doesn't enjoy it the way I do."

"You enjoy it." The doctor leaned forward. He was unwrapping a plastic spoon, scooping a bite of mashed potatoes onto it. "What do you enjoy about it?"

What could she tell him? That her body burned when she went too long between kills. That she stopped sleeping, struggled to eat. That the accumulated, unspent energy in her body seemed to eat her from the inside out and its restlessness could only be quenched by pulling a trigger. By baptizing herself in someone else's blood.

"All of it," she whispered.

27

King went back to bed after the girls left for the airport. Hours passed, but he'd felt like he hadn't slept at all by the time his phone started ringing. He sat up, the covers falling away from his bare chest. He hoped it wasn't Dani or Piper telling him there was a problem in Michigan. It was a New Orleans number he didn't recognize.

"Hello?"

"Mr. King? Mr. King!"

He struggled to place the voice, despite its urgent, desperate tone.

"Who is this?" he asked, wiping at his eyes.

"It's Geraldine. Geraldine LaPont! Those bastards came into my house and they took Tommy. They want to kill him!"

"What are you talking about?"

"I was hiding Tommy in my house. *Tommy*. He didn't feel safe at his place and so I told him to sleep over here with me, then he wouldn't be alone. Next thing I know there's a brick coming through my window and glass all over my floor."

King threw back the covers and began to pull on his

clothes. "Did you see any faces? Get any names?"

"No, it was too quick for all that, but they dragged that poor boy out of here by his hair after beating him half to death."

He got his socks and shoes on while she spoke. "Did you call the police?"

"I did, but you're likely to get here before they do."

King wasn't going to Geraldine's.

"I'll make sure an officer makes it out to you," he promised her. "But I've got to go. I think I know where they took Tommy."

"Please do," she said. "Please help that poor boy."

King ended the call and grabbed his jacket off the back of the kitchen door.

After confirming that he had his keys in his pocket, he slammed the door shut.

"What's happened?"

He turned to find Melandra standing on the landing, her face pinched with concern.

"Wexler has Tommy. I have to go."

"Alone?" she asked. "You're going to that crypt alone?"

"Yes, but it's a different crypt." King knew the first would still be crawling with police. The cult would likely be too nervous to try using it again so soon. But in Tommy's notes, he'd marked a second location that aligned with these so-called ley lines. Somewhere else this cult was known to perform rituals. King only hoped he was right and that was where he'd find Tommy.

"I'll call White on the way," King said.

But Mel was already pulling on her coat and closing her apartment door behind her. Lady started barking fiercely at the sudden commotion.

"Hush, *ma grande*," she said through the closed door.

Lady fell quiet.

King rubbed the back of his head. "Maybe you shouldn't come."

Mel threw up her hands. "First I didn't want to come and you made me, and now I want to come and you're telling me to stay behind. Make up your mind, Mr. King."

King didn't want to tell her what to do, but the danger was real now. He knew these weren't delusions and a simple insurance fraud case or even a missing person case.

"We both know I can shoot. Ask Lou," she said.

Mel had been trying to shoot her ex-husband and Lou had stepped into the bullet's path. But her aim had been true nonetheless.

"Do you even have a gun on you?" he asked as they descended the stairs, heading for the front door and the Buick parked outside.

"It's in my pocket. Do you have one?"

He did, in the Buick's glovebox.

"Then let's get out of here," she said, passing him on the stairs into Fortunes and Fixes.

The French Quarter streets weren't entirely emptied, even at this hour. They could blame that on the approach of Mardi Gras. Still, King found it easy to maneuver the Buick around the few drunks clotting the streets, dialing Detective White with his free hand.

King let it ring through to voice mail before calling a second time. When the detective still didn't answer, he left a message. "Dick, wake up. We've got an emergency. I need you to meet me at Cypress Grove Cemetery. I think Wexler is taking Tommy there. He's going to try to do the ritual on Tommy instead. I could use backup. I'll message you the map to the location."

He looked to Mel to see if he'd forgotten anything. Mel only nodded.

"Hurry," he said, and ended the call. Then he pressed

harder on the gas pedal and the Buick lurched forward.

"You're going to be glad you brought me," Mel said. "Turn left here. It's faster at this time of night."

He turned left. "Did you send White the dropped pin?"

He had to admit it was a nice trick. If Lou hadn't done it first, it would have never occurred to him to do the same.

"I did." Mel adjusted the seatbelt across her chest. "Keep your eyes on the road. We don't want to wreck and die. That won't do us or Tommy any good."

King made a note to himself to never complain about traveling with Lou again. Yes, her gift always left him nauseated and wobbly on his feet, but traveling this slow at such a crucial moment when every second counted was worse, downright painful.

"The cemetery will be locked at night. How do we plan on getting in? No chance they left the place unlocked for us, you think?"

"I'll lift you over the wall," he said.

"And what about you? Do you think I've got the upper-body strength to pull you up after me?"

The cemetery slid into view and Mel cried out, pointing. "Park as close to that wall as you can. I have an idea."

King frowned. "You won't be able to open your door."

"And that would be perfect. Do it."

He parked the Buick so close to the wall that he heard the faintest scratch of his side mirror scraping the stone. Mel opened his glove box and took the small 9mm he kept there. She checked that it was loaded and the safety was on and then shut the glovebox. She handed him the gun.

"Now, let's get on the roof of the car," she said.

"I can't stand on the roof of my car."

"We have fought Russian gangsters, unhinged vigilantes, and even my sack of shit ex-husband. It's *not* going to be the wall of this cemetery that stops us, is it?"

His face warmed. "No. I guess not."

"Then hurry up. The longer we take, the less time Tommy has."

King threw open the driver's-side door and climbed out, offering Mel a hand so she could crawl out on his side after him.

It was easy to heft her up onto the roof of the car, but he was very aware of the feel of his hands on her hips as he lifted her. Then she was on the ledge of the cemetery's wall, her feet hanging over into the dark.

It was harder than he'd expected it to be, to clamber onto the roof of his car, but once on it, he was tall enough to grab the lip of the stone ledge and pull himself up.

"Let's hope my old knees survive impact," Mel whispered, and jumped into the cemetery.

King followed, hitting the ground hard himself.

Neither of them got up quickly.

"At what age do you think it's too old to do this," she said, stumbling to standing. She steadied herself against the wall. "Whatever it is, I think we've passed it."

"Probably," he said through gritted teeth. King's own back was screaming. "Which way to the crypt?"

Mel looked at her phone's map and pointed ahead. "This way."

He followed her through the maze of stone monuments and mausoleums glowing white in the moonlight. But King knew which one it was even before they reached it.

He grabbed Mel and pulled her back into the shadows. The air left her as they hit the wall of the nearest crypt.

He pointed at the two figures standing guard outside the crypt.

She swore under her breath, then whispered into his ear, "I'll go around the back and get the one on the right. You get the one on the left."

"You're going to shoot them?" he whispered, genuinely surprised.

"I was going to bop them on the head, Mr. King. A gunshot is hardly discreet." Her breath was warm on his ear and neck. "I advise you to do the same. Choke him or something."

She turned away, but he grabbed her at the last second. She turned back, confused.

"Be careful," he said, and released her.

He stayed where he was, giving her a head start. Then he eased forward, getting as close to his target as he could. The man had only just begun to turn when King hit him hard with a right hook in the side of the head. He dropped with only a faint grunt.

The second guard opened his mouth to yell but his voice caught in his throat and his body went rigid. Then he fell like a board, revealing Mel at his back, a chunk of stone in her hand.

"Hope you didn't kill him with that," King said, taking the rock from her and throwing it away. "Remind me never to make you angry, Ms. Durand."

She nudged him and stepped into the crypt.

He stopped her with a gentle tug on her elbow. "I'd rather be in front, in case there are more guards."

"Suit yourself."

He led them as silently as his steps would allow, through the crypt, down the stairs, and into the darkness below.

He could hear the chanting before he even started down the last hallway. Mel's hand tightened on his arm and he turned back.

That's when he realized she was praying.

The first thing that struck him was the sheer mass of naked bodies. Colliding, writhing. Many of them were clearly engaged in one sex act or another, but there were too many limbs shifting in the candlelight to be sure exactly what was happening to whom.

"My god," Mel said at his back. "I haven't seen an orgy since the sixties."

Despite the shocking throb of bodies, King could tell the crowd was smaller tonight. He guessed not everyone had the desire to join the ceremony after their priest took a bullet to the head.

King's eyes fell on the altar. The boy was naked on the slab just as Jenny had been. His body was also painted with symbols that King hoped were made with animal's blood, not Tommy's.

At least one of Tommy's wrists had been slit.

Blood pumped from the wound, filling a chalice held by a hooded man.

The boy's eyes were closed, his body still.

King's heart sputtered. *I'm too late.*

"Go get Tommy. I'll cover you." Melandra pushed him forward.

The hooded man drank from the chalice of blood and put it down on the altar. King hurried across the room, narrowly missing the bodies shifting at his feet.

That's when he saw the blade, held high in the air above Tommy, ready to be thrust down into the kid's chest.

King went around the altar and body-checked the man, holding his right arm up between the blade and Tommy.

When it came down, it cut King across his arm, and blood sprang from the wound.

The two of them collided with the wall, but at the last minute, the attacker turned and slammed King against the stone.

King dropped his gun.

King kicked him hard in the shin and the hooded figure folded forward. He followed with a hook into the shadows beneath the hood and was relieved to feel the crunch of a nose breaking, lips splitting across his knuckles.

He'd half expected to feel nothing but darkness under that hood.

Pull yourself together, he thought. *Don't let all this candlelight and chanting get to you.*

The hood shifted and King saw a sliver of Wexler's face.

"I see you're playing the role of priest yourself tonight," King said, trying to throw the man off balance.

Melandra screamed, and King looked up in time to see the knife coming down, aimed at his throat.

He moved at the last second and the blade slid into his shoulder, his body erupting into fire.

He screamed as the pain engulfed him. The blade twisted and he howled again.

Then the chamber filled with a gunshot blast, the sound so loud it felt like a strike against King's skull.

Wexler collapsed, dropping the blade. King looked up to see if Melandra was all right.

But it wasn't Melandra who'd fired the shot. It was Detective White. Smoke rose from his gun as he stared wide-eyed across the room at King slumped against the wall.

The room flooded with police. Then Melandra was in front of him, praying, tying his arm with her headscarf, trying to stop the blood pouring from his shoulder.

"The ambulance is coming," she said. "Just sit here. Let them handle it. Stop moving, I said!"

King could only hiss in response, the pain in the left side of his body nearly unbearable. Even the smallest shifts made him scream.

"Robbie? Hold on, man. We'll get you out of here." Dick White's face came into view. "Then one of you can explain to me what the hell I just saw."

28

When the world came into focus again, Louie's mother was in the white room. Courtney Thorne sat in the chair across from her, her expression as cold and unforgiving as always.

"You know, I never wanted children," she said. "Even after I got pregnant with you, I only went through the motions because it was what was expected of me. But motherhood itself? It's the worst. *Absolute* worst."

"You're dead," Lou said.

"Yes, and you know why? Because I decided to marry the man who got me pregnant. I could have left him. I could have refused his proposal and got an abortion. My parents would've had aneurysms, but they didn't have to know. I could have taken so many other paths. But I did what was *right*, and now look at me. *Dead.* Is this the life you want?"

"I want her," she said.

"Ah, I suppose we're different there. Though I did want you eventually. After you disappeared in the bath for the first time—do you remember that?"

Of course Lou remembered. It was one of the rare times

in her life that her mother had shown her physical affection. "You hugged me so tight."

"Yes, well, I wanted you *then*. Maybe that was the mistake I made. But you don't have to make that mistake, Louie. You don't have to love him. You don't have to have a child with him. You're still free."

"I want her," Lou said, her lips dry again. "And I want him."

"Who are you speaking to, Louie?" a voice asked.

"My mother."

"I've been reading about her. Her psychiatric records are supposed to be private, but I have my ways. Did you know that she was being treated for anxiety? And she had a history of depression too. Her doctor was prescribing her a steady stream of Valium."

Lou remembered her parents had fought about her mother taking it.

"It's interesting, because I've long hypothesized that there was a connection between the mother's mental health and the development of psychopathy, sociopathy, or any of the personality disorders in a child."

He knelt down in front of her.

"How can you be so textbook and yet so unlike anything I've ever seen? And your child—what will your child be like, with a mother like you? I have to say, I can't wait to find out."

He giggled. *Giggled.*

The giggle was cut short by a door opening. "Sir."

"I told you not to bother me when I'm—"

His words were cut off by gunfire. Lou turned toward the sound the way a sunflower turns toward the brilliant sky.

"I'm sorry, sir, but we have a problem. I think they've come for her."

The professor stood, moving away from her. "Who?

Who's come? Not Hartford and his team. Tell those bastards that—"

"It's no one we know, sir. They're shouting in Italian."

Lou laughed. And once she started laughing, she couldn't stop.

The professor grabbed Lou by her hair, craning her neck back. "Who is it? An agency? Your handler? Who wants you?"

Lou was still laughing. She welcomed the pain. It was waking her up. She felt like she was emerging from a long, heavy slumber rife with feverish dreams.

He pulled harder. The muscles in her neck exploded with pain. "Who's come for you? Who the hell am I dealing with here?"

Lou met his gaze. "The father of my child."

KONSTANTINE STOOD IN THE PARK, watching the sun cut orange waves across the water. It made him think of home, of their view of the Arno River from their shared bedroom.

Hold on, he thought for the thousandth time in the past hours of what had been, possibly, the longest day of his life. *Hold on, Louie.*

"Here she comes," Piper said.

The girl had been at Konstantine's elbow for nearly an hour. They hadn't said much to each other. In fact, he had the distinct impression that she was trying not to speak. Perhaps she was as worried about Louie as he was.

"She'll be all right," he told her.

Piper puffed her cheeks and exhaled. "I hope so, man."

"*Man*," Stefano said, and snorted as he lit a fresh cigarette. "*Odio il modo in cui parlano gli americani.*"

"You smoke too much," Konstantine said.

Stefano only shrugged. It was an argument they'd had on and off for years.

Daniella trotted to a stop in front of Konstantine.

"All right. They're almost ready with the cameras."

"Who do they think we are?" he asked.

"A task force," she said. "Someone who's gone rogue against your agency's wishes in order to help us break this story. It helps that you came in all those black SUVs with the heavy tint."

"Yeah, very discreet," Piper mumbled.

Daniella ignored this. "Laura and her team promise they'll do their best to keep your faces out of all the shots and just get footage of Gein and his people. And the children. I'm assuming you guys can fight around them?"

"Don't blame us if your friends get shot," Stefano said.

"They're aware of the danger, but they're committed to getting the footage, so they have to go in with you. Just do your best not to kill them."

"We will be careful," Konstantine assured them. "But why did you tell them we were rogue agents?"

"There's a code about protecting your source," Daniella said. "No journalist is going to burn a bridge if they can use it to get more information later."

Piper jumped up and down in place. "Holy shit. This is happening. Okay. Okay, let's do this. I'm ready."

"*We* aren't going in," Dani told her with a stern look. "*We're* going to wait here until they come out."

"What? Why?" Piper threw up her hands. "We came all this way and we're not going in to get her? How will she know how much we love her? Then who's going in?"

"I am," Konstantine said.

Piper rolled her eyes. "Fine. But it doesn't mean you love her more than I do."

Stefano laughed beside them, turning away. "*Gli dirò di essere pronti.*"

"Wait! Uh, Stephanie! Stephan?" Piper called after him.

"Stefano," Konstantine said.

Stefano turned, his brow arched.

"Tell them not to open any of the rooms with the kids," Piper said. "The kids are like baby serial killers."

"I'm sure we can—"

"One shot Lou. She almost died," Piper insisted. "Don't let them out or you'll be fighting them too. Do you want to fight bad guys *and* baby Dahmers?"

Stefano looked to Konstantine.

"*Sì, questo è il piano.* Dr. Christfeld is sending someone to pick them up." Konstantine checked his watch. "She should be here in forty minutes."

He couldn't wait any longer. He needed to see Louie. He needed to know she was all right.

"We're coming to the house at least," Piper said. "I want to be there when she comes out."

"We will see you there," Konstantine said, before turning back to the large SUV waiting for him. Stefano opened the door as he approached and Konstantine slid into the back-seat, across the leather to the far side. Stefano entered after him.

Without comment, Stefano opened a case of guns. It held two Benellis. He loaded them and handed them over to Konstantine.

Then he opened a second case and loaded pistols for himself.

"Are we really trying to keep the journalists alive?" Stefano asked. He wasn't even trying to hide his annoyance.

"We do as Daniella asks," Konstantine said. "We are a team."

"Who?" he asked, his brows arching.

"They are Louie's team," he clarified. "And I am her team."

"*Questo stronzo romantico. Ci farà uccidere tutti,*" Stefano muttered under his breath.

"I thought you were the one that said *La Strega* made your life easier?"

Stefano threw up his hands. "*Forse ho parlato troppo presto.*"

"You don't have to go in," Konstantine said as the SUV lurched forward.

"Don't be stupid. Where you go, I go."

They were quiet for the rest of the ride as the SUV traced the last few roads between the park and the spot Lou had marked on her map before going dark.

There was nothing out here. Miles and miles of country roads and unspoiled growth.

Then the house sprang into view. A lone structure set apart from the trees surrounding it. It could have been any country house on the cover of an American magazine. A wraparound porch, large inviting windows, a cheerful, barn-like exterior.

Except for the man on the porch with the shotgun propped against one leg. Then again, this was America. And they did love their guns.

The man on the porch stood as the line of black SUVs swung into the driveway and parked.

But he didn't shoot. He only waited.

"Put this on," Stefano said.

He offered Konstantine a bulletproof vest.

"I don't need it."

"The hell you don't," he said. "She's not here to protect you. *I* am. And I say wear it."

Konstantine reached for the door, but Stefano shoved his hand away. The stream of Italian swear words that followed would have made his mother turn over in her grave.

"Put it on or I will put it on you," he said.

"We don't have time for this," Konstantine said.

"Then hurry up." He shook the vest at him. "*Smettila di parlare e indossalo.*"

Konstantine slipped it over his head.

"Take these too," Stefano said. "In case we come across these *children.*"

Konstantine accepted the can of pepper spray and the small taser, slipping them into his pockets.

"One more thing." He held up a helmet.

Konstantine knocked the helmet away and stepped out of the SUV, holding a Benelli in one hand, the other secured in the holster at his hip.

"What agency are you from?" the man called from the porch.

It said a lot that he wasn't surprised to see a bunch of men roll up in black, tinted SUVs. That meant someone was likely funding this research. When this was over Konstantine would have to find out who.

After she's safe.

He raised his pistol and shot clean through the man's skull, spilling brains across the door behind him and the porch at his feet.

Stefano got to the door first and opened it.

Then people were everywhere. They poured from the SUVs in endless supply.

"Tear the house apart. There has to be a secret entrance to the underground," Konstantine told them.

Kaia had told him that much. About how she had fought her way to the surface and out into the night, only to meet the outdoor guards before Lou arrived.

After the first forty people had entered the house, Stefano held up his hand, asking the others to wait outside on the lawn.

It was true that too many bodies would make it hard to

move around in the space. Besides, they needed the reinforcements in case this went sideways.

Crashing and banging echoed through the house as each room was searched.

Over the heads of his people, Konstantine spotted the camera crew on the lawn, filming the house at a different angle. A tall brunette was saying something into a microphone while looking into the camera. Dani and Piper stood close by, watching, their expressions worried.

"We found something!" someone called from inside the house.

These words were swallowed by an explosion that rocked the world under Konstantine's feet.

Konstantine saw only the swell of red-hot fire rushing toward him before Stefano's body fell on top of him, pinning him to the ground.

"THE FATHER OF YOUR CHILD?" Gein asked. "*The father of your child* is slaughtering my team!"

"Then you'd better let me go," she said. "Or I might just have to break the promise I made to Kaia."

"The promise you made to Kaia?"

The ground under Louie shook.

"Sir, that's the trip wire. They've breached the interior."

"Kaia," the professor repeated. "She must have told him how to get in and out. Did we even decimate their numbers in the blast?"

"No," he said. "It looks like he has twice as many waiting on the lawn. What about the subjects?"

"Lock the doors. No one in or out."

"And the intruders?"

"Arm everyone," he said. "Make him fight his way through."

"I think that's his intention, sir. Wouldn't it be better if we just—"

"No!" the professor screamed. "This is *my* show! *My* research! We do what *I* say!"

The other voice said nothing. Lou kept trying to focus on the form in the chair. It kept slipping in and out of focus.

"Someone is here," she said. "Someone wants to speak to me."

And why not. All the other ghosts of her heart had visited her tonight. Why not the last one?

Louie, the spirit whispered.

"I'm here," Louie said. "I'm right here."

"He can't hear you," the professor said. "And he'll never find you. I'll make sure of it."

"Sir, they're in the first hallway."

"Then let's start the shift sequence. Let's see if he can get through this maze."

29

K onstantine and Stefano helped each other to standing. Konstantine's ears rang, but he seemed otherwise unhurt. The same couldn't be said for the first wave he'd sent into the house. At least ten bodies lay piled outside a hole in the wall.

Most of the others were injured, struggling to stand.

"Get the wounded outside," Konstantine said.

He stepped over the bodies and peered down into the dark. Stefano struck a flare and threw it into the hole, revealing a dark hallway.

"More flares," he commanded, and the remainder of the team lit their flares and pitched them into the black. The tunnel glowed red, revealing another door at the end of the hallway.

"We have a pipe bomb in the car," Stefano said.

"Get it," he said. "We'll take out that door."

Kaia had said that if Lou was being held in the white room, she would be far from the first entrance. He was betting on that now, that she would be too far from the blast to be hurt.

It wasn't until after the pipe bomb was set off at the door that Konstantine could finally see the labyrinth waiting for him.

"Get the others," he said. "We're going in together."

In the winding hallways, he found no shortage of killers. Creatures who were more instinct than human. If they attacked, they were shot in the head. If they fled, they were shot in the back and then the head.

Konstantine had no time to waste. His sole aim was to find Louie and see that she was all right with his own eyes.

He couldn't rest until he did.

But what followed was madness. Endless doors that would not open and corridors that looked exactly like the one before. After thirty minutes of falling over themselves, they had no choice but to start tearing the doors down one by one.

They'd blasted eight doors off their hinges before they found the first child. A little boy with hollow black eyes and sharp eyeteeth.

He ran at Konstantine with his hands hooked like an animal's. But it was Stefano who hit him with a cattle prod, electrocuting him into unconsciousness.

"Carry him up to the surface and give him to Dr. Christfeld. She should be here by now."

The light from the cameras shone down on the boy, highlighting his skin in a pale glow.

To their credit, the filming crew had stayed out of the way despite being right on Konstantine's heels as he tore down door after door.

They found more than thirty children behind such closed doors, neutralizing them before sending them to the surface to be secured by Christfeld and her team.

"This is more than we thought," Konstantine confessed when it was only he and Stefano outside a door. "Something is wrong. Send someone to speak to Dr. Christfeld and make sure she can take more. We were far off by our estimates."

And with each door that did not reveal Louie, Konstantine's fear grew.

After the last empty room, he couldn't take it anymore. He went to the closest camera protruding from a corner of the wall and screamed into it.

"You know who I'm here for! Give her to me or I will tear this place down brick by brick!"

A woman approached him at a run. Konstantine shot her through the chest and watched her drop. They were at another dead end. Another corridor with no way out.

"We killed the power to the building, but the lights are still on," Stefano said.

"Find the generator and destroy it," Konstantine said. "We can—"

His words fell away as a door slid open and a man stepped into view. He looked taller in real life than his photos had suggested, but Konstantine knew exactly who he was.

Beside him huddled a slender man with a tablet. He clutched it so hard, his fingers had bleached to the color of bone.

"*You*," Konstantine hissed through gritted teeth.

A bullet tore through the man's shoulder. He spun, falling back. Konstantine turned to see that Stefano's gun was up, his finger closing in on the trigger again.

"If you kill me you can't get in the room!" Gein screamed, holding his hand up as if this would stop a bullet. His other hand grasped his bleeding shoulder.

"Seal the room," Gein called out. "Seal it!"

The door to his right slammed shut.

Louie.

Konstantine was on Gein, yanking him up to a sitting position. "Open it! Open it!"

"I have to be alive for it to open!"

Stefano shoved his gun against the temple of the assistant with the tablet.

"Oh my god, oh my god, oh my god," the assistant blabbed.

"Open it," Konstantine told him.

"Paul, don't you—"

But Paul was already pressing buttons on the keypad by the door with shaking fingers.

The door opened.

And what Konstantine saw stopped his heart.

LUCY WAS TRYING to talk to her. Lou was sure of it.

"I can't hear you," she whispered. "I can't hear what you're saying."

"Sir, is it normal for her to be speaking like that?"

"Hallucinations are a common symptom of prolonged sensory deprivation," Gein said. But their voices were distant. They might as well have been speaking underwater. "I'm surprised she's lasted this long. The children can only handle an hour before they're inconsolable, screaming about monsters and boogeymen and—"

"Lucy, I can't hear you," Lou whispered.

"Who's Lucy?" Gein asked.

"I said that you don't have to worry about him," Aunt Lucy said.

At last her face came into view. And it was Lucy. Aunt Lucy as Lou remembered her before she'd gotten sick. Before she'd started losing her hair and had become so thin, frail, and light that she could have blown away in a breeze.

Tears slid down Lou's cheeks. "Lucy."

"You have nothing to fear, my love."

"Konstantine will kill him," Lou said.

"Sir?"

"Ignore her."

"I'm not talking about *him*." Lucy nodded at Gein and laughed, rising from the chair and kneeling down in front of Lou.

Her hand felt so cool on Lou's face. The chill of it was refreshing against her burning skin.

"I'm talking about Konstantine, my love," she said. "You don't have to worry about *Konstantine*."

Lou sagged against the chains, straining at the end of their tether.

"Sir."

"They'll hold. They could hold a fucking elephant."

"Are you sure, because—"

"Shut up. I'm trying to hear what they're saying in the video. They've just entered quad four."

"Konstantine," Lucy whispered again, still pressing her hands lovingly to Lou's cheeks. "You're afraid he will leave her. That he will abandon her the way your father abandoned you. That he'll break her heart into a thousand pieces the way your heart was broken into a thousand pieces. But he won't."

"He won't?" Lou's voice caught in her throat.

"No, my love. He will never leave her. Never ever."

Lou's chest compressed so hard it stole the air from her.

"You don't have to be afraid. Don't be afraid, my sweet girl. You're strong enough for this."

Tears spilled from Lou's eyes and the last of her will left her. A profound relief consumed her.

"Aunt Lucy," she cried. And collapsed.

KONSTANTINE SAW Lou on the floor. A dark smudge against the stark whiteness of the room.

But what stopped his heart was the sound of her crying.

He'd never, not once in their years together, ever heard or seen her cry.

"Louie?"

He was across the room in an instant.

"Louie. *Amore mio*. Look at me. Look at me."

When he pushed back her hair he saw her face, wet with tears, but she would not look at him.

"Santa Madonna," Stefano swore, and crossed himself.

"Find a way to undo the chains."

"What has he done to her?" Stefano asked.

"*Rimuovi queste fottute catene!*" Konstantine screamed.

"*Sì, sì.*" Stefano turned and ran from the room.

He returned holding the assistant by the back of the neck.

"I don't have the key. I don't have it! It's in his desk in his office," the man wailed.

"Then take me there."

"All right. All right! Please just stop putting that gun in my face. I can't think when you do that."

"Lucy. *Lucy.*"

"I'm here. Louie, I'm here. I'm right here." Konstantine tried to gather her in his arms, but she was too heavy. She'd always had a gravity to her, but with the chains, she was nearly impossible to lift. It felt as if he were trying to lift a car with his will alone.

The straitjacket hid her upper torso, but he could see the chafing at her ankles from the shackles. And there was the blood. There was a smear of it across her legs and the floor beneath her. But he could find no cut.

"*Amore mio*, I'm here. I'm here. Please look at me. Louie, *please.*"

He was still holding her when Stefano returned with the keys, dragging the assistant by the neck. The assistant unshackled her with shaking hands, working one lock after another.

The ankle shackles fell away, then the cuffs and locks at the back of the straitjacket unhooked, releasing her.

With frantic fingers, Konstantine undid the back of the jacket, freeing her arms. The lights in the room suddenly went out, bathing them in blessed darkness. Emergency floodlights kicked on to take their place.

"They finally found the generator."

"Louie. Louie, please answer me."

"Konstantine."

"Yes, my love. Yes. *Yes.* I'm here. *Amore mio.* I'm here."

She placed her hands on the sides of his face, but she didn't stop crying.

"I'm here. I'm right here," he said, lifting her from the floor. He carried her like a bride from the room.

"Where's that bastard?" he asked Stefano, still holding Lou in his arms.

Stefano was already lighting the end of another cigarette. "They've taken him up. They've got him bound and gagged in the back of the SUV. The journalists want to question him before the police arrive. You want to leave before the police arrive, no?"

"Yes, but—" The weight in his arms disappeared.

Louie was gone.

30

Lou couldn't stand. Her legs shook then folded, but she had enough strength in her to call out, "Isadora! *Isadora!*"

The tile under her hands and knees was cold. The sound of feet rushing came to her.

"Santa Madonna." Hands touched her gently, lifting her face. "What's happened? *Strega*, speak to me."

"Is she okay? Is she okay?"

"Who?" the doctor asked. "Who are you talking about?"

"The baby! Is she okay?"

Recognition dawned in the doctor's eyes. "Let's see then. Let's see. Come on. Can you stand? Come on."

Lou tried, but her legs wouldn't cooperate. She was too dehydrated.

"Hold on," the doctor said. "Hold on."

The doctor began shouting in Italian. "*Qualcuno mi porti una sedia a rotelle. Di corsa! Questa è un emergenza!*"

A wheelchair appeared and Lou was eased into it.

Her stomach was cramping horribly, but she couldn't tell

if that was from her own fear or if something was wrong. And she was losing consciousness again. She couldn't stay awake.

"Why can't I stay awake?" she said.

"Did you hit your head?" Isadora asked.

"No, I just—the drugs. I think it's the drugs he gave me."

"Drugs? What drugs?"

But Lou couldn't answer her. She was already falling back into the dark.

THE DRIVE to the airfield had been long and silent. Konstantine was allowed to lose himself in his thoughts of Louie while Stefano completed the business with Dr. Christfeld and the Ravengers.

Stefano tried to cheer him, telling him it had worked in their favor that no one had seen *La Strega* as she was. Bound and in tears. The rumor of her as the unconquerable boogeyman would live on.

But Konstantine had seen her. And he couldn't get the image of those wet cheeks out of his mind. It burned like an afterimage, as well as the desperate regret that he hadn't wiped them away.

He'd been too stunned to see her like that—so much like the girl he'd first seen, fourteen years ago, crying out her murdered father's name in her sleep.

I should have held her tighter. Maybe then she would have taken me with her.

Konstantine's phone rang just as they arrived at the airfield. He answered it as he stepped from the SUV and began walking toward the waiting jet.

"It's me," Isadora said. "I just wanted to let you know that she's here. And she is fine. Dehydrated, but she is okay. The drugs he gave her are wearing off."

The air left Konstantine.

"Konstantine?"

He forced himself to speak. "What drugs did he give her?"

"Sedatives. *Qualcuno voleva mantenerla debole.*"

Konstantine opened and closed his fist. "I am glad she came to you."

And he meant it. He wanted Lou to prioritize her well-being above his comfort.

"Take good care of her, whatever she needs. Please. Tell her to rest and I'll be there soon. Thank you, Isadora."

The doctor hung up, and Konstantine was left standing beside the plane holding his phone, looking from Stefano to the jet as if unsure what to do with himself.

"*La Strega?*" Stefano asked.

Konstantine slid the phone back into his pocket. "She went to Isadora. She will be fine."

"And your other problem?" Stefano asked. "Is it even a problem anymore? Surely a rescue like this must be worth something."

Konstantine hadn't come all this way in order to woo Louie. To assert in some indirect way that he was still in love with her, that he would do anything for her. That she should choose him above any other potential lover.

He had come only because he could not live in a world without her in it.

He could not bear the thought.

"Get on the plane," he said, waving Stefano toward the stairs. "Let's go home."

KING KNOCKED on the hospital door.

Tommy looked up from his phone. "Hey."

"How are you holding up?" he asked, coming into the room and pulling up a chair. "I heard Jenny and Carrie came by to see you."

"Yeah," he said, his smile sheepish. "They brought me clothes and my phone and everything."

"That was nice of them," King said, taking a seat.

"Yeah, they've been real nice to me since—well, since the truth came out."

"The truth does that," King said. "How do you feel?"

It was hard to look at the kid. Half of his face was the color of an eggplant, one eye swollen entirely shut. His slit wrist had been bandaged. He looked like someone who'd been through hell.

"Better," he said. "So much better now that I'm not a suspect anymore."

"I have to ask," King said. "What was up with that pig's heart in your fridge?"

Tommy laughed. "Oh, that. It was meant to be a prop on one of the tours. Just a scare. But I forgot all about it. I couldn't sleep because of the sound the fridge was making and I unplugged it and—I just forgot. Is it still in there?"

"No, it was confiscated," King said. "If I had to guess, it's in a landfill somewhere."

"That's fine," he said. "They're not hard to get. There's a butcher over in Treme who sells them."

King tried not to wrinkle his nose.

A knock at the door made them both turn. Geraldine stood in the doorway holding a large Styrofoam container.

"Why, hello there," she said. "Tommy, baby, I brought you some lunch."

"You didn't have to do that, Gigi," Tommy said, his hands touching his bandaged arms self-consciously. "I already ate."

Geraldine clucked her tongue. "You know this hospital food ain't no good. This here is shrimp and grits and collards and cornbread, baby. And you better eat it all. You's too skinny."

Tommy took it. "Thanks, Gigi."

They helped him sit up so he could start picking at the food. They looked cozy, the pair of them. King didn't want to intrude.

"I just dropped by to let you know that even though your uncle is dead, they want to reopen your mother's case. They found her bloody clothes in the attic at his house. They have enough evidence to prove he did it. It can't bring her back, but I hope it gives you some peace."

"It does," Tommy said.

Geraldine patted his arm. "It's still hard losing your momma, I'm sure, baby. Eat your grits."

King stood. If he left now he could still make his dinner date with Beth. A promise was a promise, even if what he really wanted to do was go home to Mel and eat lasagna. Watch TV and pet their dog. "I'll leave you to it. But if you ever need me, you've got my number."

Geraldine laughed. "Yes, should I happen upon another cult, Mr. King, you'll be the first one I call."

31

"Are you sure about this, *La Strega?*" Isadora said. "If you tell him, you can't take it back. You can't *unknow* such a thing."

But Lou was sure. She wanted to do this. It was time.

"I'm sure," she said.

"You better be, because he's supposed to be here in ten minutes. *Ten minutes.*" The doctor shook her hands at Lou. "*Dio aiutami. Voglio essere viva alla fine della giornata.*"

In fact, it was closer to seven when Konstantine knocked on the door of the clinic and was escorted back to the room where Lou had been ordered to rest.

"*Amore mio,*" he said, coming in. "How do you feel?"

Then he was in her arms, and she was holding him so tight, he made a little sound of protest.

"He has to breathe, *Strega,*" Isadora said. "His face is turning red."

Lou forced herself to relax her hold, but only a little. And he wasn't trying to escape her. Instead, he covered her ear, her cheek, her neck with kisses.

"I'm so glad you're all right," he said. "You scared the hell out of me."

Isadora met her gaze over Konstantine's shoulder and Lou gave a faint nod.

"I'll give you two a moment and I'll be back," she said, stepping from the room.

"Did he hurt you?" he asked. "You were bleeding. I will kill him."

"I promised—"

"Yes, Kaia told me about your promise, but that doesn't mean I won't make his life a living hell while he is in prison. There are many, *many* ways to hurt a man without taking his life."

How to explain that it was the room that hurt her more than that man? That it had been the hours she spent at the mercy of ghosts, face to face with her worst fears.

"Konstantine," she said. "I have to tell you something."

He grew very still in her arms. "*Amore—*"

"I'm pregnant."

Whatever words were forming on his lips died. He pulled back from her and searched her face.

"You're pregnant," he whispered. "And it's mine?"

"Yes, it's yours. It can only be yours."

His eyes widened. Then widened again.

"And I want to keep her."

He stood, throwing his hands up in the air. "*Oh, signore mio. Pensavo volessi un altro uomo!*"

"In English, please," she said.

He buried his face in her stomach, squeezed her tightly around her waist.

Finally, he lifted his head, revealing a heart-stopping grin. "I knew it. I knew you were distracted. I thought you were in love with another man or wanted another lover or—*Oh mio dio.*"

Lou pushed her fingers through his hair. "Technically there is someone else. There will always be someone else. For the rest of our lives."

"I can share you," he said. "I will share you. It would be my *honor* to share you. But please, only with our children."

"Make me a promise. If anything happens to her—to us—I can't—No."

Lou's throat was too tight to say more. Konstantine's expression softened.

"*Amore mio.*" On his knees, he took her hands. "*Certo. Certo*, we can do this. There is nothing I would not do to keep you both safe. *Niente.* Niente *in questo mondo.*"

"Promise me," she said. "Promise me you won't die. You have to fight, because if she loses you—"

He stood and covered her lips with his so that the words couldn't even be uttered.

"It won't happen," he said. "It will never happen, I swear it. I will love her. Maybe even more than I love her mother."

"And if she's like me? If she's different like me—"

"It changes nothing." He kissed her forehead, her cheeks, the backs of her hands. "It changes absolutely nothing."

A knock came at the door. "*Siete pronti?*"

"Go away," Konstantine said.

Lou laughed. "Come in."

The door was pushed open, and Isadora entered with a medical cart. She tapped the top of the transabdominal machine and smiled. "Ah, you two look happy. *Bene.*"

"*Sono l'uomo più felice del mondo.*"

Isadora closed the door behind her. "Then are you ready to see your baby, signore?"

"*Sì*," Konstantine said, squeezing Lou's hand. "I'm ready."

EPILOGUE

Piper couldn't tell if she was enjoying herself or if her eardrums were splitting in half. It was strange to have an entire bar full of people singing happy birthday to her, but she grinned and bore it like a champ. She refused to be a killjoy at her own party. It helped that an adorably tipsy Dani was hanging off one arm and a bedazzled drag queen was on the other. They only let go of her to clap along with everyone else.

"How does it feel to be twenty-seven?" Dani asked, squeezing Piper's waist.

"A lot like twenty-six," Piper said. "No discernible differences as of yet."

"You wait," Henry said. The glitter covering his eyelids sparkled in the overhead light. "Yesterday I sneezed too hard and pulled something in my neck. Aging is crazy!"

"I don't think we're old enough to say things like that," Piper said.

"You're right. Let's have another drink."

"Let's!" Dani cried.

Henry waved down the bartender.

"Are you sure about that, babe?" Piper pushed the hair back from her face. "If you keep going at this rate, Henry and I will have to carry you home."

"Nah." Dani dismissed the idea with a wave of her hand. "Just get Louie to do her *swoosh-swoosh* thing."

"Excuse me? Her what?" Henry asked with a laugh.

"Hail a taxi," Piper said. "Lou's really good at, uh, hailing taxis."

Henry raised a brow. "I'm sure she is. Looks like she takes taxis all the time."

"Now who's spilling secrets," Piper whispered into Dani's ear.

Dani giggled and pretended to lock her lips with an invisible key. She was in too good of a mood to realize how her words had affected Piper.

For the hundredth time that night, Piper looked around the bar and didn't see Lou's face. Had something come up? Had she changed her mind about coming to her birthday party?

Henry slid two Malibu and pineapple cocktails toward them. Piper asked the bartender for two large waters too.

She drank her drink despite her sinking spirits. She'd just about given up when Henry tapped her shoulder.

"Speak of the devil," he said, and nodded in the direction of the far wall.

Piper turned, following his gaze.

There she was.

In her leather jacket and mirrored shades, Louie cut through the crowd toward her.

Piper's heart lifted. "You made it."

She wasn't about to admit how scared she'd been that Lou wasn't going to show.

"Happy birthday," Lou said. She handed Piper a small box.

"Oh, what is it? Can I open it here? Whatever it is? Because some things can't be seen by witnesses."

Lou smiled. "Open it."

Piper tore the red ribbon off the white box and lifted the lid. On a bed of tissue paper was a small photograph of an ultrasound.

Dani, who'd been leaning over her shoulder, cried, "Oh, it's a *baby*. *I* want a baby."

"I thought you wanted a Pulitzer," Piper muttered.

"My set is about to start, birthday girl." Henry kissed her cheek. "I'll talk to you after."

Piper accepted the kiss and turned back to Lou. "When is this from?"

It was impossible to discern any details from the photograph in a dark bar with flashing lights.

"Today."

Piper put it back in the box. "*Cool.* What do I do with it? Do people, like, put unformed offspring on the fridge or something?"

Lou laughed. "Look under the photograph."

Piper did, and her breath hitched. It was a keychain showcasing a photo. Not of the ultrasound but of Piper, Dani, and Lou, from a road trip they'd taken out west to the beach.

"Read the back," Lou said.

Piper had to strike a lighter in order to see the words. "To the best gay aunt in the world."

"You're the reason I decided to keep her," Lou said.

Piper's head snapped up. "What?"

"Aunts are really important. Every kid needs a great aunt. And mine will have two."

"Oh my god, you can't say things like that to me. My heart's gonna explode." She buried her face in Lou's neck. She felt like she was going to cry. Hell, she *was* crying.

"Don't explode," Dani said behind her, trapping Piper in a three-way hug. "It's a nice gift."

"You don't seem surprised."

"Who do you think she got the photo from?" Dani asked, still holding on to her.

It was nice to be trapped between two of her favorite people.

Lou released her first. "Why are you so drunk?"

"I'm not drunk." Dani flipped her hair over one shoulder. "It doesn't count if you're celebrating."

"I saw that your story is doing really well," Lou said.

"Hell yeah it is," Piper agreed, twirling the keychain on her finger. "I haven't been able to open a web page or turn on the TV for weeks without hearing about that asshat Gein. I'm just glad they gave him two life sentences. But what happened to those murder kids you had squirreled away in a cabin?"

"Kaia and Elijah were adopted," Lou said. "Konstantine knew a couple in Chicago who really wanted kids."

Piper hissed. "Hope they know what they're getting themselves into."

"I've checked on them. They're okay."

"Did Konstantine ever find out who was funding the bastard?" Dani asked. "It still boils my buttons that we couldn't track the source. I don't believe he funded that whole facility with just his inheritance."

"Whoever it was, they dropped Gein as soon as he was caught," Lou said.

Piper pulled Dani close.

"Boils your buttons? Babe, seriously. Drink this water. No, here. *Drink* it."

Dani only drank about four sips before she cried, "Oh! Let's get a tarot reading done for the *baby*."

"It's like two in the morning. Mel's asleep," Piper said.

"You have your cards. You do it!"

It was true. Piper had brought her cards to the Wild Cat because Henry had wanted a reading.

She fished in her bag and found her deck. Slipping the cards from the pack, she shuffled.

"Let's see," she began. *What can you tell us about this kid?*

Lou placed a hand over Piper's, gently urging her to stop. "Don't."

Piper cocked her head. "No?"

Lou shook her head. "No. If it's bad, I don't want to know. And if it's good, then I'll let the universe surprise me."

"Fair enough," Piper acquiesced.

"Come dance with me!" Dani cried, pulling Lou to the dance floor. "You'll be glad you got your movement in now before you're the size of a watermelon and can't even tie your own shoes."

Lou allowed herself to be pulled toward the dance floor.

Piper planned to join them, but as Lou turned away, she saw that two cards were sticking up from the center of the deck. She took them, just out of curiosity.

Leaning against the bar, she turned them over one at a time.

She wasn't surprised to see the Death card. Lou was always represented as Death. A card with a lone figure surrounded by infinite darkness. But the second card *was* a surprise.

The Sun card.

A card full of light. So much light. Happiness. Hope.

Centering the figure of a child reaching up to the sun, calling it down to her.

Piper put the cards away.

Darkness giving birth to light, she thought as she moved toward the dance floor. *How interesting.*

. . .

DID you enjoy One Foot in the Grave? Louie Thorne's story continues in the next novel, ***Blood Rain: Shadows in Water #11.***

GET YOUR THREE FREE STORIES TODAY

Thank you so much for reading *One Foot in the Grave*. I hope you're enjoying Louie's story. If you'd like more, I have a free, exclusive Lou Thorne story for you. Meet Louie early in her hunting days, when she pursues Benito Martinelli, the son of her enemy. This was the man her father arrested—and the reason her parents were killed months later.

You can only read this story by signing up for my free newsletter. If you would like this story, you can get your copy by visiting ➜ www.korymshrum.com/lounewsletteroffer

I will also send you free stories from the other series that I write. If you've signed up for my newsletter already, no need to sign up again. You should have already received this story from me. Check your email and make sure it wasn't marked as spam! Can't find it? Email me at ➜ kory@korymshrum.com and I'll take care of it.

As to the newsletter itself, I send out 2-3 a month and host a monthly giveaway exclusive to my subscribers. The prizes are usually signed books or other freebies that I think you'll enjoy. I also share information about my current projects, and personal anecdotes (like pictures of my dog). If you want these free stories and access to the exclusive giveaways, you can sign up for the newsletter at → www.korymshrum.com/lounewsletteroffer

If this is not your cup of tea (I love tea), you can follow me on Facebook at → www.facebook.com/korymshrum in order to be notified of my new releases.

ACKNOWLEDGMENTS

Here we are with our *tenth* Shadows in the Water book finished and done.

This is where we drop the curtain and share a round of applause.

First off, many thanks to my amazing production team. Hats off to The World's Best Editor: Toby Selwyn. A round of applause The Most Excellent Cover Designer: Christian Bentulan.

And we certainly can't forget my ever-enthusiastic critique group, The Four Horsemen of the Bookocalypse. Katie Pendleton, Angela Roquet, and Monica La Porta. Monica in particular does a great job correcting all the Italian and of making sure I understand Italy's food culture. *Grazie*!

And we can't wrap up these thank-yous without acknowledging my lovely street team. Thank you for reading the books in advance, reporting those lingering typos, and posting honest reviews. Your continued support makes the work worth it.

Everyone listed above is perfect and can do no wrong. Therefore, any remaining errors in the book are my own.

ALSO BY KORY M. SHRUM

Dying for a Living series

Dying for a Living

Dying by the Hour

Dying for Her: A Companion Novel

Dying Light

Worth Dying For

Dying Breath

Dying Day

Shadows in the Water: Lou Thorne Thrillers

Shadows in the Water

Under the Bones

Danse Macabre

Carnival

Devil's Luck

What Comes Around

Overkill

Silver Bullet

Hell House

One Foot in the Grave

Castle Cove series

Welcome to Castle Cove

Night Tide

2603 novels

The City Below

The City Within

The City Outside

Standalone Novels

Jack and the Fire Eater

Blade Born: A Borderlands Novel

Nonfiction

Who Killed My Mother? a memoir

Learn more about Kory's work at: http://www.korymshrum.com/

ABOUT THE AUTHOR

Kory M. Shrum is author of more than twenty novels, including the bestselling *Shadows in the Water* and *Dying for a Living* series. She has loved books and words all her life. She reads almost every genre you can think of, but when she writes, she writes science fiction, fantasy, and thrillers, or often something that's all of the above.

In 2020, she launched a true crime podcast "Who Killed My Mother?", sharing the true story of her mother's tragic death. You can listen for free on YouTube or your favorite podcast app.

When she's not eating, reading, writing, or indulging in her true calling as a stay-at-home dog mom, she loves to plan her next adventure. She can usually be found under thick blankets with snacks. The kettle is almost always on.

She lives in Michigan with her equally bookish wife, Kim, and their rescue pug, Charley. Learn more about Kory and her work at www.korymshrum.com